9/23/05

To Mrs. Carol,

A fighter for God's

Way! I love

you will!

God Bless!

FINDING LIFE

A NOVEL

JAMES GRAHAM

authorHOUSE™

1663 LIBERTY DRIVE, SUITE 200
BLOOMINGTON, INDIANA 47403
(800) 839-8640
WWW.AUTHORHOUSE.COM

First published by AuthorHouse 03/29/05

ISBN: 1-4208-3866-0 (sc)

Printed in the United States of America
Bloomington, Indiana

This book is printed on acid-free paper.

For my mother, Bonnie Graham, you will
always be my world. Without question,
you are the greatest person I know.

For my father, James L. Graham, Sr., you've faded
so fast. I pray this book is finished in time.

For Leslie, my wife and my future, a child will soon take
the place of those we have lost. They are waiting for us.

Acknowledgements

This book had no future until the day Dr. Fred Stephenson entered my life. Thank you for inspiring me to write the story God placed in my heart. Your passion has afforded success in everything you do. And though you are a celebrated teacher and author, your character remains your most amazing accomplishment.

To Beth and Monty Montgomery, you are North Carolina's brightest, not to mention Harvard's. Thank you for your editing expertise and Biblical insights. I treasure your friendships.

"…rejoice in our sufferings, knowing that suffering produces endurance, and endurance produces character, and character produces hope…"

The Apostle Paul

Prologue

This is a story about me, Chance Gordon. It's a story I tell on this date each year, of how my life was saved by the genius of friendship and the small miracles of everyday life. And though I may never be the person I was before my accident, I awake each morning with a purpose. And when I start to feel sadness fill the image looking back at me in the mirror, I think of my friend, Charlie Robbins. I am telling you this story today simply because he gave me the chance. Charlie has been my best friend since we were knee high - but don't let me get ahead of myself.

Today I sit at the place where I was reborn. An old oyster shack sitting on the banks of a river may not seem to be the best place to start life over, but for me it was a salvation. I still come back here every morning. There's a peacefulness in an early morning sun, a cool breeze through the marsh, the aroma of salt in the air and a cup of coffee that combine to make you sense a new day and another chance to rectify your mistakes of yesterday. I watch the fishing boats trudge slowly out to sea, becoming smaller until they disappear into the sun, as if it were calling them home. A few eager seagulls joyfully sing as they follow the boats, excited about another day of swindling fish from the rising nets. Small waves gently collide against the concrete dock upon which I sit, as hundreds of small fiddler crabs hurry back and forth into their holes, timing their pace perfectly with the tide.

There's not a more peaceful place on earth.

Charlie and I used to come here as kids. We had a ritual each day: We'd walk down to the E-Z Check and buy a Soda Pop and a bag of peanuts. We would then come back here, sit on the edge of the dock and let our legs dangle in the water below. There was nobody here to bother us, as all the fishermen were out in the river catching whatever was in season. There were clams and shrimp in the summer and oysters in the winter. Charlie and I would talk for hours, eating peanuts in our sodas, throwing shells at the scurrying fiddler crabs and occasionally taking a nap in the warm sun.

The afternoon was always an exciting time. The fishing boats would come in, tie themselves to the dock and unload their catch. Charlie and I got paid for carrying the bags to the house. We also shared the same grandpa, who happened to own the place. This allowed us a lot of freedom, making it the best job around.

I'll always remember one late afternoon when Charlie and I were here trying to hit fiddler crabs with our BB guns. There was a hunter sitting out near Crab Point waiting for the ducks to fly in for the evening. As a flock flew out over his head we watched as they got closer to us. The hunter stood in his skiff, aimed his shotgun, and squeezed off two shots. For a second all was quiet; then a few yards away on the riverbank we watched one duck fall at the edge of the water and another fall twenty feet behind it. The duck at the water's edge didn't move. The other duck was obviously injured but able to get up and flap its wings wildly until it suddenly stopped and looked down the bank at its mate. It flopped the short distance to the lifeless duck and as we watched in amazement, it sat beside its mate and wrapped its good wing over him. Charlie and I stood there for a while until we saw the hunter make his way to the shore to collect his kill. By the time he got there both ducks were gone. Charlie rushed the injured duck back to his house as I buried the other near our sitting spot.

Charlie kept watch on that duck day and night. I remember his dad saying there was no way he would ever get a wild duck to eat, but Charlie didn't listen. Charlie showed up at our grandfather's steps and said, "Gramps, we've gotta save this duck."

Gramps looked down at the tears in young Charlie's eyes and gave his typical saying, "Let's see what we can do."

It took two weeks to mend that duck. Charlie nursed her, exercised her wing, and never lost faith that she would fly again. That duck bit him so many times that he wore bandages around both hands - but he never swayed. Charlie kept that duck on course the entire summer until early one Saturday morning, as Gramps and I watched, he let her fly away.

Charlie gave that duck a new life. He would one day do the same for me.

———————

As for growing up with Charlie, he was always the smart kid - but not the kind of smart kid that didn't have friends. Charlie was a thinker; he would always make the right decisions. Whenever the gang and I came across a problem, we went to Charlie. He seemed to always come up with a plan to save our skin.

There were a bunch of us kids that grew up together: Albry, Scotty, Joe, Phillip, Shaun, Bubba, and a few others occasionally tried to join in our group. Charlie and I were the closest. I couldn't think of anything more fun than sleeping over at his house. He had a big oak tree with branches that traveled right along the side of the house. At night we would climb out of his attic window and to the top of that tree. Peering out from that massive oak we could see clear across the Newport River to the houses along Crab Point. No matter how hot the night was, the breeze coming off the river made it comfortable. Charlie would talk about everything; he had a gift for conversing. Even at that young age of twelve he could bring down a powerful subject with the local adults. I was always ready to see him pull out a smoking jacket and pipe when he sat back, crossed his fingers and began his treatise on the marvels of life.

Charlie was also just a plain kid. Nothing was more entertaining to him than to hear someone, if not himself, make strange noises from a certain part of our back ends. We had heated competitions to see who could fake one the best by blowing on our forearms. Charlie was a master. Once when there was a big homecoming crowd in church, Charlie crawled under the pews and hid underneath where my dad was sitting. He made a subtle flatulence noise with his arm and then rolled back to his seat. Dad looked around trying not to laugh until he realized that everyone in church thought it was him. When he said, "Excuse me," we all started giggling, which landed us in a heap of trouble that day.

We were silly kids. Most of us went our separate ways after high school. Albry went off to a Christian college in Florida. Joe went to a law school in New York. Scotty settled down and began his own landscaping business. Josh moved out to Phoenix and became a cowboy. The others trickled out and settled down in the comforts of Morehead City and Wilmington.

As for Charlie and me, we lived out our childhood ambitions to attend the University of North Carolina at

Chapel Hill. Charlie, of course, received a full scholarship and would eventually earn early acceptance into medical school after his second year. Chapel Hill brought about a new chapter in our lives, and that's actually where this story began to unfold. Life was good and love abundant in Chapel Hill…I had no hint of the hell filled days to come.

Part One

Chapter 1

There are those days in our lives that carve their memory a notch deeper than the others, visiting our minds frequently, stirred to life by seemingly innocuous smells of summer or sounds of children playing in the surf. It is the smells and sounds of these happy times that carry my thoughts back to Jordan Lake - for it was there that I first met Wendy Summers.

Jordan Lake was the hot spot for students that hung around Chapel Hill during the summer. It was the closest thing to a real beach that we could find. I was there with a group of guys on that fateful day when a playful co-ed game of volleyball put Wendy and some of her sorority sisters across the net from us. I was instantly captivated; she had beautiful blue eyes and long blond hair pulled back in a ponytail. It's hard to say exactly what it was about her that drew me in; there was just something about her that I couldn't stop staring at. Well, there were a couple of things. She had a way of shyly turning her head towards her shoulder and showing off her perfect smile. And then there were her eyes of summer blue. I had heard people talk about eyes dancing, but I always dismissed it as silly romantic ploys to win over a naïve girl.

But Wendy's eyes did dance. And from the first time I saw her walk onto that sandy volleyball court I knew that she was perfect, even in her imperfections. Just by looking at her I knew, she was something special. I was never a romantic, but on that day I reconsidered love at first sight.

As I stood there dreaming about a life with someone I had only laid eyes on thirty seconds earlier, she looked at me, smiled, and said, "Hi, I'm Wendy." I have never forgotten the feeling of that exact moment. I was completely at a loss for words.

"The lady just introduced herself Chance; don't be a poor sport," Charlie blurted out from somewhere behind me.

"I'm sorry. I'm Chance. Do you go to school at Chapel Hill?" I managed to squeeze out.

"Yes, we all do," she said, looking back at her group of friends.

"Come here a lot?" *Did I really just say that? Do you come here a lot? Good grief…could I use a cheesier conversation piece?*

"Not really. We just wanted to enjoy a day at the beach and get some sun. What about you?"

I was relieved that she would even continue the conversation after such a scripted line. "Yeah, we try to get here on weekends to play volleyball."

She gave me the most innocent smile and said, "Oh, I bet you're good."

I wasn't sure how to reply to that question. On one hand, I didn't want to seem overconfident. But, again, I didn't want to be passive and unsure of myself. Girls like confident guys. At least that's what I had always been told.

I decided on moderation. "I'm okay, I guess."

I'm not sure I hit that volleyball even once during the game. All I could concentrate on was Wendy bouncing around, looking so adorable that I had to stop and shake the fog out of my head. She was, in a word, mesmerizing.

Of all the years that Charlie had known me, he had never seen me so tongue-tied and unsure of myself. For the next hour I spent my time racing across the net every time Wendy would slip or fall. I grabbed her hand and helped her up while the guys just looked at each other, wondering what in the world had gotten into me. Charlie knew that something special was happening. He gave me an occasional wink or a thumbs-up when our eyes crossed.

As the afternoon wore on I dreaded hearing the most devastating words that I could possibly hear..."It's been fun guys. Maybe we'll run into you again." Charlie sensed my desperation and made sure the day would not end so easily.

"How would ya'll like to join us for hotdogs on the grill? It's a perfect afternoon for a cookout," he asked unassumingly.

Charlie had this special way of seeming like someone you had always known. Girls, in particular, always felt safe around him. Everything about Charlie was approachable and honest; you rarely heard him say a negative thing about another person. You could take the most abusive, nastiest, hateful bully in school and Charlie would say, "He just has some problems to work out."

Charlie had big, innocent, puppy dog eyes that often made him look half awake. His curly brown hair never swayed. He wasn't a tall or intimidating guy; in fact, he was probably no taller than 5'7." Charlie was simply a likeable person. In high school he was voted homecoming king, an award normally coveted by the quarterback or star basketball player. And when it came to dating, Charlie was always an overachiever. He didn't look like a lady's man, but looks can be deceiving. Charlie always got the pretty girls, proof that nice guys do win sometimes.

––––––––––––––––

The girls looked around at each other. One girl, I think her name was Tammy, was obviously not interested in being at the lake any longer. "I really need to get back," she said without giving an excuse.

Not to be defeated, Charlie went right to the heart of my desires as he looked at Wendy and what appeared to be her closest friend and said, "What about you guys? It'll be fun. The sunset will cool things down soon."

Before they could answer Charlie stepped closer to them and lowered his voice so no one else could hear him. I saw him say a few words and then as his voice volume increased he said, "We'll even drive you home in the Jeep since you don't have a ride."

Without answering Wendy looked over at me and asked, "How old are you, Chance?"

Her question caught me off guard. I stared at her for a few seconds, hoping that she would clarify her question. In a split second Charlie slipped behind the girls and with his eyes and hands spread wide open, he mouthed the words, "It's your birthday!"

"Oh, yeah," I stumbled, "I'm 21."

"When was your birthday?" Wendy inquisitively asked.

Uh oh. When was my birthday? I knew better than to lie to a girl; somehow, someway, they always nailed me with the truth. There were no nervous ticks or flickering eyes, but I always got caught.

In a quiet panic, I turned to Charlie. The question must have been obvious in my eyes as he said, "Uh…tomorrow. Tomorrow he'll be 21."

With an interrogating smile, Wendy gazed at me and said, "Does that sound right to you birthday boy?"

Like a president stuck in a lie, I mustered as much confidence as I could and replied, "That's right. Tomorrow I'll be 21. I lose track after so many years." A crooked smile fought its way across my face.

"Hot dogs sound good. What do you think, Jess?" Wendy said, turning towards her friend, both knowing there was no birthday.

"Sounds like fun."

God couldn't have painted a more beautiful sky that afternoon. The hot sun immersed itself into the lake as the white clouds and blue sky transformed to orange with streaks of red running through them. Charlie prepared the grill as Wendy and Jessica walked the other girls to their vehicles. I'm sure they were questioning the decision to stay with five strange guys, whom they had only known for a few hours. When I saw Wendy grab her bag out of the car and say goodbye to her friends, I felt my heart skip to a different rhythm. I believe I could have hugged Charlie, but I wasn't much for hugging guys.

As afternoon faded into night, we all sat around a small fire laughing and talking. Wendy settled in next to me and occasionally looked over and smiled, her eyes glittering in the moonlight. The fading sun brought a cool breeze along the lake. I noticed chill bumps on Wendy's arm and asked her if she would like a blanket from the jeep. She grinned and said, "Only if you share it with me." It was a perfect ending to a perfect day. Wendy and I sat closer together as Charlie entertained us with stories that only he could tell.

The drive back to Chapel Hill nearly froze us to death, prompting Wendy to snuggle closer to me. I wished that night could have lasted forever; it would turn out to be one of the happiest moments in that tragedy I called life.

As I walked Wendy to her apartment, I knew I had to see her again. When she paused at the door, I struggled to keep my calm – and failed miserably.

"So, can I share a blanket with you again sometime?" I asked.

Good grief, Chance! Is there any wonder why I don't ask girls out? I just asked a girl that I don't really know if I could share a blanket with her.

"I'm sorry…." I stuttered. "What I meant was…."

Laughing at my struggle Wendy grabbed my hand and said, "Of course, I would love to."

Chapter 2

I had been dating Wendy for almost a month when I brought her home to Carteret County; although, I'm not sure you could really say we were an item, giving the fact that I had not even kissed her yet. One month and no smooch. It was a bit strange, at least for college kids. Wendy would later say that she was as confused about that situation as she was about anything else in life. She would discuss the situation with friends: Was it her breath? Did I just want to be friends with her? Was there somebody else in the picture that I felt guilty about?

The truth was I had never felt so strong for anyone before. I had dated many girls before Wendy, but nothing even remotely came close to my feelings for her. Everything just had to be perfect. The first kiss would be one that she would never forget. She may forget me, but not that first kiss.

The most terrifying thing about bringing Wendy home was her meeting Big Daddy Gordon. That's what we called my father. He was always the X- factor. I never knew if he would be a perfect gentleman, or a flirt, or who knows what else. All I could think about was the last girl I took home; her name was Sandy. She and I were sitting on the couch as Dad stood in front of us talking. In his constant need for comfort he wore an old pair of pajamas, barely attached to his waist by a tragically dysfunctional button. I was all too familiar with that button; I had seen it fail to do its job more times than I cared to remember. It would fail again that night, as Dad stood there in front of us. The look on Sandy's face clearly revealed our future together. She never spoke to me again.

Dad was also a practical jokester, and Charlie was his favorite target. Once when Charlie was walking past our house, Dad hid behind a tree and shot him with a BB gun. The sting caused Charlie to dance around slapping at his butt. Somehow Dad controlled his laughter and stepped out from behind his cover. "Charlie, did one of those hornets get you?"

"Son of a gun!" Charlie said. "Something tore my rear end up."

"You danced pretty good, son. Reminds me a lot of that Michael Jackson fella."

Once Charlie was sure that whatever stung him was gone, he proceeded down the road again. Dad pulled the BB gun from behind his back and shot Charlie in the rear again, but this time he didn't even attempt to conceal his guilt. As Charlie jumped around, again slapping at his butt, Dad laughed out loud and said, "Sorry, Charlie, I saw that hornet flying at you again, so I tried to shoot him."

"Yeah, a hornet. Well, you missed!" Charlie blurted at Dad. "I'll get you back, Mr. Gordon. You just wait."

Now, as I said, Charlie was one of the nicest guys you could ever meet, but when it came to practical jokes, he was king. About a week after the shooting incident, Dad was putting up Christmas lights, standing on a ladder with both hands above his head. Charlie just happened by and saw his opportunity. "Need some help hanging those lights, Mr. Gordon?"

"Yeah, Charlie, help me hook this light cord on these nails. I can't let go or the whole thing will fall off."

"You don't say," Charlie grinned.

As Dad stood on the top of that ladder, both hands above his head holding the light cord, Charlie walked up behind him and pulled his pants down to his feet.

"Why you little...sorry good for nuttin'...boy you better march over here and pull my pants back up!" Dad demanded. "Charlie, I mean it. I can't let go of these lights." Dad danced around in a futile attempt to get his pants up with just his legs. "I'll bury you in the mud, boy," he growled.

"Sorry, Mr. Gordon, I see one of them h-o-r-n-e-t-s coming. I better go before he stings me again."

Charlie left Dad there that day – pants around his ankles, standing on a ladder with his hands in the hostage position. Any sane person would have dropped those lights and pulled their pants up – but not Dad. He struggled for at least five minutes trying to release one hand from the lights long enough to bend down and grab his pants. With each attempt, a section of lights would drop off. Dad mumbled to himself as he tried to figure out a solution to his breezy predicament. Every time a car passed by it slowed down and gawked as Dad stood there with his posterior exposed.

As Charlie walked back home, he flagged down some teenagers and informed them of Dad's situation.

"Let's go see this!" The car full of boys sped off. A smile ran across Charlie's face as he heard the sound of a blowing horn and screams of laughter in the distance. "Nice legs, Mr. Gordon," one boy hollered. "Work it, baby..."

———————

One thing was for sure – I needed to keep Dad and Charlie away from each other with Wendy around. The last thing I needed was another of Dad's southern exposures.

I waited until the weekend of the Morehead City Seafood Festival to bring Wendy home. I played the weekend through my head a thousand times. I wanted her to have the memory of a perfectly romantic first visit to my hometown.

The Seafood Festival was always a big time in Carteret County. There would be bands playing, games, thousands of people walking around, and, of course, great food. Along the boardwalk, vendors of all types set up and showed off their merchandise. Reporters ran around talking to people; sometimes you would even run across a celebrity looking to get away for a few days. But the best part that year would be setting up the first kiss with Wendy Summers.

Charlie managed to get a weekend away from his rounds at the hospital and the long hours of study that medical school required. It was always great to hang out with him back home again. Jessica also wanted to come down with us; it was obvious she had a crush on Charlie and wanted to spend a weekend around him. Charlie, in his innocence, was oblivious to this fact.

It was a flawless fall day when we piled into my Jeep and headed for the coast. We could feel the sun beating down on our skin, but the slight breeze seemed to arrest any sweat from our pores. We cruised down Highway 70 with the top off the Jeep, leaving any worries behind in Chapel Hill. The wind was whipping Wendy's hair across her face and eyes. She looked like a picture flexing her head forward and peering through the tangled strands at me. Charlie was in the back with his head extended over the seat, extracting figures from the white, puffy clouds.

He lived for weekends away from the stress of the hospital and classes.

The trip home seemed to fly by. Wendy decided to play DJ as she went through my collection of tapes, picking out her favorite songs. It was great until Jessica started singing "Sweet Home Alabama." Actually, everybody was singing, but Jess kept increasing her volume, making sure everyone could hear her voice – which reminded me of a wounded goose. When Jess got really out of hand with a particular song, Charlie lifted his head and glared at me in my rear view mirror. The words "you owe me" seemed to slowly drip from his mouth.

We arrived in Morehead just as the sun was setting. As we drove across the high-rise bridge and into town, we saw a full view of the majestic star floating over the water, signaling the eventide of day. Its yellow and orange brightness made the gray clouds glow with a pink hue. Its beams raced across the sound making it seem more like a mirror than a body of water. The sun hit some spots at angles that blinded its passing admirers. The water was as blue as I had ever seen it, contrasting perfectly with the orange-yellow and fading pink glow of the sun. I drove slowly making sure Wendy had a chance to fully revere the beauty of where I grew up.

The marshes of the Newport River attracted a lot of wildlife. White cranes and ducks flew out of the long grass marshes, barking a song of the wild until finally disappearing in the brightness of the sun. In the distance, shrimp boats were slowly making their way back to shore after a long day of trolling. Seagulls flocked around the nets hanging high above the boat, picking off any shrimp that were not released with the catch. You could hear the distant cries of the birds as they competed for a chance at the net. My grandfather always said it was the most peaceful noise on earth, the low roar of boat engines fighting through each wave, birds singing, ducks quacking, and little marsh birds that seem to cry the saddest songs.

Nobody said a word as I pulled down the remote dirt road where Charlie's parents lived. The girls remained quiet, speechless from the natural beauty of our little paradise. It was the exact way I wanted to introduce Wendy to Carteret County.

Charlie's dad was sitting on the edge of his dock as we pulled up to the house. Mr. Robbins lifted his feet from the water and waved as Charlie and Jess grabbed their bags and headed for the house.

"Hey, guys, you picked a perfect weekend to come down. There should be a good turn out for the festival."

———————————

Charlie was nothing like his dad. We used to jest him by saying that Bobby Seffers was his real dad. Bobby was mentally challenged and had a bad habit of walking in the middle of the road. He walked everywhere he went, mostly because no one wanted to pick him up. The combination of hot humid days and miles of walking made Bobby strong in more ways than one.

We never could figure out how he got around so fast. You would pass him walking, but by the time you reached the old Red and White in town he would be sitting there eating an ice cream cone. We got so curious one day that we decided to just follow him around all day.

"What do you boys want?" he would growl at us.

"Nothing, Mr. Bobby, we just wanted to smell you around...I mean follow you around," Scotty would joke.

"Yeah, you think you're funny, boy?" Bobby would shoot back. "You look funny."

We lasted about an hour before collapsing from exhaustion. Bobby was the walkingest man we had ever seen. He was probably in his seventies at that time; it's still a mystery how he could walk and beat a vehicle into town.

————————————

Bobby was a good man. Charlie and I knew that. Even though we occasionally joined in, we felt bad when the other kids would harass and poke fun of him.

He also had a son by the same name. People called him Junior, although some called him much worse. He, like his dad, was mentally challenged but had a heart of gold.

The kids in town were ruthless in their treatment of Bobby Junior. The older kids would throw sticks at him as they chanted, "Retard." Being much younger and easily influenced, they would often pressure us to join in the ridicule. Charlie and I would never forgive ourselves; it was the only time I ever heard Charlie make fun of someone. I knew by the regret in his eyes, after seeing young Bobby cry, that he would never do it again.

————————————

Mr. Robbins made his way off the dock to greet Charlie with his traditional handshake and face slap.

"Hello, Mr. Robbins. Are we going to see you at the festival tonight?" I asked.

"Young Chance, shouldn't you know by now that there is no festival without me?"

"Yes Sir, just didn't want to miss you," I replied.

"And who is this pretty little lady?" he asked flirtatiously.

"I'm Wendy Summers."

Mr. Robbins pulled his glasses down to the tip of his nose and peered at Wendy. His forehead crunched upwards as he lifted his right eyebrow in an inquisitive manner and asked, "And, Ms. Wendy, why are you hanging around the likes of these guys? You seem to be a woman of taste."

Wendy chuckled at Mr. Robbins question. "I guess they have me snowed. Maybe you would make better company," she shot back.

Mr. Robbins smiled with one side of his mouth as he continued to study Wendy, completely avoiding me. "I think I like this one, Chance. Then again, the last time I saw you with a girl was when you went to the prom with your sister."

"That is not true," I said defensively, looking at Wendy.

"Oh, Chance, it's nothing to be embarrassed about," Mr. Robbins replied as he continued a coy smile at Wendy.

"Ms. Wendy, I trust tonight you will honor me with a dance?"

"Sounds like fun," Wendy unwisely accepted.

"Maybe I'll let you dance with Chance first. It's tough to dance with another after I swing you around."

Now, I may not have been Sammy Davis on the dance floor, but one thing was for sure - Mr. Robbins, along with my dad, were the two worst dancers ever seen. Every year was the same embarrassing scene: Dad and Mr. Robbins would sneak off to the festival and partake in the consumption of some ritualistic concoction they called Captain Silly. I'm not sure what they put in that stuff, but they became oblivious to the world around them.

Then they started to dance.

Dad looked an awful lot like a stud chicken as he jutted his head back and forth, his lips pursed out like a kid going to bed without dessert. After he got his neck loose, he began to flap his arms and jerk his knees up and down like he was walking through a busy cow pasture. And for the next two hours he walked in a circle doing the same thing over and over.

Mr. Robbins' dancing skills were also about as sharp as a bowling ball. He had one move that he had done since we were kids: he reached both arms straight in the air, like he was reaching for the heavens, and then proceeded to swivel his hips, as he slowly moved his arms down, and finally hugging himself. If he stopped there it wouldn't be so bad.

But he didn't.

He continued swiveling his muddled hips around while he reached down and grabbed his socks. At that point he had the seat of his pants aiming straight at who ever the unlucky person was dancing with him. With his head down towards his knees, hands grasping his shins, he began to roll his posterior around in a figure eight position. I couldn't imagine a more embarrassing way to introduce your parents.

"We really need to get to my parents' house for dinner," I said in an effort to save any dignity I had left.

"It was nice meeting you, Mr. Robbins. I look forward to our dance tonight," Wendy said in her sweetest voice.

Mr. Robbins gave a confident nod and walked back toward the house. "It's a date of infamy, sweetheart."

As we drove off, Wendy turned to me and said, "He's a bit weird...but in a cute way. Is that Charlie's real dad?"

"Well, let me tell you who I think his dad is..."

Chapter 3

It was a short drive along a meandering shore-side road from Charlie's house to mine. In between were a few acres of woods with a connecting path that we made as kids. My house sat forty yards off the bank of the river; and, like most others in the area, we had a wooden dock that extended 150 feet onto the water. At the end of the dock was a square gazebo where we kept our wooden skiff. Before the luxury of driver's licenses entered our lives, this rickety old boat served as our means of transportation to the mainland of Morehead City.

I could tell Wendy was a little nervous about meeting my family. To be honest, I was nervous for her, too. She didn't say a word as we drove down the long dirt path to the house. She quietly looked up at the line of live oak trees that occupied both sides of the road. The overgrowth of the trees joined at some places to form a tunnel of leaves that only allowed small rays of sunshine to pierce through.

"It's beautiful here, Chance. This must have been a great place to grow up."

I smiled back at her, knowing that she was probably just trying to make conversation. "It's still a great place to grow up," I replied.

When we finally made it through the tunnel of trees, the sprawling yard appeared, bringing with it the aroma of freshly cut grass. I turned the engine off and listened for a moment as the sound of roaring crickets began to reach a fevered pitch and then, in unison, became suddenly quiet. Dad was walking down the dock with a wire crab pot in each hand, while Mom sat on a wooden swing reading a book. There was nothing more enjoyable to Mom than reading with the river breezes of late afternoon.

Dad dropped the crab pots and waved as I opened the door for Wendy. "The yard looks great, Dad," I yelled while Wendy took one last look at herself in the mirror.

Dad hurried towards us with Mom close behind, nursing her glass of sweetened tea. "You must be Sarah," Dad said when he reached the Jeep.

Wendy looked embarrassed and unsure of what to say.

"Oh, I'm sorry," Dad said, a stealthy grin across his face. "This is Debbie then...no?"

Wendy caught on to Dad's feeble joke. "No, I'm Sally. It's nice to meet you, Mr. Gordon."

Dad leaned his head back and let out a stomach-shaking laugh. "She may survive this weekend after all." He then winked at Wendy and asked, "Did you meet Mr. Charlie Robbins yet?"

"Yes, he was very sweet."

Dad looked confused. "Are you sure you met Charlie Robbins, kind of an unattractive guy with an unstable personality?"

"I'm sure I did," Wendy smiled back.

Dad looked disappointed. "So I take it he has already asked you to dance tonight?"

"Yes sir."

"Well, just between you and me, he's the second best dancer in town. I'd be happy to show you the best."

"I'll take you up on that," Wendy volleyed.

Seeing that the conversation was headed to dangerous territory, I interrupted: "Wendy, would you like some of Mom's famous sweet tea?"

"Sounds wonderful."

I glared at Dad as I walked Wendy to the house with Mom. "Be good," I mouthed.

"I'll grab your bags," Dad said, shrugging his shoulders.

Mom poured Wendy a glass of tea and then took her on a tour of the house. Things never changed; the kitchen was well lit with garden windows that had all different kinds of plants growing on them. The living room was a darker, more comfortable room with soft leather furniture. Bookcases lined the walls and were full of books my mother had collected over the years; she was a voracious reader. Nautical decorations dominated the room. Mom hung old steering wheels from boats and metal lanterns on the walls, while oil paintings of vessels at sea hung near each entrance, illuminated by soft lights. One wall had a fish net with seashells scattered through it.

But the best part of the room was the large glass window looking out across the Newport River. At night you could lie back on the couch and watch the lights from trawling boats travel up and down the river.

"Your house is beautiful," Wendy said after seeing the place.

"Thank you," Mom said, knowing that Wendy's house was probably three times the size of ours.

Hoping to enjoy what was left of the daylight, I suggested Wendy and I go for a walk on the dock. Dad was finagling with a fishing rod when we reached the end of the gazebo.

"Whatcha doing, Dad?" I hesitated to ask.

"Oh, just testing out my new reel," he said as he tossed the line out into the water.

"So, Wendy, do you like seafood?" Dad asked.

"Sure."

"What about crabs?"

"Yeah, I've had she-crab bisque many times."

Dad raised an eyebrow as he looked over at me. "Have you ever seen a crab?"

"Of course," Wendy quickly answered.

"Alive?"

Wendy stopped for a second, pursed her lips, and pondered Dads question. "I can't say I have, Mr. Gordon."

Excitement ran across Dad's face. "Well, honey, today you will catch your first crab, right here with me."

Wendy looked a little concerned as her eyes glared upwards at me.

"It'll be fun," I said in my most convincing voice.

Dad disappeared into the garage and returned a few minutes later with a large bucket and an old fishing rod with a piece of string tied to it.

"What's he going to do with that?" Wendy whispered.

"You'll see."

Dad stomped his way down the dock and set the bucket down in front of Wendy. "Okay, crab class begins, young lady. First, some philosophy behind the art of crab catching."

"Come on, Dad, is this really necessary?"

"Eh…" Dad cut me off. "I'm teaching this class. I don't need you disrupting those who desire to learn. As I was saying, the philosophy behind catching crabs can be a heated debate. Some people are happy just setting traps out in the river and checking them every few days. There's no sport in that. I believe it should be man against crab - mano a crabo, if you would."

Wendy stared blankly at Dad, not sure if she should take him seriously.

"You see, Wendy, what would happen if there was a nuclear storm and all the boats were destroyed? Hmm? How would you get out to the crab traps?"

"If it was that bad there wouldn't be any crabs left, not to mention people," I said with a sarcastic tone.

"What did I say about disrupting the class?" Dad said, staring down like a professor at a chatty student.

"Allow me to apologize for my son's rudeness. He has a lot of qualities in common with the mailman," Dad said as he rolled his eyes at Wendy. "To catch a crab you must think like a crab. And crabs have only one thing on their minds." Dad allowed his question to soak in. "Chicken."

"Chicken?" Wendy repeated, trying not to laugh.

"Chicken," Dad repeated with emphasis. He then pulled a piece of chicken breast out of the bucket, sliced a small piece with his knife, and carefully tied the string around it. Like a soldier with a sword he held the apparatus up in the air and said, "Let it begin."

A blank stare covered Wendy's face when Dad looked over at her and exposed his white dentures. "Okay, Wendy, what I need you to do is lie face down with this bucket in your hand. Just let it hang gently over the water trying not to move it too fast. I'm going to sit next to you and show you how to do this. Chance will stand behind us and let us know if he spots anything."

Like a good sport Wendy did just as Dad asked. With the rod in his hand, Dad slowly lowered the chicken into the water. "Watch as the chicken fat disperses through the water. It won't take long for those old crabs to come sniffing around."

It was quite the sight. As I stood on the dock behind them, I couldn't help but giggle at the sight of Wendy lying face down on the dock with Dad hanging a raw piece of chicken in the water below; if only her sorority sisters could have seen her.

For the next five minutes we sat there staring at the water. It was mesmerizing listening to the waves break, one after the other. Cool breezes rustled through the marsh making it dance in perfect rhythm, while the salty air filled our noses, leaving a fine grit on our skin. In the distance we could see the silhouettes of fish, and the occasional porpoise, jumping back and forth against the backdrop of a fading sun set. It would have been an ideal time for our first kiss, except for one thing – Dad pulled a cigar out of his pocket, "Beautiful afternoon, isn't it, kids?"

Just when I had given up on any crabs hitting the line we heard a familiar splash in the water. It was a sound I had heard thousands of times as a kid crabbing off the docks.

"Don't move Wendy. I think there's a crab in town," Dad said as he slowly pulled the string up to reveal what was biting at it. The muddy water made it difficult to see below the chicken, forcing Dad to keep pulling the string up as he gave instructions to Wendy.

"Okay, Wendy, now try not to move too fast. I want you to get that bucket as close to the surface of the water as you can."

Wendy did just as Dad said.

"When I pull this chicken out of the water, there's going to be a crab hanging on for dear life. All you have to do is get that bucket underneath it, and I'll knock it into it," Dad said confidently.

As that crab came out of the water, claws dug deeply into the chicken meat, Wendy must have thought it was the Loch Ness Monster. She screeched in terror, dropped the bucket in the water, and began sliding backwards across the dock - away from the terrified crab, which quickly let go of the chicken and scurried back into the water. Wendy scooted back about four feet before I could tell her to stop, but it was too late. All Dad and I saw were her feet spread apart in the air as she splashed into the water, back first. I rushed over to see if she was okay. Wendy stood up in the waist deep water with river mud adorning her face. I struggled to look horrified instead of humored. Dad didn't put forth as much effort as he grabbed his belly and began hooting and hollering.

"I don't know who was faster getting in the water, you or that crab," Dad said in between bouts of laughter.

"The crab's in the water!" Wendy screamed as mud shot from her mouth.

Now I know they said Jesus was the only person that had the power to walk on water, but Wendy sure came close that day. She made it to the shore and began slapping at her legs and back like she was covered in fire ants.

Dad stood up on the dock and gazed out at Wendy dancing around. He took a long puff off of his cigar and blew it in the air. "I tell you, son, that girl ain't right."

Chapter 4

Going to the seafood festival had been a tradition for Charlie and me since we were small children. Not a lot happens in Morehead City, so the festival brought an excitement to the town that would rival Oscar night in Hollywood. Everybody's happy and cheerful, much like children anticipating gifts at Christmas.

Mom and Dad always went to the festival early to help sell tickets. It was Mom's way of helping the community; Dad just liked cutting up for a few hours before the big band started playing.

Because the increase in traffic made parking difficult, Charlie and I always took the wooden skiff across the river inlet to the festival. We would tie the boat under the waterfront boardwalk and walk the short distance to the vendors and games. It was a routine that never changed, and sometimes brought as much excitement as the festival itself.

―――――

Charlie and Jessica were due to pick us up at the end of the dock at 7:30 pm. Wendy and I waited at the end of the old wooden structure and allowed our feet to hang down into the water below.

Wendy studied her feet skimming the surface. "It's wonderful here, Chance."

"I'm sure your hometown has a lot more to offer than a yearly festival," I said.

"I would have loved to grow up on the coast like this. It's so peaceful. Things don't seem to matter as much here. I bet you love to escape here after the stress of exams: the water, the breezes, the sounds and smells...it just puts everything in perspective."

Wendy pulled her legs out of the water, wrapped her arms around her knees and began to slowly rock back and forth. Everything was quiet and still. I felt like this was the perfect time to at least hold her hand, but I couldn't muster up the guts to make a move. *Maybe if I started to face her more it would make it easier.* I pulled one leg out of the water and rotated toward her. Wendy must have caught on to my plan. She seemed a little shy as she tilted her head downward and glazed up at me.

"So what were you doing last year at this time?" Wendy tried to ignore the awkward situation.

"Oh, probably the same thing, just waiting on this dock for Charlie to pick me up. It seems that I'm always waiting for Charlie to pick me up."

"So is Jessica, if you know what I mean," Wendy said with a smile.

"So, she really likes him?"

"Of course she does. He's a great guy."

"Yeah, the girls have always thought he was cute. I guess he's an easy guy to like."

"Well, maybe so, but I know someone that blows him away," Wendy said with a sweet smile across her face.

My eyes lightened up to Wendy's subtle playfulness. "Oh really? Tell me about him."

"Well, he's very sweet. He sometimes plays volleyball at Jordan Lake. He has a really pretty home with lots of birds and beautiful sunsets. He has innocent blue eyes and the most adorable shy smile that I have ever seen. I haven't known him long but he seems almost perfect."

"Wow, sounds like a cool guy," I said with a playful sarcasm.

Wendy began fishing for some feedback. "He is. I just wonder what he thinks of me."

"Oh," I said off guard, "he probably thinks that you're the most wonderful girl in the world."

Wendy cocked her head to the side. "You think so?"

"Ab-so-lute-ly." I was starting to get the hang of this. My brain started to reel off all the movie lines I had heard over the years. "Yeah, he probably thinks your eyes dance when you smile at him. And that the air smells so sweet when you walk by him. In fact, I bet he watches you walk and wonders if you will just float away like an angel."

Wendy's smile seemed to grow further across her face. Everything became quiet again, even the wind stopped blowing. I looked up at Wendy, and this time without a plan for my words, my heart completely took over. "He thinks you're beautiful."

Wendy gazed up at the fading sky. "So, do you really think John feels that way?" A sly smile crawled back on her face.

"Yes, whatever his name is, I'm sure he feels that way."

Wendy and I broke out in laughter, which ended as fast as it began. We sat there looking at each other, studying the movement of each other's eyes. In an instant, all my hesitations cowered away. I was going to kiss the most beautiful girl on earth.

The anticipation raced my heart. I just knew that if I could kiss her once, the feeling would last a lifetime. I leaned in just a bit to instigate the event and Wendy followed suit. Slowly our lips got closer until…

"Whoa! Hold on Jess, it's going to get a little bumpy."
Perfect timing.

Charlie came flying around the riverbank with the boat skimming sideways. Jessica was in the front holding on tightly while life preservers and clam rakes almost went flying out into the river.

Charlie slowed the boat down just in time to pull into the dock. The wake from the skiff's rapid deceleration came crashing to shore, causing Wendy and me to quickly stand up in an effort to avoid the splash of the salty water colliding with the dock poles. Charlie gently bumped the boat into the dock and came to a complete stop.

Jessica's hair was sticking every way but down as she tried to erase the frazzled look on her face. While she busily patted her hair, Charlie stood up and grabbed the edge of the pole, stabilizing the boat against it.

"Okay, guys, stop looking at each other's teeth and get in," Charlie said, clueless of his ill-timed arrival.

My head dropped in disbelief.

"Terrible timing. Sorry, Chance," Charlie said, realizing what he had interrupted.

Wendy, obviously embarrassed, tried to play it off. "It's okay, we were just talking."

"Well, there's plenty of time for talking, or whatever you guys want to call it, later. Let's roll," Charlie said as he gave Wendy a wink.

The trip to the boardwalk took longer than usual due to some large swells that were likely running away from a storm rolling across the Atlantic. If the ocean seemed vast in the daylight, it was a thousand times that when darkness became it. You couldn't help but think of all the great ships that were defeated by its vastness, becoming part of what is known as the Graveyard of the Atlantic. Running across the inlet in an eighteen-foot skiff didn't have the most calming effect on us, but we trusted in Charlie's nautical wisdom to get us across safely.

After securing the skiff, Charlie and I helped the girls onto the dock and began walking towards the impressive crowd of people. There was a chill in the late summer air, a hint that fall would soon be arriving.

As we made our way into the festivities, the smell of fried seafood greeted our senses. Music could be heard from all directions, slightly less audible than the sounds of children screaming and laughing. I always loved the lights; everywhere you looked were bare light bulbs hanging from draped wires.

"Hey, Charlie, isn't that P.J. Daniels up ahead?"

"Of all the people to see first," I replied with a sigh.

Wendy smiled at Jessica. "Sounds like an old girlfriend sigh to me."

"What's her story, Chance?" Jessica asked without hesitation.

Before I could muster a word, Charlie obliged. "That's the one that got away. Chance asked her to be his girlfriend in the second grade. Boy, did she love him. Probably would have ended in marriage if that incident hadn't happened."

Charlie waited for a reply.

"What incident?" Wendy and Jessica asked in unison.

"Oh, it was nothing, really, nothing at all," I said.

"Now, Chance, I wouldn't say nothing at all. Look, it could have happened to anyone. You see, P.J. was about a foot taller than Chance in the second grade; you know how girls grow faster than guys. Everyday on the playground she would chase her man down, that being Chance of course, wrestle him to the ground and tickle him until he cried Uncle. Well, one day she tickled young Chance a little too much and he soiled his pants. He was so humiliated that he wrote her a letter ending the affair and informing her that she was not allowed within three feet of him or she would be arrested."

I laughed at myself. "Charlie told me about seeing that on *The People's Court*. I figured if they protected people from being harassed, they would certainly protect me from being tickled to the point of urinating on myself."

Charlie again jumped in, "Anyhow, she bought it and left Chance alone. But she never lost the flame for Chance. She even called him before she got married to make sure there wasn't any chance of getting back together again."

We quieted our voices as we passed P.J. with some other girls. There was an awkward acknowledgement as our eyes met.

"Hey, Chance," she said in her squeaky voice. "How's school been?"

"Great, P.J., thanks, I hope you're doing well. Any kids yet?"

"Not yet, but we're trying." P.J. turned her attention to Wendy. "So is this your girlfriend?"

I wasn't sure how to respond. "Um, well, this is Wendy Summers. She's from Charlotte. We go to school together at Chapel Hill."

P.J. glared at Wendy. "Well, good. I was a little worried when you took your sister to the prom. I'm glad to see you're finally getting over me."

My eyes widened. "I did not go to the prom with my sister!"

Wendy looked at me with a confused smile.

"Wendy, I did not go with my sister. We went stag, but my mom drove us to the prom."

"Well, technically..." Charlie started to say.

"Shut up, Charlie."

————————————

The next few hours flew by as Charlie and I ran into old friends who had, like us, made the trip back to Morehead City for the festival. You would have thought Charlie was the mayor, as he seemed to know every other person that passed by us. Charlie, truly, had never met a stranger in his life.

After making our way through the conversations and vendor shopping, we decided to try some of the famous Carteret County seafood. Being from the city, Wendy and Jessica had never experienced real seafood beyond tuna or salmon steaks. I had Wendy ready to eat some squid until Charlie decided to allow the tentacles to hang down his lips.

As the jelly-like legs dribbled down his chin, Charlie lifted one of the greasy delicacies toward Jessica. "If I had to describe it, I'd have to say that it tastes a lot like the South American spiders, you know, with the long legs," Charlie said with a look of innocence on his face.

"You're gross, Charlie," Jessica said with disgust.

"Is there something less slimy that I could try, Chance?" Wendy softly asked.

"Sure, let's try the fried soft shell crabs. They're my favorite."

"Are they going to hang out of Charlie's mouth too?" Jessica asked.

"Probably," I replied.

As we made our way to the soft crab vendor, we saw Dad and Mr. Robbins in line ahead of us.

"Well, well," Dad said in a slow voice, "Looks like the city girls are going to try some of the Crystal Coast's fine dining."

"Hi, Mr. Gordon, Mr. Robbins. I hope you're enjoying your festival," Wendy said.

"Yes, Ms. Wendy, and we expect that we will enjoy it more-so once the music begins," Mr. Robbins replied.

Dad grabbed a soft crab and began inspecting it. "It's funny, you know. This may be a distant relative to that crab you caused to have cardiac arrest today." Dad spoke to Wendy without taking his eyes off the crab. "Now that you know the art of capturing one of these beautiful creatures, it's time to learn how to eat one."

Dad removed the grease-filled napkin covering the crab and turned its face towards his. "I prefer to look it right in the eye, and these do still have their eyes attached, and…" Dad opened his mouth and shoved half the crab in, face first.

Wendy grabbed her stomach with one hand and placed the other over her mouth. She quickly gained control of herself, yet continued to hold a few fingers over her mouth just in case. Jessica didn't do as well as she ran for the waters edge and began heaving.

Dad looked at Wendy and then Jessica as he chewed like a cow eating grass. "I don't guess you girls want me to save the other half for you?"

Mr. Robbins pulled his glasses down, as he always does before talking. "Oh, no worries, girls. I'll have you eating fried eel and sliding oysters down your throat in no time."

Wendy contemplated her options. "Do you have hamburgers here? I'm really in the mood for a regular hamburger."

———————

By the time we found some *regular* food for Wendy and Jessica, the sun had completely disappeared, leaving behind a blanket of twinkling stars. The four of us had settled down at the end of the boardwalk, away from the action of the festival.

"The sky is beautiful tonight," Wendy admired. "Those stars look like diamonds."

Charlie looked around at the clear sky. "There's gonna be a storm tonight."

"I didn't see that on the weather channel," Jessica said. "How do you know?"

"It's an old saying that a storm out on the ocean will suck all the energy from around it, leaving clear skies in the areas surrounding it."

"That's true," I added. "My dad always said when you see beautiful stars, along with angry waves crashing to shore, look for a storm to come rolling in."

"Is it gonna be bad?" Wendy seemed a little nervous.

"Nah, probably just a shower," Charlie answered confidently.

We sat there staring at the sky for a few more minutes. Suddenly, from the north, a light shot across the darkness, only to flicker out before reaching the ocean.

"What was...was that a shooting star?" Wendy screeched with excitement.

"Is that the first time you've seen that?" I asked.

"Well, no, but never across the ocean like that. That was so amazing." Wendy clasped her hands together and smiled like a child seeing a puppet show.

"You know what that means don't you?"

Wendy and Jessica looked at each other. "No."

Charlie squeezed his lips together and shook his head. "That means our dads are dancing. God's laughing so hard that he's crying. That's really what shooting stars are – God's teardrops at night."

I grabbed Wendy's hand. "Let's go check them out."

———————

Walking toward the band area we could hear the chorus of *"Carolina Girls"* as a group of people surrounded the dance area.

"How much do you want to bet that Dad's in the middle of that circle?" Charlie asked.

"I have a feeling he isn't alone," I answered back.

We made our way through the layers of people only to discover that our suspicions were correct. Dad and Mr. Robbins were the only people on the dance area. It was obvious they had already warmed up. Dad hadn't missed a beat in twenty years; his head jutted back and forth, stopping occasionally to wink at a pretty girl, while his arms flared like a bird with a wounded wing.

Mr. Robbins was also playing the crowd as he grabbed a woman from the crowd and began his routine of lifting his arms in the air before hugging himself and rotating his hips like an Elvis impersonator.

Wendy and Jessica looked at each other with bulging eyes before laughing out loud. "They are so cute," Wendy said between laughs.

"Yeah, it's cute when they're not your parents. It's completely humiliating," Charlie said, averting his eyes from our parents.

I looked down at the ground in an effort to conceal my face. "You'd think after twenty years of watching them that I would get used to it. But it just gets more embarrassing every year."

Charlie agreed.

We stood there watching, mortified at the sight, while the girls started hooting at the old men. "I think Mr. Robbins has been watching MTV, seems like he's got some new cuts this year. Isn't that...yeah...that's one of the old MC Hammer dance moves," I taunted.

Charlie looked up in the air and turned his eyes toward me. "You're not helping, Chance."

"Sorry. I guess I should be thankful Dad's still using the original moves."

Before we knew it, Dad and Mr. Robbins had Wendy and Jessica in the mix of things. Jessica danced just as bad as our parents; pinching her nose and pretending to go under the water - a move I believe my Dad created twenty years earlier.

Wendy was simply amazing. She twisted and turned, making her long hair frolic from one shoulder to the other. Her smile was so natural; I couldn't picture her without it. It revealed the most genuine kindness I had ever known. And for the first time I knew, love was something real, a feeling I couldn't explain.

Wendy pranced her way to me and grabbed my hand. "Think you can steal me away from your dad?"

"I hope so. Do you know how to shag?"

Wendy shrugged her shoulders. "Want to teach me?"

"Anything to see you laugh," I said, swinging Wendy into the dance area.

We laughed at each other for the next hour, dancing and shagging, not caring if we looked like fools. Wendy grasped my arms making me feel weak and intoxicated by her presence. I was living in the moment, the one split second when a rollercoaster first drops. Nothing else mattered; no one else existed. There was only her.

"Let's get out of here," I said when Dad and Mr. Robbins motioned for us to join them in a line dance.

"Where do you want to go?"

"There's a special place I want to show you. Charlie and I used to go there a lot as kids."

I took Wendy's hand and led her through the crowd that had grown into thousands. As the hanging lights dimmed behind us, we ventured through the dark, breezy night a few hundred yards to the entrance of the Morehead

City port. Large container ships effaced the concrete loading docks while towering cranes stood still after a long day of lifting cargo out of the great vessels.

Wendy seemed unsure when I led her through a gaping hole in the chain-linked security fence that surrounded the port. "Are we allowed in here, Chance?"

"Sure, I have a special pass. It's good as long as nobody catches me."

The buildings in the port were steel structures that jutted the skyline and seemed more appropriate for an industrial city than a coastal town. For security reasons, there were lights everywhere, making the port look like a miniature New York City when darkness fell. The only escape was high above the port, at the top of the buildings…and that was exactly where I was heading.

The two highest structures in the port were the phosphate domes, measuring two hundred feet tall and dominating the skyline from miles away. A narrow ladder was built into the side of the great domes, leading to the top where a flat platform rested.

At first Wendy seemed distrusting of the intimidating ladders. "Chance, I'm a little scared of heights. I'm not sure I can do this." She extended her head to look at the towering dome before her.

"It'll be okay, Wendy. I promise I won't let anything happen to you. It's a different world up top. I want you to see it. It's really special."

Wendy again looked up at the two hundred foot climb and then back at me. "I'll try, for you."

In the distance we saw headlights driving toward us through the main street of the port.

"Hurry, Wendy, the port authority is making his rounds."

Wendy climbed up first as I followed behind her with instructions not to look down.

"Just keep climbing, it'll be over in a second."

"That's what I'm afraid of Chance, that it'll be over in a second," Wendy said with a nervous voice.

As we climbed higher into the night air, the noises below became more and more faint. The sound of the wind dominated and strengthened with each step up we took.

When we reached the top, Wendy crawled on her hands and knees to the center of the platform. As she slowly stood up, her mouth gasped at the sight; she could see for miles into the night sky.

"Oh, Chance, this is so beautiful. I feel like I can touch the stars."

Looking out across the ocean, it seemed to be a never-ending expansion of darkness with millions of perforations that made up the stars. Through the black night, there were lights from ships, marching their way through the unforgiving sea.

Wendy circled around the platform, taking in the majesty of the moment. To the north she noticed a beam of light that blinked on and off in an unrelenting pattern. "What's that light doing?"

"That's the Cape Lookout lighthouse. It warns ships not to come too close to the rocky bottom. There have been a lot of ships swallowed by this ocean; even Blackbeard's pirate ship is out there."

As Wendy continued to soak in the view, I fiddled in my pocket to retrieve a French fry I had stashed from the festival.

"Is the boy still hungry?" Wendy said jokingly when she saw me pull the crumpled fry out.

"Very funny," I said. "These are actually for you, Missy."

"For me?"

"I want you to do something for me."

"Please don't say that you want me to eat a French fry that's been in your pocket for the last hour."

"No, silly. First, I want you to trust me. Then I want you to stand with your eyes closed while holding this fry above your head."

"Chance, this is not the place for you to start going weird on me," Wendy said, staring at the French fry I was holding.

"Just do it, please. It's really important."

Wendy grabbed the fry and did as I said. The wind whipped through her hair as she stood like a statue in the middle of the dome.

"Okay, I'm going to walk over to the edge and talk to you as you continue to keep your eyes closed."

I walked about twenty feet away from Wendy, coaching her along the way. "Now, don't move. I'm going to use my special powers to make that French fry jump out of your hand and fly all the way across to mine."

"Okay Chance you're officially weir-..." Before she could finish her sentence Wendy opened her eyes and stared at her empty hand. "Where did it go? I felt it leave my hand." Somewhere in the distance the screeching of birds pierced through the night air.

Twenty feet away I was squatting, tossing a French fry up and down in my hand. "I told you I was going to us my special powers."

"How on earth did you do that, Chance?"

"Let's just say I have friends in high places," I said with a broad smile.

"Are you telling me God did it?"

I took a second to lower my head and laugh at her innocence. "Not quite that high. Let me show you."

I pulled a few more fries out of my pocket and walked back to the center of the platform where Wendy was standing. "I want you to do the same thing, but this time keep your eyes open."

Wendy smiled suspiciously while she held the fry back over her head. "Now what?"

"Be patient. You'll see soon enough."

In the background the screeching calls of seagulls began to fill the quiet night air. "Those birds are going crazy over something. Are they always that loud?"

Before I could answer her question a streaking seagull snatched the single fry from Wendy's hand. Wendy's eyes swelled to the size of silver dollars as a flock of other gulls swooshed over her head in pursuit of their fry-carrying leader.

"Chance Gordon, I'm going to kill you. You turned a bunch of crazy birds on me!"

"Pretty cool, isn't it?"

"Wait until I tell your Dad that you allowed a pack of killer seagulls to attack me," Wendy said, giving me a playful hit.

"Killer seagulls?"

"First, a vicious crab, and now a pack of hungry birds. Do you impress all your girlfriends this way?"

I took a second to give her words a second thought. Wendy bent forward to wipe her knees and legs off, for no good reason, being that they weren't dirty. I wondered what she meant by "my girlfriends." Was she implying that she was mine? Or was I reading way too far into that. Without considering what I should say next I blurted, "Just the ones I like."

Everything became silent, even the seagulls stopped fussing and switched their attention to us.

Wendy waited for me to say something further, but nothing would come. She rose up from cleaning off her clean knees. She put her hands on her hips as she stood only inches away. "How many other girlfriends do you like?"

I struggled for words as a burst of thunder erupted from the sky.

"It looks like that storm Charlie talked about is here," Wendy said as she looked up at the dark silhouettes of the clouds. Rain began softly tapping on the steel platform before increasing to a suddenly frantic pace.

"Should we get down Chance?"

I stood silent, not deciphering Wendy's words as sheets of soaking rain battered our heads. I knew we needed to get away from the lightning that would soon be there, but I just had to kiss her before the moment got away. My courage swaggered back and forth. Just as I was on the verge of going through with it I suddenly back away. The raindrops became larger, each one seeming to soak my entire body.

Wendy's eyes squinted as the wind began pushing rain into her face. "Chance, what's wrong? Shouldn't we climb down now?" Wendy said with a sense of urgency in her voice.

"Yeah, let's get out of here," I shouted above the deafening sound of rain battering the rooftop.

Wendy turned to go to the ladder. "Wendy, wait… I…I need to ask you…" Realizing that she could no longer hear me over the storm I gently pulled her arm around to look at me. As the rain continued to fall upon our heads we kissed for the first time. Drops of rain ran down my face and chin. I could feel Wendy's lips smile as we stood there on top of the world.

I know God doesn't show us the treasures and joy of what heaven is like, but I had to believe, that at that moment, I was as close to heaven as this earth would allow me to get. In that second, my life became complete. I knew I had found what so many people search their entire lives for and usually never find.

After saying goodnight to Wendy, I went back to the guest room and opened the windows. The storm passed quickly, leaving behind a cool breeze.   Gusts of wind lifted the curtains, making them dance back and forth before falling softly back to their rightful positions.

It was 3:00 in the morning as I laid on the bed, hands behind my head, staring at the vast night sky and smiling at God for the gift he had given me. I played the moment over and over in my head. I had never been so happy.

Chapter 5

"Rise and shine sleepyhead!" Dad came charging into the room with his usual obnoxious wake up call.

"Dad, it's seven o'clock. Let me sleep a little longer. Besides, Wendy's probably exhausted from yesterday."

About the time I got repositioned on the pillow Wendy poked her head inside the door. "Yeah, get up sleepyhead. You've already wasted half the day."

I looked up at Wendy and Dad as they peered down at me from the doorway. "Okay, yep, rise and shine. Ready to roll," I said before covering my head with the pillow.

———————

After breakfast Dad took Wendy and me on a short boat ride down the coastline. Wendy had really begun making herself at home with Mom and Dad; she even jumped into the driver's seat for a while as Dad coached her on avoiding the shoals.

When midday approached we packed the jeep and said our goodbyes. Mom gave Wendy a big hug and a wink as she said, "I hope we get to see more of you Wendy. It has been such a pleasure having you around this weekend."

I could tell Wendy was touched by my mom's sincerity. "I hope so, too. I just love your home, Mrs. Gordon. You made me feel so comfortable. Thank you for everything."

Dad was also surprisingly polite when he said goodbye. He stood in front of Wendy, pursed his lips together, and said, "It has truly been a pleasure meeting a young lady as classy as you. I'm not sure the crabs feel the same, but, as for me, I really enjoyed having you. You take care of yourself and remember us when you become a big time CEO somewhere."

Wendy showed Dad her brilliant smile and lifted herself up on her toes to give him a big hug. "I'm sure no one ever forgets you, Mr. Gordon. You're just not the forgettable type."

Dad smiled and said nothing as he wrapped his arm around Mom, something I noticed he always did when he was especially pleased.

The dust rose from beneath the jeep tires as we rolled away from the house and down the long dirt road that led to the main highway. Wendy waved at Mom and Dad until they disappeared from sight. She then turned around and let out a big sigh.

"Thankful to be escaping here?" I said with a laugh.

"No. I don't want to leave, Chance. This has been the best weekend of my life. I'm just sad that it has to end."

"We could drop out of school and live in my old room. I'm sure you could make a good living catching crabs and such."

"Very funny, Chance. You're just making fun of me. I really had a great time with your family. They are just so incredibly nice. You won't have nearly as much fun with my family."

"Are you saying I'm going to meet them?"

"Of course, I want everyone to know how wonderful you are."

We reached the end of the road just as Wendy finished her sentence. The jeep sat idle for a second while I let a couple of cars pass by. There was an uncomfortable silence, which was quickly broken when Wendy leaned across the seat and kissed me on the cheek.

"What was that for?" I asked.

"It's for showing me a great time this weekend."

"So am I going to have to bring you back here every time I want you to kiss me?"

"Of course not. You can kiss me anytime you want to," Wendy said.

"Anytime?"

"Anytime I say you can."

"Of course. Look, Wendy, there's one more person that I want you to meet before we pick Charlie and Jess up."

Wendy perked up in her seat. "I'd love to, who is it?"

"Someone very special."

Wendy and I drove down around the bend overlooking the marshland and riverbanks. About a mile later we pulled into an old church parking lot with an old rusty pick-up truck parked in the front.

"Are we going to church?" Wendy asked.

"There's someone inside I want you to meet."

As we made our way into the front doors we were greeted by the familiar rows of pews that sat amidst the excessively air conditioned room. The hardwood floors looked as if they had just been cleaned. The smell of wood polish filled the air as the echo of the door closing traveled through the room. From the front an old man limped through one of the side doors. The hunch on his upper back and the protrusion of his lower jaw gave clue to his longevity.

"Hello, Chance."

"Hey Gramps. I wanted you to meet someone." I looked over at Wendy, who was already smiling at the old fellow. "This is my Grandfather. We call him Gramps around here."

"They call me much worse in most places," Gramps said as he held an arthritically deformed hand out. Wendy gently grabbed it as she started to introduce herself.

"You must be the Wendy I keep hearing about." Wendy seemed a little surprised that Gramps knew her.

"That's right…," Wendy was unsure how to address him. "May I call you Gramps?"

"Of course you can, darling. I hope you've had a good time during your stay. Did Mr. Gordon treat you okay?"

"I've had a great time, and yes, he treated me very well."

Gramps was very sharp for any age, but especially so, given that he was quickly approaching 84 years. It was obvious that he was quite advanced in age as his thin frame showed the burden of many years of working in the river. His face was wrinkled but still showed the sincerity and humbleness that made him an influential figure around the community. He always wore a smile on his face that would put the entire room at ease, no matter the occupants. He spoke with a slow, yet clear, drawl. And after talking to him a short time, it was clear by the way he smiled while he conversed, that he was the spitting image of Charlie.

"I sure am glad that you two stopped by to see me before going back to school." Gramps looked like he had just remembered something as he turned and said, "Chance, would you mind climbing up into the attic and getting down some of those white candles before you take off? I'll show Wendy around while you do it." Gramps patted me on the back before putting his arm around Wendy and leading her around the church.

"He's a special boy, that Chance."

"Yes he is. I'm starting to see it more each day," Wendy agreed.

Gramps pointed to some stained glassed windows along the side of the church. "Chance's father made all of these windows. He's a very talented man." He turned back around to walk toward the back of the church. "I raised him, you know."

Wendy tried to figure out whom Gramps was talking about. "Mr. Gordon, you mean?"

"Well, I call him Robert," Gramps smiled. "His daddy was my best friend growing up. He died when his boat went down in a storm. His mama never cared much about him, God bless her soul, so I took him under my wing and raised him as my own. Never gave me a minute's trouble, him or Charlie senior."

Wendy began to catch onto the family connections as Gramps walked her to the back pew of the church and patted his hand for her to sit beside him.

"Chance thinks a lot of you. That's nice to see. He's a fine boy." Gramps looked down at the floor for a second and then back at Wendy. "And I can tell that you are a fine young lady, too."

"Well, thank you," Wendy responded back.

"They share a special friendship, Chance and Charlie," Gramps continued. "They've always been that way; always looked out for one another. Their dads were the same way, could never be separated by anything. They're still that way."

Wendy spoke up, "I could tell by the way they danced at the festival."

Gramps shook his head in disbelief. "That's one way they should be separated. Child, they are the worst dancers you have ever seen."

Gramps crossed his leg and interlocked his fingers as he sat back against the pew. Wendy noticed the similarity to the way Charlie talked.

"I'll never forget it," he started back, "the day we thought we were going to lose young Charlie."

Wendy continued to listen intently.

"He was so sick and we had prayed for a miracle. Doctors said he needed a kidney transplant to survive. And with God's blessing we found that Chance would be a perfect match. The boy was only six, but he was so brave."

"Did Chance give Charlie a kidney?" Wendy asked.

"Actually, we called him Robert Junior back then."

Wendy looked confused, "You did? Is that his real name?"

Gramp's persistent smile grew larger and his eyes twinkled like a child as he continued with his story. "Charlie was hooked up to a machine. He was so miserable. He just couldn't stand not being able to play with Chance and the other kids. He was a tough kid but he would sometimes get so frustrated that he would cry. And when he started crying, Chance started crying. Before you knew it, we'd all be crying."

Gramps smiled and shook his head as he continued staring at the old wooden floor. Wendy turned more towards him as she brought her legs up and sat on them.

"What happened next?"

"Well, it was just tearing Chance up having to see Charlie trapped in that hospital bed. He would have done anything to get Charlie out of there. So when he found out that he could give him his kidney, he didn't waste a second saying he would do it."

Gramps again paused and looked back up at Wendy, humored by the way she held her knees up against her chest, completely attentive to his every word.

"So the doctors said that Charlie would have a very good chance of surviving with the new kidney."

Gramps sat straight up in the pew and again crossed his fingers as his smile began to travel further across his face. "It was the darndest thing, I tell you. The night before the surgery, I went over to see how young Chance was doing. I found him packing his bags in his room, and I noticed that he was packing a lot of his little games and such. So when I asked him why he was packing so many toys, he sighed and said, 'Gramps, it's going to be pretty boring hooked to that machine for the rest of my life'."

Wendy slightly closed one eye as she tried to figure out what Gramps was saying. "Why did Chance think that?" she asked.

Gramps again shook his head. "You see, Wendy, Chance thought that he was trading places with Charlie. He didn't know that they would both be healthy. He was willing to give up his life to make Charlie happy again."

A tear ran down Wendy's face. "Oh my gosh. That's the sweetest thing I have ever heard."

"A special relationship I tell ya," Gramps said as he pulled a tissue from the hymnal holder and gave it to Wendy.

"After the surgery the doctors started calling him Chance, because of the chance he gave Charlie to live again. We've never called him anything different since that time."

––––––––––––

After a long series of hugs and pats, we said good-bye to Gramps. Wendy's smile had now become persistent as she looked at me. I wasn't sure what Gramps had told her, but it was working. She grabbed my hand as we headed out the front doors and gave a final wave to Gramps.

It was always tough leaving my family behind, but it was easier knowing I had Wendy to accompany me.

Chapter 6

Fall in Chapel Hill was a wonderful and refreshing time. Orange and yellow leaves began blanketing the ground and perching themselves up the steps to the old Wilson library. A familiar crunch of desiccated foliage followed wherever you stepped. The sticky humidity of summer became a faded memory as the cool autumn breezes made it more fashionable to wear long-sleeved fabrics and worn-out jeans.

Wendy had a fondness for light turtlenecks; she always looked beautiful wearing those with her meticulously ironed jeans. I would often sneak up on her as she made her way across campus. Hiding along the way, I called her name as faintly as I could, and then concealed myself behind the nearest tree. It was a pretty corny thing to do, but Wendy always fell for it.

I would like to say that it was a wonderful season of love without any hitches, but that would leave out a very important detail. His name was Jack Armstrong. He was a well-groomed socialite from Massachusetts with strong features, broad shoulders, and deep brown eyes. He spoke with an easy drawl that brooded of confidence and attracted the attention of others. For the most part he seemed like your average fraternity guy, wearing mostly khaki pants and a T-shirt with a plaid shirt tied around his waist.

The girls in Wendy's sorority found Jack quite handsome, and it didn't hurt that he was also the star baseball player for the Tarheel's most talented team in history. Needless to say, he was a strong presence on campus.

It turned out he also had very good taste in girls. He let it be known around the Greek circles that Wendy was just the kind of girl that he would like to date. The fact that I was around was only a mild inconvenience.

I first met Jack on the steps of the library as Wendy and I finished our lunch. He was making his way up when he noticed Wendy. He had a contagious smile that almost seemed like a frown, but was obviously nothing of the sort.

He made his way toward us, acknowledging only Wendy as he said, "Hey, Wendy. I just realized that we share the same political science class. I was wondering if maybe we could get together to study sometime." Before Wendy could answer he looked over at me. "I'm Jack Armstrong." He held his hand out and gave me a stronger than required shake before turning his attention to back to Wendy.

Wendy was obviously smitten by his request, but also cognizant of the fact that I was sitting beside her. She looked over at me with her mouth half open, not sure which words to let out. She continued looking at me and the somewhat concealed shock on my face as she let out a slow answer. "Uh, well, I guess we could do that, sometime, in the library...sure."

"That sounds great, Wendy. Let's do it Monday after class." Jack looked back at me again, lowered his head a bit and asked, "What was the name again?"

I smiled, trying not to show any animosity, "Chance, Chance Gordon."

"Right. So Chance, do you like baseball?"

"Sure, I've actually seen you play."

"Great. I hope I didn't disappoint you. Look, if you and your friends ever need tickets, just let me know. I'll be glad to hook you guys up."

"That's very kind of you," I said, trying my best to find some flaw that would at least make him somewhat human.

Jack gave Wendy a wink, patted me on the shoulder, showed us his perfect politician smile and galloped back up the stairs toward the front door. Before he could make it in another student pushed his way to him with a pencil and piece of paper. Jack gladly signed it and continued on his way.

"Yep, I tell ya, people are always asking me for my autograph, too. Gotta take time for the kids you know," I said jokingly as Wendy turned her eyes off of Jack and back toward me.

"Look Chance, maybe I shouldn't…"

"No, no," I interrupted, "it's always easier to study with someone else. Certainly I would prefer him to not be so…," I struggled for a diplomatic adjective, "so…perfect, but I'm sure he's a great guy."

"Chance, you are so wonderful," Wendy said as she leaned over and wrapped her arms around me.

I closed my eyes knowing Jack had the potential to challenge our young relationship.

Chapter 7

It had been about a month – who was I kidding – it was exactly 27 days since that first encounter with Jack. I had the opportunity to learn a lot about him, due mostly to the fact that he and Wendy studied together often and, secondly, because Jessica could not stop talking about him. He was from a wealthy family in Massachusetts. He turned down a chance to turn pro right out of high school and instead accepted a full academic scholarship to Carolina. Even better was the fact that it was the Morehead scholarship, one of the university's most prestigious awards, given to bright young leaders of tomorrow. It was the same scholarship Charlie had won, which had given him the opportunity to get to know Jack through some of the award ceremonies and mandatory meetings.

"I'm telling you Chance, the guy's bad news," Charlie said as he stared down at his shoes on the brick walkway.

"What can I do, Charlie? I mean, if I say something I'm going to look like the bad guy here."

"I know. I do, but this guy is a devil in disguise. At one of our meetings last summer he bragged about stealing three of the cheerleaders away from their boyfriends, and they played on the football team."

"Well, maybe you should tell her, since you know him."

"That probably won't be a good idea either. I told Jessica about a few of his escapades with the ladies and she blew me off as a jealous boyfriend. The guy just has the wool pulled over so many people's faces. He's amazing."

I gave Charlie a sudden elbow to the arm. "Ouch, man," Charlie rubbed his arm, "what was that for?"

"Charlie Robbins. Mr. Morehead scholar himself." Jack was just happening by with one of his teammates when he noticed Charlie and me sitting on the brick wall in front of the cafeteria.

"I didn't know you two knew each other," Jack said as he looked over at me.

"Been friends our entire life," Charlie responded as he shook Jack's hand.

"No kidding. That's quite lovely." Jack's demeanor was much different than when he was around Wendy.

"So yeah, Chance, I'm taking Wendy out for a study dinner tonight. Not sure how much studying we'll get done, though," Jack laughed through puckered lips as he looked over at his friend.

"Really? She didn't mention that to me," I said with an obvious confusion on my face.

"I'm sure there're a lot of things she doesn't tell you about us," Jack shot back.

"Why don't you lay off, Jack. I'm sure there are plenty of other girls for you to fool with your good old boy routine," Charlie said, completely out of character.

"Easy, Robbins. Nobody owns Wendy. If Chance is the upstanding citizen he leads on to be, I'm sure he doesn't mind letting Wendy decide who she'd rather be around."

Charlie stood up and glared at Jack. "This is a game to you, Jack. Chance really cares about her."

I had heard enough. "You know what, you're right. If Wendy wants to be with a guy like you, then I don't need her." The words seemed right, but they felt so wrong. I couldn't imagine Wendy being with a guy as shallow as Jack Armstrong. *Why would he want to steal the girl I had just fallen in love with? He could have just about anybody.*

"That's the Chance I keep hearing about. May the best man win – right?" Jack slapped me across the back. "And, Robbins, you ever talk to me with that tone of voice again and you'll need one of your buddies to stitch you up." Jack walked backwards a few steps and extended his head back with an antagonizing nod. "Don't try me, beach boys." And with that he slapped 'fives' with his friend and disappeared into the sea of students hurrying to their classes.

Chapter 8

The cafeteria was hopping with the usual lunchtime rush. Students were slinging their book bags in between tables, trying to avoid hitting anyone as they scoped out the area for an open table, or at least a familiar face. In the back right corner was a long table filled with a rowdy bunch of guys. Food flew back and forth, occasionally missing its intended aim and hitting an innocent bystander.

"You boys just don't have it figured out yet." Jack Armstrong sat at the head of the table acting more like a CEO than an elite athlete.

"Look, the way I see it, we have two more years left here. To optimize your time, you must improvise. You guys have your trophy girls, and that's just fine. I mean, hey, I have four or five of those." The other guys broke up in laughter as they threw their remaining portions of food to the head of the table.

Jack flicked a pepperoni off his shoulder. "Now seriously, my dad and older brother have passed this important information to me and I'm kind enough to give it to you morons."

"We don't need no smart girls. I like my girls to be on my level," a husky fellow yelled from the end of the table.

"No wonder the football team can't remember their plays. Girls on your level don't go to school, they go to prison," Jack said, regaining control of the table.

"Look guys, if you can get one smart lady, who isn't bad looking – if she's not in your league it becomes obvious – she can save you a ton of time. Do you guys enjoy going to class?"

A unanimous "No" came from the table.

"It's simple, you find a smart lady who shares a lot of your classes and presto – instant grades with no fuss."

"You're such a jerk, Armstrong," came the reply from John, a star football player who knew it was guys like Jack that gave serious student-athletes bad names.

"Chill out, John. You're just jealous of us guys that can play the game," replied Jack.

"Whatever, Armstrong. Why don't you go toss a ball with your boyfriends," John said as he quickly sat up, knocking his chair over.

Jack leaned back and placed his arms behind his head as he watched John trample his way through the narrow isles to the exit. "Look, I don't care what you guys do. I just delivered you the goods. Do with it as you wish."

Back at the sorority house Wendy sat on her bed as a crowd of sisters surrounded her four bedposts.

Suzie Parlor, the daughter of a famous Georgia senator, made it well known that only society's elite would have a chance of dating her. She also made it well known that Jack Armstrong was a much better choice than lowly Chance Gordon.

"Wendy, seriously, is this really a decision for you? What is Chance going to do after college, go home and fish with his father? Jack Armstrong is going to make a lot of money one day as a professional football player. And then he's going to retire and become a politician…and let me just tell you from experience, politicians make a good living."

"First of all, Jack plays baseball, not football. And second, Chance may not come from a lot of money, but he does have a wonderful family. Suzie, you're never going to experience true love if you keep looking at a guy's bank statement and not his heart."

Another sister jumped in, "I'm willing to look at Jack's heart, his checkbook, his eyes, his chest…."

Laughter erupted throughout the room. "I know, I know. It's just not that easy. I really care for Chance. He's sweet and gentle and…and cute. All the things a girl could want. And just when I think I've found the perfect guy, in walks Jack Armstrong. Not only is he a dream, but he's also a genuinely nice guy. Just the other day he took time to sign his autograph for a little boy at the coffee house."

Suzie piped in again, "And so the question remains, is there really anything to consider here? You have the perfect man after you. Guys like Chance Gordon are a dime a dozen. Just come back to Sandy Springs with me and I'll show you a town full of nice, cute guys. Jack Armstrongs don't come around every day; Chance Gordons do."

Wendy sighed with indecisiveness. "I'm just not sure about that. Chance is special. I truly believe that."

Jessica sat alone on the other bed pretending to be deep in study. "Well, you better figure it out soon. I invited Jack to your birthday party this weekend."

"You did what?" Wendy suddenly awoke from her thoughts. "Jess, why would you do that?" Wendy couldn't believe the predicament Jessica created.

"I'm throwing the party. Besides, Jack Armstrong is totally hot. His friends are scrumptious, too. And the more hot baseball players we have, the better the party."

Cheers again erupted from a few of the girls. Jessica walked over to Wendy and sat next to her on the bed. "Look, Wendy, just think of this as the perfect opportunity to decide who it really is that you want to be with. Having both of them there will only help you decide who you feel more comfortable with." Jessica grabbed Wendy's hands and quickly dropped her shoulders. "This is a good thing Wen. You're going to thank me. Just wait."

Chapter 9

It had been two of the longest days of my life. I had called twice and she didn't return either of my messages. I had not heard her voice, smelled her perfume, or watched her smile in almost 48 hours.

Unable to sleep, I reached over and grabbed a small box off my desk. Inside was a tiny lighthouse, a replica of Cape Lookout, the same lighthouse that Wendy saw the night we first kissed. It wasn't much, but I thought it would mean a lot to her. I was excited about it until I learned from Charlie that Jack would also be at the birthday party. It was obvious that Wendy was falling for him. Why else would she go two days without calling me?

I had just begun a fitful slumber when the phone startled me awake.

"Hey, stranger," Wendy's voice came through the receiver.

"Wendy, I'm glad you called. Gosh, I feel like I haven't talked to you in days."

The line went silent for a long second. "I know, Chance, I'm sorry. I've just been studying a lot for midterms next week."

I didn't need to ask whom she was studying with. Charlie saw her and Jack walking out of the library together the previous day.

"Well, I hope you're making progress. I've been putting in some long hours also, you know, getting ready for exams myself."

Truthfully, I was putting in long hours thinking about Wendy and the painful realization that I was slowly losing her.

Wendy changed her voice to a more serious tone. "Chance, I have to tell you something." *Oh no. Not the "we need to talk" talk.*

I braced myself for the big let down.

"Chance, I miss you. I've missed seeing you the past few days. I want you to know that."

"I've missed you, too, Wendy. I'll see you at the party tomorrow night."

Again Wendy became quiet. I heard a few breaths come through the phone. "Look, Chance, I need to warn you about the party. Jack will be there."

"And?" I said innocently.

"And we've been spending a lot more time together recently."

"And?"

"And, well, I just wanted you to know ahead of time. His friends can be kind of rude and ugly sometimes."

I almost choked. "His friends?" *What about Jack?* I thought. "Don't worry about me, I'll be fine," I said without elaborating on my recent run-in with Jack.

"I know you will. I just don't want it to be weird with Jack and you both being there," Wendy said.

I thought about what she said for a long moment. "Why should it be weird?"

Wendy again struggled for the appropriate words, "Well, just with the way Jack is and all. He seems to have feelings for me, even though he knows about us."

"That's very big of him," I said sarcastically, though not on purpose.

"Now, Chance, don't be like that. Jack's a nice guy, just like you."

"Just like me," I repeated with an obvious distaste. I started to go further with the conversation, but realized it would be a futile effort. There's nothing worse than being the bad guy, and that's exactly where I was heading.

"Look, Wendy, I'm sorry. It's just difficult not seeing you as much the last couple of days. I guess I'm being silly. You know how I feel about you and I trust you. I really do. No matter what happens I promise I won't go changing on you. If Jack Armstrong is the kind of guy that you want to be around, then that's just the way it is – and that's that."

I had to admit that it was a bit of a baiting for a strong confession of her love for me. But it didn't quite turn out that way.

"Oh, Chance," Wendy again sighed but couldn't complete her thoughts. "I'll look forward to seeing you at the party tomorrow night."

Sometimes, an answer not completed is an answer still the same.

———————

Charlie and I met the next morning for our usual Friday workout. The swelling in his eyes gave proof that he was up all night studying for some medical exam.

"Late night, buddy?" I asked as Charlie took one last sip from his coffee cup before venturing through the gym doors.

"Blood-born diseases," Charlie mumbled without elaborating further. "What's your excuse?" he chided back after noticing my inflamed eyes.

"This Wendy and Jack thing is just killing me. I can't sleep, I can't study, and I can't eat. I'm just useless, Charlie."

"It's easier said than done, but maybe you should just let it happen the way God has planned. You're doing your part, now put it away and have faith."

"Sounds nice, Charlie, but if everything was God's plan, some people wouldn't choose eternity separated from Him."

Charlie looked in the bottom of his coffee cup to ensure that not a drop was left and then threw it into the garbage. "I know. But still the same, I've never known someone to worry enough to make another person have feelings for them. Love has to be a freewill decision; that's how we were created."

I opened the door for Charlie. "Let's get this workout done, Dr. Phil."

Charlie loaded up the bar and took his position on the bench. But instead of grabbing the bar and beginning his presses, he closed his eyes and folded his arms.

"Are we going to workout or take a nap?" I jokingly asked.

"I can lift more asleep than you can awake," Charlie shot back. "So what did you get Wendy for her birthday?" he asked, continuing to waste time.

"I got a replica of the Cape Lookout lighthouse. She fell in love with it the night I took her to the phosphate domes."

Charlie didn't say anything. He grabbed the bar and began lifting the weight off its support. "That's nice. I'm sure she'll love it."

"I hope she's more impressed than you are," I said with dejection.

"She'll love it, Chance. I have no doubt that she'll love it."

"What's that mean?" I asked.

"Nothing. Why don't you spot me so I don't cave my chest in."

As I leaned over to guide the weight down, a dreadful, yet familiar, voice came from behind me.

"It's the beach boys." Jack Armstrong walked to the front of the bench as Charlie struggled to lift and look at the same time. "How many beach boys does it take to lift 95 pounds?" Jack asked sarcastically.

"What do you want, Jack?" Charlie and I asked simultaneously.

"Just checking on my boys. I'll be over at the squat rack if you ladies need a spot. I wouldn't want you to hurt yourselves with that heavy weight." Jack smiled as he took time to look both of us in the face. "Ta-ta fellas."

"That guy has some audacity," Charlie said as he sat up on the bench.

"It just makes me sick that he deceives so many people," I responded. "Just wait, tonight he'll be the most courteous gentleman to grace the campus of Chapel Hill."

"Yeah, speaking of gentlemen, Scotty will be coming up this afternoon. He'll be here for the weekend."

"Scotty Foreman?"

"Yeah, his grandmother is in the hospital here. He's going to be staying with us."

Scotty was part of our group growing up. He was by far the craziest of the bunch; there was never a dull moment with him.

"He'll be coming to the party with us," Charlie said, shaking his head as he thought about it. "I'll make sure he behaves himself."

"As if it wasn't stressful enough," I said. "Not that it matters. Besides, it'll be nice to see someone from back home."

Chapter 10

For at least a couple of hours that afternoon, all was well in my world. Scotty made it to the "big city" without getting too lost. The three of us sat around catching up and reliving old times. The stories took me back to a more peaceful and simple time in my life. Our biggest worries were getting in trouble with our parents. Beyond that, life was a breeze.

Of all the guys, it was Scotty who got into the most trouble as a kid. It just seemed that words flew out of his mouth without any sense of control. His vicious sense of honesty and fairness often left him in a sticky web of verbal matches with folks. Quite simply, trouble seemed to follow Scotty. I'd have to say that he was probably the best kid to ever get in the amount of trouble that he found; but a good kid he was.

————————

"So this girl has some hotshot putting a bucket over her head?" Scotty said with his strong coastal accent. He sat back into the beanbag chair and leaned his head against the sliding glass door, taking in the surroundings of a real life college apartment.

"Don't get the wrong idea. This guy comes across as really nice and morally upstanding. If Charlie or I even tried to convince Wendy or Jessica of anything different, there's no way they would believe us."

"So why worry about them? With all the girls on this campus I'm sure somebody will feel sorry for you again," Scotty said in his predictable joking way.

I crossed my arms and sat back in the chair, allowing the sub par joke to clear the air. "She's special. I know it's hard for someone like you to appreciate the fact that some people are just perfect for each other, but it's true. Wendy is the perfect girl for me. I don't care about anyone else; I don't want to talk about anyone else; I don't want to hear about anyone else. All I care about is Wendy, and I don't want her to get hurt by some guy who could care less about her feelings. She's too special for that to happen."

Scotty sat up and looked as if he were digesting what I had just said. He scratched his head in deep thought. A few moments passed by as we both sat silent.

"What do you mean 'someone like me'?" Scotty asked. "Charlie," Scotty screamed to the back of the apartment, "Chance is making fun of me. When you finish curling your hair, I'm ready to go."

"Are you going to change?" Charlie screamed back from the bathroom.

"Change? I've got my dress clothes on. You boys are just jealous that you can't look this good."

Scotty stood up and pressed his pants and shirt with his hands. From the time we were kids, Scotty wore the old styled straight-legged Wranglers with boots. And although this was perfect for back home, it was far from the fashion at Chapel Hill. Regardless, Charlie and I knew that we couldn't ask him to change because of other people. That simply would not make sense to Scotty. Accept him as he was – there was no other option.

Charlie walked out of the bathroom with khaki pants and a light sweater on. Scotty looked up from pressing his pants and gave Charlie a look over. "Whoa, Robinson, I didn't know we were going to a funeral."

Charlie laughed as he slowly shook his head. "We may be if you irritate some of those baseball boys tonight."

Charlie loved Scotty in all his imperfections. We both did. And, as always, we accepted him as he was.

"Watch out, college ladies, here comes Scotty Foreman," Scotty roared as he led the way out the door.

Charlie looked over at me and rolled his shoulders. I couldn't help but laugh as Scotty walked bow-legged through the parking lot. It was looking like an interesting night already.

Charter 11

Wendy lived with three other sorority sisters in a small two-bedroom apartment, which sat only twenty feet away from the large main house. Each year, the new president took over the hut and picked three of her closest friends to join her. That year the president was none other than Suzie Parlor.

It was somewhat of a mystery to the sisters as to how Suzie achieved this honor when no one seemed to remember voting for her. It became apparent however, that the same money-driven power that provided her father's re-election in Georgia also had a lot to do with her appointment as sorority president. *Could he have bought the votes from the state officers?* The sisters tossed this question around often, but no one cared enough to investigate any further. The questions, however, became significantly less mysterious when Tammy Bogart, the North Carolina officer who tallied the final votes, arrived at the first statewide meeting in a new Hummer. Coincidence or not, Senator Parlor happened to own the largest Hummer dealership in Georgia.

Regardless of how this most unlikely of candidates became the head of household, she was official and therefore had to pick from over one hundred sisters, of which none could be defined as her friends, to become her new roommates. And since Jessica was the closest to tolerating Suzie's intolerance of the average folk, she happily accepted when the offer came her way. Jessica's closest friends were Wendy and Dana Watson, who completed the inhabitants of the president's sorority hut.

There had been no rain for weeks in Chapel Hill, leaving the ground and fallen foliage desiccated and wilted. As we walked along the declining gravel driveway that led to Wendy's house, the crackling of leaves dominated the conversation, which had been minimal to begin with. The streetlights flickered along the path, providing only enough light to reveal the leaves somersaulting across the desolate road. Scotty shuttered with each gust of wind and let out a repetitive "brr" as he shoved his hands farther into his jacket. The clicking of his boots only added to my anxiety, which was enough to bring on a headache. I found it amazing that in only a few short days I had gone from someone who felt completely comfortable around Wendy, to a level of nervousness that would rival the most insecure of schoolboys asking for their first date.

Why was I feeling so funny inside?

My question was quickly answered when I noticed the oversized SUV parked at the front of Wendy's door. The dozens of other vehicles parked around it were dwarfed by its intimidating size. Any possibility of it not being Jack's truck was erased when I saw the Carolina Baseball sticker plastered to the back windshield.

I stopped at the midway point of the rocky slope and stared at the white albatross that occupied two parking spots. The wind picked up again and shot a leaf across Charlie's face.

"What's the hold up, Chance?" Charlie said, clearing his face of any possible debris.

"Yeah, let's hurry it up, I'm freezing," Scotty joined in.

"Maybe I shouldn't even bother. I mean, how early do you think Jack got here to steal the front door parking space?" I said with a defeated tone. "I just don't feel good about this. Maybe I should just make this whole thing easier and go back home. I can call her and tell her I'm not feeling well, which is actually very truthful at this point."

"I'm not going to let you do that, Chance. There's only one way to know for sure and that's for us to go in there and simply be ourselves."

Scotty let a belch out. "Yeah, you tell him Charlie."

"That didn't include you," Charlie quickly corrected himself before turning his attention back to me. "You may regret not going in there for the rest of your life. What if Wendy decides that you don't care for her as much as Jack does?"

"I believe the truth will show itself eventually," I responded.

"Well, don't you think you should be standing around when it does?" Scotty surprised us both with his rhetorical question.

I looked down the hill at the parking lot full of cars. A sickening feeling continued to grow deep in my bowels as I fixed my eyes on Jack's SUV parked right next to Wendy's car. "Let's do this."

———————————

Jessica greeted us at the door and gave Charlie a kiss on the cheek.

"I prefer mine on the lips," Scotty said, closing his eyes and puckering out his chap lips.

"Jess, this is Scotty Foreman. He grew up with Chance and me back home."

Jessica hesitated for a second as she looked over Scotty's wranglers and boots. "Maybe I'll just shake your hand instead," she finally let out.

"You'll be kicking yourself later," Scotty replied, ignoring Jessica's displeasure with his substandard humor.

"I'll take my chances." Jessica finally broke a smile.

My anxiety hit a new level when I peered into the small dwelling and saw people squeezed in every possible cavity of the house. The congestion made it necessary to raise our arms in an effort to maneuver through the ocean of students with more efficiency.

Scotty was beside himself with enthusiasm. "Sweet mother of Elvis, there's more people stuffed in this little place than our entire town."

"Just keep moving, Scotty. I need to use that bathroom straight ahead," Charlie directed.

We squeezed ourselves into the line of people that traveled along the far wall of the house. Through the crops of hair I caught an occasional glimpse of Wendy greeting her guests, receiving their gifts with her intoxicating smile. She always reminded me of a beautiful picture when she smiled, a masterpiece that any of the great artists would love to capture with their mixed oils. But this picture quickly changed; a few bystanders moved their positions, leaving a clearer pathway to see Wendy sitting on her footstool, and Jack kneeling beside her like a prince comforting his princess.

"There she is, guys," I managed to choke out as a flush of nausea and chills consumed my body.

"Sweet mother of...," Scotty paused to think about who would fill in the sentence this time, "whoever. She's awesome!"

"Thanks, I think."

"How'd you get a babe like that to talk to you?" Scotty asked with more honesty than I cared for.

I stared over at her, amazed by her beauty, completely jealous that Jack was at her side and not me. For a moment I gave up on ever holding the key to her love again. I faltered and flapped wildly in my mind, only to tire and drift to the depths of utter defeat. Jack was in control, and there wasn't much I could do about it.

Scotty gave Charlie a slight elbow in an effort to encourage his bladder a little more. "You know, Charlie," Scotty took a serious tone, "I don't know who dresses prettier, you or that guy beside her."

Charlie quickly forgot about his urinary urges and focused on Scotty. "Pretty? A guy? I think you've been in Chapel Hill too long," Charlie said.

"No, seriously, I've never seen a guy dress so pretty. He almost makes me look average – almost."

"That's my buddy Jack," I added.

"No, can't be. He looks like a nice enough fellow," Scotty replied. "Could use my help with picking out a wardrobe, but not everyone can look like me."

"God never gives us more than we can handle," Charlie said under his breath.

The bathroom door suddenly opened and Charlie moved in quickly, but not before Scotty slid in with him.

"What are you doing?" Charlie said as he squeezed his knees together.

"I'm not staying out there with those people," Scotty answered.

Charlie's eyebrows followed his eyes in a pose of confusion. "You're not doing what? Get out of here, you weirdo, I'm going to pee on myself."

"Nope."

"Chance is out there; he'll hold your hand."

"Nope. He's going to leave me by myself and go over there with Wendy."

Charlie was speechless. He turned his back to Scotty and began to carry on with his business.

"Just pretend like I'm not here."

Charlie rolled his eyes. Nothing happened.

"Here, let me help you out," Scotty said as he turned the water on.

"I don't need help, you goofball. Wait until I tell everyone about this."

Scotty ignored Charlie's comment and began looking through the medicine cabinet. "Wow, there's some cool stuff in here."

Charlie looked up at the ceiling in disbelief, still unable to empty his aching bladder. "Stop looking through their stuff, man. What's wrong with you?"

Charlie was finally able to complete his business between Scotty's steady chatter. Scotty grabbed a bottle off the top shelf in the cabinet. "What's Ka, ka – nep – kip," he asked, struggling to pronounce the word on the bottle.

"It's nothing. It's just for constipation," Charlie answered with boiling agitation.

Scotty tossed the bottle up a few times. "I tell you what - I certainly don't need any of this stuff. I go at least…"

"That's nice. I'm happy for you," Charlie interrupted Scotty before he could finish.

"But my dad uses it - a lot. Mom's cheese biscuits just kill him."

Charlie pushed Scotty aside and began washing his hands. "Tell him to put two tablespoons in his coffee. Make sure it's very hot. It irritates the intestines and causes a very quick and efficient movement."

Scotty looked confused for a second and then smiled as he nodded his head and began laughing. "Gotcha, Charlie. It'll cause diarrhea, right?"

"Yes, tell him to use it sparingly."

Scotty patted Charlie on the back. "It's good to see all these years of medical school are paying off. Dad will be very proud of you."

Charlie hesitated before he opened the door, knowing it wouldn't look good when he and Scotty came marching out of the small bathroom together. After a deep breath Charlie quickly opened the door and walked out, trying not to acknowledge the long line that had grown by twenty people during his visit. Scotty appeared behind Charlie and stopped at the entrance of the door. The next guy in line quickly backed away from the door as he analyzed the situation.

Scotty gave him a friendly nod. "Goes a lot faster when you go two at a time. Just make sure you wash the sink out, if you don't get the toilet."

"Geez, Scotty, come on. You're embarrassing me. Let's go find Chance."

"Told you he was going to leave me."

───────────

I was around the corner saying hello to the faces I recognized when Charlie and Scotty came up behind me. Charlie placed his arm around my neck. "Okay, buddy, let's look like we belong here. I'm going to find Jessica again. I'll be over to help you out in a few minutes."

I took a deep breath and blew out the butterflies that had harbored in my gut. "What are you going to do, Scotty?" I asked.

"I guess I'll hang with you. I've seen enough of Charlie for a while."

As Scotty and I made our way through the congested room, Wendy saw us and stood up in anticipation. Jack also took the liberty of standing as a big brother smile ran across his face. When we finally reached her, Wendy gave me a big hug, which lasted a lot longer than I expected.

"It's so good to see you, stranger," Wendy whispered in my ear.

"The feeling's mutual," I whispered back.

"I'm Scotty Foreman." Scotty took the liberty of introducing himself to Jack since Wendy was temporarily occupied with me.

"Hey, Scott, great to meet you," Jack replied with his fabricated gallantry.

While Wendy and I continued to catch up, Jack proceeded in his fake interest of Scotty. His voice was remarkably congenial, but the ferocity in his eyes could not be concealed as he peered at me talking close into Wendy's ear. His appetite for control made him progressively venal, to the edge of explosion. During the moments that my eyes would meet his, a coldness traveled through the layers of my spine, leaving me somewhat dazed by his wickedness. *How could a guy be so evil and fool so many people?* The thought kept racing through my head. I wondered if Hitler ever courted.

"So Scott," Jack began to coax himself into a shortened name relationship with Scotty, "how long have you been friends with my buddy Chance?"

"Ever since the doctor slapped us on the rumps," Scotty replied.

Jack couldn't help but giggle at Scotty's slang vernacular. "I take it that means all your life."

"Yep, I've known Chance and Charlie ever since we were tapping toes in the crib."

"That's really nice. I'm sure you guys have built a strong relationship."

At this point Scotty was losing interest in the small talk and began to study the people around the room. Jack noticed his diversion. "So, Scott, do you like baseball? Maybe you've heard of me."

———————————

"I didn't know how much I missed you until I saw that sweet smile walking to me." Wendy continued to whisper in my ear.

"That sounds so good. I've been afraid that Jack was stealing you away."

"Jack's a nice guy, too. I have to admit that it's been confusing."

"So you do have feelings for him?" I felt the despair begin to feel my chest.

"I just don't know what I feel. I know it sounds weak, but I have feelings for both of you. And it's even worse living around so many voices that have fallen for Jack's gentleness and confidence."

"Gentleness," I repeated without going any farther.

I took in a deep breath, trying to focus my scrambled thoughts. My head began to spin. I looked around the room, filled with Jack's friends and the girls from the sorority who were smitten by their presence. I looked back at Scotty as he demonstrated to Jack and his friends how to catch clams with your feet. Every time Scotty put his head down to demonstrate the sliding of his feet - which was how he caught thousands of clams - the guys would elbow each other and mock his jovial innocence.

"Chance, are you okay?" I heard Wendy's voice enter my temporary solitude.

"Yeah, I'm fine. Look, I think we're just going to get out of here. This is just a little too uncomfortable for me."

Wendy's eyes began to moisten. "Chance, please don't be mad at me. I've been so afraid of letting you down. You mean so much to me. I love our time together. These feelings are just horrible. I just need some time to figure things out. Please understand."

I looked up and made eye contact with Wendy. "I do understand. There are just some things about Jack that I don't like. I think he's playing games with you."

"Oh, Chance, he's been nothing but nice to me. He's really a good guy. The only thing we do is study together. I have gone to a couple of classes for him, but that's all."

Wendy was not a weak person. She was only being honest. And who wouldn't be flattered to have the most eligible bachelor at the university after her? At least Wendy was being candid about it.

I didn't want to upset Wendy any more than I already had, especially considering that it was her birthday. *How bad would I look if she started crying?*

Wendy's emotions were suddenly thwarted by a girlfriend who pulled her over to wish a happy birthday to her. As they talked I felt a bump come from behind me.

"Excuse me," Jack said with politeness until he saw no one was listening. "I'm surprised you had the guts to show up here tonight."

"Well, surprise," I answered back.

Scotty walked up to me. "I've been showing Jack and his buddies how to catch clams. I think these boys could feed themselves if they were put in a good river."

"Yeah, thanks for wasting fifteen minutes of my life with that useless babble. And, by the way, the next time you come to one of my parties, don't wear those giddy-up cowboy pants. And lose those boots while you're at it."

Scotty's face turned red with anger. He puckered out his lips as his pupils became dark and telescoped. "Why you...if you ever do go clamming I hope a flounder bites your..."

"This is not your party, Jack, it's Wendy's; so why don't you at least give her the courtesy of not being yourself for a while," I responded, cutting Scotty off.

"Let me correct you, clam boys. Any party Jack Armstrong goes to is his party." Jack stuck his fingers in both of our chests as he said, "Don't forget that."

Jack walked off, but not before placing his hand on the small of Wendy's back and whispering in her ear. He looked back at us and gave a sinister grin.

"I can't believe that guy. There I was thinking you and Charlie were off your rockers about him, and then he turns into the poltergeist," Scotty said, still in shock at what just took place.

"I told you he was unbelievable."

"Everyone gather around, and bring your gifts. It's time to honor the birthday girl." Jack's voice suddenly became calm and gentle as he spoke out over the chatter.

"Oh great, they're going to want me to give my gift to Wendy in front of everyone," I said to Scotty.

Without time or warning Jack said, "Where's our friend Chance hiding?" He acted like he didn't know where I was even though he had been watching me since he left.

"This guy is unreal," Charlie said as he pushed his way to us.

"You don't even know," Scotty replied. "I think we may be witnessing the anti-Christ."

Wendy made her way to the front on Jack's directions and sat in the chair he had pulled up for her. Everyone who knew me, which wasn't many, turned to let me go through. I tried to swallow the progressive lump in my throat as I stepped up in front of everyone. Wendy gazed at me and smiled. I took a deep breath before reaching in my pocket and pulling out the small box.

"Well, Wendy, I didn't plan on doing this in front of all these people, but here it goes." I handed the box to Wendy. "I hope it reminds you of a time that is as special in your heart as it is in mine."

Wendy's eyes glistened with tears as she opened the box and pulled out the replica of Cape Lookout lighthouse. Wendy's smile broadened as she held it tight against her chest and said, "It is special. Thank you, Chance."

Jack's voice suddenly cut us off, "Okay, nice gift, Chance. Who's next?"

Before Wendy could finish thanking me another gift was thrust upon her. She continued to smile at me and mouthed the words, "I'll never forget." Jack didn't miss a thing; the fury raged in his eyes when I smiled at him.

For the next half hour Jack acted as the host of the party, handing gifts to Wendy and placing them in a pile beside her after she finished thanking the givers. I couldn't help but notice that Wendy kept uncovering the lighthouse that Jack would smoother with wrapping paper and ribbons after each gift.

"Somebody needs to teach this guy a lesson," Scotty said, still fuming from the exchange with Jack.

"Just let it go, Scotty, he's not worth the trouble. Besides, his true colors will come out soon enough. He can't play this charade forever."

"I wonder about that," I said.

"Is that everybody?" Jack asked as he surveyed the room. "Okay, now I have a little something I would like to give the birthday girl." Jack looked to the back of the room and one of his friends brought a shoebox to him. "Wendy, it's been really nice getting to know you the last couple of weeks. And, well, I just wanted to say thank you for helping me out with my classes and..." Jack put his head down trying to look somewhat uncomfortable and shy, "and, I just think you're a really special girl. Thank you."

Jack carefully handed Wendy the box and pulled the top off. A cute little kitten popped his sleepy head up and let out a half-hearted cry. The room moaned with approval as Wendy picked up the little guy and melted him into her chest.

"I hope you like him," Jack said.

"He's adorable," Wendy replied. She stroked him a few times before squeezing him onto her shoulder. "Oh, how cute, he's got a little collar on."

Wendy took a closer look at the collar and froze at the sight. She suddenly became quiet as she placed the kitten back on her lap. Jack looked back at me and winked. Wendy spread the fur away from the baby kitten's neck and began searching for a way to remove it.

"Oh my," Wendy managed to let out. And with that she held up a sparkling diamond tennis bracelet. Everybody began squeezing in to take a closer look as Wendy placed the resplendent bracelet around her wrist.

"It's beautiful Jack. I don't know what to say," Wendy said, continuing to stare at the gleaming diamonds.

"No need to say anything. You deserve it." And with that he leaned over and kissed her on the forehead.

As everyone continued to rush in to see the beautiful bracelet, Charlie, Scotty, and I were left standing like an isolated island. Jack stood up on his toes to see over the crowd. When he found us he mouthed, "Maybe you should leave now – losers."

Scotty blew him a kiss. "This guy is out of control."

"I think he's right," I replied.

Charlie put his arm around me. "I know it doesn't look good, but remember it's in God's hands."

"This guy may have God fooled, too," I said.

"I assure you he doesn't. Hang in there. If Wendy's worth having she'll be there in the end."

"It doesn't look good," Scotty said with his unrelenting honesty. "I'll be back in a few minutes."

"Where are you going?" Charlie asked curiously. "I thought you were scared to walk around by yourself?"

"I'm becoming a big boy," Scotty said with a smile.

Chapter 12

Scotty had been gone for over ten minutes when Jack made his way over to us.

"Didn't know what you were up against, eh, Chance?"

"Guess not," I replied.

"And Robbins, just so you know, if I wanted your girl," Jack mustered up his lips before finishing, "wouldn't be a problem."

"And Jack, just so you know, if my girl wanted you, I'd have her committed."

"Thanks a lot, Charlie," I said feeling the hits from every direction.

"Where's the cowboy at?" Jack asked.

Before we could answer Scotty came walking out of the kitchen wearing a towel around his waist and carrying a tray with four cups on it.

"What in the world is he doing?" I asked.

Charlie let out a noise that was part huff and part laugh. "I think I know. We can't let him serve that coffee."

"How do you know it's coffee?"

Charlie began making his way to Scotty when Jack placed his hand on his chest and said, "Hold it, Robbins. I'm running this party. If your cowboy friend wants to serve coffee, I'll decide if it's okay or not." Jack squeezed his chin with his hand and focused his eyes upward, as if thinking over the pros and cons. "Hmm, you said he couldn't, so I think I'll say that he can." Jack let out an evil laugh and quickly walked over to Scotty.

I looked over at Charlie. "What's going on?"

"I tried to stop him," Charlie said, shrugging his shoulders.

———————

Jack made his way to Wendy and Scotty. "Hey, buddy, what do you have there?"

Scotty smiled and said, "Oh, I just made a few cups of coffee for my new friends."

Jack placed his arm on Scotty's shoulder and looked down at the cups. "Is one of those for me?"

"Certainly it is, like I said, for my new friends."

Scotty handed Jack the yellow mug and then proceeded to pass the other two to Wendy and Jessica. He then lifted up his cup in a toast. "To a very," he paused for a moment in thought. Jack put his head down in an effort not to laugh. Scotty's eyes twinkled as a toast entered his head, "To a very moving evening."

Jack smirked and then quickly played it off as a cough when Wendy looked at him. "Yes, my friend Scott, to a very moving evening," Jack repeated.

"Thank you, Scotty, you are so sweet. Are all the boys like you back home?" Wendy asked.

Scotty took a sip from his cup. "Some sweeter than others," he said and then gave a nod to Charlie and me as we watched from across the room.

———————

"Maybe I should fill you in, Chance," Charlie said as he nodded back to Scotty.

"I made the mistake of telling Scotty about some laxatives in the bathroom. When you mix them with hot liquid, especially caffeine, it makes them, well, very strong."

"You're kidding me," I replied.

"Wouldn't do it."

Scotty came scooting across the room with a mischievous smile plastered to his face. "Hated to do it, guys, but the guy made fun of my boots. He shouldn't have done that."

We both stared blankly at Scotty. He tried to avoid looking us in the eyes. "He also gave Chance's girl a kitten." Scotty took another sip from his coffee. "Shouldn't have done that either."

Charlie and I continued to glare at Scotty. He did his best to avoid eye contact.

"Eye for an eye, right?"

"Turn the other cheek," Charlie responded. Jack began making his way back over to us.

"Somebody's gonna be turning some cheeks shortly," Scotty said. "How long does it take for that stuff to kick in?"

"Not long," Charlie answered.

Jack stopped suddenly. His eyes grew large and his hand went limp, causing some of the coffee to spill on the floor. He gasped and placed his cup in a stranger's hand beside him. The crowd had thinned out some, but there were still fifty or sixty folks standing around. He placed his hands on his stomach and then surrendered one to grasp his backside.

"This stuff is going to help my dad so much," Scotty said. Charlie and I glared back at Scotty. "Science uses rats all the time to do research," Scotty said blowing us off.

Jack stumbled with a strangely familiar gait that we had all experienced at some point in our lives. His head turned and focused on the bathroom nearby. With the concentration of a surgeon during a delicate procedure, he began to walk, one step at a time, towards the bathroom.

"Gotta go," Scotty said as he flew away from us. Before we could stop him he made his way over to Jack and smacked him solidly on the back.

"Hey, buddy," Scotty said as he landed the friendly, yet firm pat to Jack's fragile back. Jack's body gyrated and his knees buckled under the pressure; a mortifying noise filled the room.

"Whoa," Scotty said as everyone's attention turned to where the high-pitched explosion emerged.

"I'll be quick, I promise," Scotty said. And with that, he scurried into the bathroom and locked the door just before Jack could reach the handle.

With sweat pouring down his forehead, Jack squeezed his stomach harder and leaned back against the wall outside the door. As everyone watched, his true colors finally escaped his dying escapade.

"Get out, you idiot. I swear I'll kick your butt when you get out," Jack screamed as he plastered his face against the door.

"It's just going to take longer if you make me anxious," Scotty's sarcastic voice came muffling from behind the door.

"You redneck cowboy!" Jack bellowed. "Get out now. You don't know who you're dealing with."

"Sure I do. Jack Armstrong, the guy who uses girls to do his homework so he can do more important things, like make fun of people."

"I'll make fun of anyone I please. You're finished, you back-woods punk. I mean it."

"Almost finished, but not quite yet," Scotty replied.

Another horrifying grunt jolted Jack back against the wall. The commotion drew a large crowd around the bathroom door. Wendy stood speechless at the monster that materialized before her eyes.

Jack turned around and screamed at the crowd of people surrounding him. "What are you people looking at?" He kicked at the crowd and then slid down the wall and onto the floor. The crowd shuffled in to take a closer look. Another revolting noise ripped from Jack's quivering body and a rotten smell washed over the stale room. The crowd groaned in unison and abruptly dispersed away from the fallen hero.

Scotty's muffled voice again echoed from the bathroom, "That wasn't me."

The night was officially over, and so was the reign of the great Jack Armstrong.

Chapter 13

I had no more trouble with Jack Armstrong after that night. In those few moments, catalyzed by Scotty's actions, Jack relinquished the sway that had so many people under his mesmerizing influence. He suddenly appeared less attractive as his fabricated smile was replaced with his more natural irascible smirk. Jack Armstrong's windows were finally opened for everyone to see through.

Before Scotty could escape the small house that felt more like an epic battlefield, he was greeted by dozens of handshakes and approving nods from the baseball players and other athletes. He had accomplished what all of them had wanted to do, but were unable to, in the spirit of team unity.

When we reached the front door, Wendy, Jessica and a few other sisters were standing there, giving their goodbyes and well wishes to those that were exiting. Scotty stopped in the doorway. He looked back at Wendy and said, "I'm sorry I messed up your party. I guess you won't be inviting me to any of your birthdays in the future."

Wendy smiled. "After tonight I'm not sure it would be a party without you. And there's nothing to be sorry about; in fact, I need to thank you."

Scotty nodded his head at the other girls and said, "Goodnight, ladies. It was a pleasure meeting you."

"Wait," Jessica spoke up. She walked up to Scotty and gave him an enraged look. Scotty froze, anticipating a barrage of nettled words. "There's one more thing." She leaned up and gave Scotty a kiss on the cheek. "Just didn't want to regret missing my chance."

Scotty beamed as his cheeks turned red for the first time in his life. As he walked out the door and down the steps he said, "That's right. You boys need to stop worrying about Jack Armstrong and start worrying about Scotty Foreman."

––––––––––––––

From that night forward Wendy and I were inseparable. We began a ritual each evening of walking through the campus together, holding hands and telling each other about our day. We'd dream about our future after graduation and the goals that we would someday reach together. And with each day and each new dream, I found myself falling farther in love with her. Those days were magical for us both.

As the year came to an end, I found that the crowning dream of my life was Wendy Summers. Her radiance never dulled. Unlike the entropies of life, she only became better, more appealing, and more loved.

Wendy began to hint about the decisions we would make in the coming months that would complete our college years. Where should we look for jobs? Should we look in the same cities? Would we just try to remain within a few hours of each other? How much would we see each other with real jobs to deal with? What would the future hold for us?

––––––––––––––

On spring break of the last semester we would have as college students, I packed up the jeep and headed home to Morehead City with the rest of my life lumped in my throat, eager and nervous to release it. I had called Charlie and he would have everything ready - and then some.

It was later that sunny, yet cool, afternoon that Wendy and I walked down the road to the dock where she was first introduced to crab catching. The late sun was going through its typical color mutations from yellow to orange, and as we walked to the end of the rickety old dock, it began to bleed pink around the clouds that covered it.

Wendy's beauty always amazed me, but on that defining day, against God's most beautiful backdrop, she seemed to shine. All of our struggles seemed far behind us, and only our future remained.

At the end of the dock I stood behind Wendy and placed my arms around her. Holding her close seemed to take the slight chill out of the calm, quiet air. The usual business of the coastal wildlife had not yet arrived for the season, but I knew that as we stood there a northern journey of birds, ducks and shellfish was making its way to us. Those peaceful noises would soon awaken us in the morning, and rock us to sleep in the evenings.

Wendy placed her head back and nestled it on my shoulder. I felt her deep breath of contentment before she whispered, "I love you, Chance."

Those words had become more frequent over the past few months and I easily repeated them back to her. "I love you, too, Wendy. Isn't this just perfect?"

"Yes," Wendy said as she tried to cozy up even closer to me. "I wished I could stay in this moment forever."

"That would be nice, but you know what seagulls do to statues."

My joke was missed and I was glad it was. Wendy wrapped her arms around me and kissed me on the cheek.

I squeezed her tight and stood there in silence, listening to the perfect repetitions of the breaking waves.

"Do you know what scares me the most?" Wendy broke the silence with her question. "It scares me to think about my life without you in it. I think about last year and how close I came to losing you. I hate thinking about those days."

"Then don't think about them. They're over. But you know what? I think it made us closer to go through all that."

"Really," Wendy said, pulling away slightly and looking up at me. "Do you really feel that way, Chance?"

"I do."

"I don't want to ever be without you again. You're perfect for me." Wendy again laid her head upon my chest and allowed her arms to hang limp as I held her tighter. "I just hope you feel the same about me."

I kissed Wendy on the top of her head, taking a second to smell the sweetness of her aroma. I always loved the way she smelled.

A few feet away I spotted a string hanging off the edge of the dock. "Looks like someone has been crabbing up here," I said, changing the subject. "Wendy, how much do you trust me?"

"With all my heart Chance. Why do you ask?"

"I'm thinking there might be a crab on the end of that string. Can you see it moving?"

Wendy stared down at the string for a second before saying, "Chance, you know how those things scare me. Remember last time?"

I laughed. "How could I forget?" I grabbed Wendy's hand and led her to the string. "The crabs are beautiful this time of year, when you can find one."

"I'm not sure how you can say crab and beautiful in the same sentence," Wendy responded.

I grabbed a net off the end of the dock and walked back over to where Wendy was standing. "Will you trust me, Wendy?"

"I don't know Chance."

"I promise you, it will be worth it. Their shells sparkle in the early spring; it's amazing," I said, continuing my coaxing.

"Okay, but promise me this is the last time I have to pull a crab out of the water."

"I promise – last time."

I coached Wendy on how to pull the string up slowly. "An inch at a time," I said. And as Wendy sat on the edge of the dock I lay beside her with the net cast just over the water. "When did you know that you loved me?"

"Oh wow," Wendy said as she continued to concentrate on the slow moving string. "I'd have to say that I knew I didn't want to ever live without you on the night of my birthday party. That was when I knew how nasty boys could be and how wonderful you were. I'm sure I loved you before that, but that was when I knew how deeply I loved you. How about you? When did you know?"

"I've fallen in love with you a hundred and ninety-three times."

"What?"

"Every day since I first heard you talk I've loved you. But each day I see you, I feel like I'm falling in love again. Just when I think my heart won't beat fast when I see you, or that my hands won't sweat, they do. Each day it gets stronger."

Wendy smiled and leaned down to kiss me. I stopped her from moving any further. "Hold on, you're almost to the surface."

As she closed both eyes and continued lifting I suddenly sat back up and threw the net behind us on the dock. Wendy opened her eyes, confused by my sudden movement.

"What's wrong? Did I drop it?" she asked.

"Nothing, it's just an old box on the end of it," I replied in an agitated voice.

"How did a box get on...," Wendy became suddenly quiet and lifted the covered box onto the dock and began removing the plastic wrapped around it. As she began opening the small black box I shifted onto my knee and faced Wendy. Inside the box was a diamond ring I had bought one month earlier. Tears began to stream down Wendy's face as we faced each other, both on our knees. Wendy leaned forward and hugged me. "I think you're supposed to stand up," I whispered.

"I've spent 193 days falling deeper in love with you, and, today, I know with all my heart, that I want to spend the rest of my life doing this – loving you."

I gently took the box out of Wendy's hand and removed the sparkling platinum band. And, with her hand in mine, I asked the question I had practiced a thousand times in front of the mirror: "Wendy Summers, will you marry me?"

"Yes. Yes, of course I will," Wendy sobbed. "You've made me the happiest girl to ever crab off a dock."

As we stood on that historic spot holding each other, fireworks began shooting off from the far end of the dock and along the shoreline. The initial fright of the noise quickly changed to laughter as we held hands and watched the raining explosions of lights fall from the sky. With each blast we laughed harder.

"I can't believe you did all this," Wendy said as she again wrapped her arms around me.

"I didn't," I replied. "There's only one person I know that's cheesy enough to do all this."

From behind us I could see the bushes rustle as Charlie crawled away. Just before he got to the road he lifted his arm out from the brush and gave a thumbs-up.

Chapter 14

It was only four months later, after a flurry of planning, that Wendy and I walked into the Calvary Chapel to become Mr. and Mrs. Gordon. Having the ceremony so soon – only a week after our graduation - allowed all of our friends to partake in one last celebration before beginning our busy lives.

Gramps made the trip to Chapel Hill to give us our vows. The chapel was quite a change from his tiny church back home with the creaking wooden floors that announced each person's arrival. Gramps was completely at ease as he talked to the congregation about the beauty of the chapel and compared it to the little church he had spent his life in.

Everyone immediately fell in love with the old man, looking so physically feeble, but sounding so strong. His laugh alone was enough to make the entire gathering laugh with him; Gramps was always a hit. Everything went off without a hitch until he got to the part of the vows that said, "till death do us part." Gramps missed his wife terribly, as did we, and even after twelve years the pain still silenced him at times. But he made it through the remainder of the service and sent Wendy and me off as husband and wife.

Dad and Mr. Robbins were on their best behavior at the reception, however, they did dance. Their addiction for embarrassment was simply too strong. But when we saw Wendy's mom pull Mr. Summers onto the dance floor and start copying Dad's moves, well, misery just really loves company. Mrs. Summers had a blast doing Mr. Robbins' Elvis dance and even did a pretty good chicken dance with Dad. Mr. Summers, a stern bank CEO, didn't look quite as pleased to be humiliating himself in front of so many strangers.

Before long, all the parents were out there dancing. Wendy's sorority sisters were horrified by the sight of their gawky parents losing all inhibitions and enjoying life for a few minutes. Wendy and I had never laughed so hard. Soon a line formed, and with Gramps leading the way, they traveled throughout the room picking up the younger folks. Wendy and I thanked God that we were able to sit at our table and watch the annihilation of our friends.

Words could not do justice to the happiness and contentment I felt at that moment, sitting with my new wife, as we watched our family and friends celebrate the joining of our lives.

Chapter 15

After the honeymoon, Wendy and I settled down in Kennesaw, Georgia, a suburb of Atlanta. Wendy began her job as a journalist for the *Atlanta Constitution*, while I landed a position with Delwood Tooling Company. We both quickly climbed the corporate ladder and soon found ourselves wrapped up in a new house and logging twelve-hour days. Although busy, we still found time to enjoy our new life together.

I guess it was my determination to become somebody that Wendy's parents and friends thought I couldn't be that eventually led to my downfall. I wanted to prove them all wrong. I may not have grown up with a silver spoon in my mouth, but I sure knew how to find one, and his name was Walter Clayton.

Clayton Industries was one of the nation's largest commercial builders, and by far, the biggest in the southeast. Three generations of Claytons had run the company, each holding steadfast to the 'good old boy' way of doing business. They poured millions of dollars into the few tooling companies that were lucky enough to earn their account. Getting them to bring Delwood into their world had proven a futile process, one which had long before been abandoned. Delwood, it seemed, was too fancy and did not meet the criteria for 'good old boy' ways of doing business.

I was hired to change that.

Nobody knew much about Walter Clayton, only that he came from Georgetown, South Carolina, and loved eating seafood. Over the years, many different people from Delwood had tried to schedule dinner with Mr. Clayton at the best seafood joints in Georgia. But the requests went unanswered. The only feedback from his secretary was, "Mr. Clayton is not interested."

The solution, however, was simple, and I was certainly the one to solve it. I knew the surest way to insult a true coastal native was to invite them to a seafood restaurant hundreds of miles from the ocean. When you grow up on the coast, seafood was either fresh or shipped off to inland restaurants. I quickly thought of an offer Mr. Clayton couldn't resist.

————————————

"Make sure you tell him they're salty," I reminded the secretary at Clayton Industries.

"Salty, you say."

"That's right, and I just caught them myself on Saturday." I had just returned from a weekend trip back home.

"And you're cooking them?"

"It's an oyster roast at my house. I'll be happy to pick him up."

"I'll get him the message."

I sat back and watched the clock. No more than three minutes had past when the phone rang.

"Yeah, this is Walter Clayton."

"Good morning, sir," I replied.

"Just how salty are these oysters?"

"You'll need a glass of sweetened tea between each one."

"Six o'clock?"

"Yes, sir."

"Send me a limo."

———————————

Within a month Delwood Tools signed its largest account in the history of the company, a seven digit deal with Clayton Industries.

———————————

Through hard work, long hours and schmoozing the right people, namely Mr. Walter Clayton, I became manager of the southeast district after only one year at Delwood. By all standards I was successful. My time had arrived and I took full advantage of it. Even though the hours were longer and travel was more frequent, Wendy and I were very comfortable. The only thing that seemed to bother her were the more frequent binges of drinking that came with entertaining customers. I, too, was unaccustomed to this lifestyle but found it necessary to succeed in the corporate world. I assured Wendy that everything was under control.

On my one year and six month anniversary at Delwood I received word that my boss, Mr. Farlow, wanted to see me in his office. Mr. Farlow never invited someone in his office unless there was something terribly wrong or terribly good to discuss. Even though I was the top producer in the company and the youngest to ever reach managerial status, I was nervous.

I walked into Mr. Farlow's office, which overlooked the skyline of Atlanta. He was turned around in his chair, staring out the window with his back towards me. "Have a seat, Mr. Gordon."

"Yes, sir."

Mr. Farlow spun around and placed his feet on the glassy oak desk between us while placing his hands behind his head. The wrinkles of his forehead seemed to travel to the apex of his bald scalp. After a slow, deep breath he said, "You're 24 years old. You've climbed the ladder faster than anyone in the company's history. That's pretty impressive for a young man like you."

"Thank you, sir. I believe it was just your good coaching," I replied.

"Don't patronize me, son. You've kissed your share of butt; you can stop puckering up every time I pass by you."

"Sorry, sir. I'm obliged to never kiss anyone's butt again."

Mr. Farlow chuckled at the remark. "Faster than anyone in our history. Do you know what that means, son?"

"I'm not sure I do, sir."

"That means you've climbed faster than even me. How do you think that makes me feel?"

I swallowed hard before saying, "Proud?"

Mr. Farlow quickly sat up in his chair, leaned his chest forward on the desk and peered across at me. "That's right – proud. Because of your hard work, I can now relax a little and feel certain that things will be properly managed."

"Yes, sir, I assure you they will."

"I like you, Chance. I knew when I hired you that you would do well." Mr. Farlow stood from his chair and walked around the desk. I stood up when he made his way to where I was sitting.

"There's one more thing I need to say to you today, Mr. Gordon." Mr. Farlow's hand extended and firmly gripped mine. "Welcome to the six-digit club."

My body went numb with the words. I could no longer feel below my knees, but somehow they continued supporting me. "What are you saying, Mr. Farlow?" I asked rhetorically.

A smile rolled across his round head. "Your next paycheck will reflect the raise. We need to take care of our star performer. We'll keep you at one and a quarter for the next year, then bump you up to higher rates the year after. I suspect you'll be at a quarter of a mil in the next five years."

One hundred and twenty-five thousand dollars! I grew up believing that twenty thousand was a lot of money. "I'm not sure what to say, Mr. Farlow…thank you."

"Thank yourself, son. You've earned it."

———————

I rushed back to my office and called Wendy. My adrenaline was making my ears throb.

"Hello," Wendy answered the phone.

"Hey, sweety, it's me. If you don't like your job, quit. In fact quit today if you want. I need to tell you something wonderful. I got promoted. We're rich. We're going to celebrate tonight – maybe even tomorrow and tomorrow night…"

Wendy interrupted me with her laughter. "Slow down, Chance. I can't keep up. All I heard was the word 'rich.' What happened?"

I took a few deep breaths and tried to contain my energy. "Look, just put on your nice dress and I'll pick you up at 6:00. And don't eat any lunch. We're going to eat like the rich and famous tonight. And shave your legs. I love you."

Chapter 16

One month later...

"**W**hat's going on, baby? I got here as soon as I could." Wendy was waiting at the corner café where she had asked me to meet her. I noticed tears beginning to fill her eyes.

"I'm pregnant," she said before throwing her arms around me. Elation filled my body like a vacant house with floodwater. My chest tightened and the water began to spill from my eyes. We cried as we held each other, refusing to acknowledge the onlookers. We had reached the pinnacle of happiness, our completion of contentment. Life had shined upon us with a thousand suns.

I took the rest of the afternoon off and joined Wendy for some "preliminary shopping." Holding hands was something we never seemed to do enough of, but on that day we never let go. The anticipation was simply too much; if only our miracle could have arrived that same day.

We browsed through cribs, decors and monitors. No detail would be missed for our baby. It would have everything waiting for it. Two thousand dollars later,

Wendy and I left the store and headed home. The fact that we dropped that kind of money on preliminary shopping never concerned me. I would have gladly starved to provide for our child.

While Wendy went upstairs to take a nap, I decided to call home with the news.

"Hey, Mom, guess what I did today?"

Mom was unable to think of a response.

"I went shopping at the *Nursery Warehouse*."

Mom remained quiet, although I could almost hear the wheels turning in her head. "Chance, don't give your mother a heart attack, but why did you go shopping at the baby store?"

"Oh, you know, just wanted to get ready."

I could sense that Mom was doing her best not to get excited until she knew for sure. "Get ready for what? Are you and Wendy planning to start trying already?"

"There's no trying left."

Mom screamed. "Would you stop beating around the bush and just tell me. Is Wendy pregnant? Am I going to be a grandmother?"

"Do you prefer Granny, Grandma or Me-ma?"

Mom screamed again.

In the background I heard Dad yell out, "Who the heck are you talking to? Ed McMahon?"

Mom screamed back, "We're going to be grandparents."

I heard some commotion with the phone before Dad's voice came through. "Listen, Chance, first of all, nice job. Second, there are a few things you have to start doing today. Are you listening, son?"

I laughed at Dad's enthusiasm. "Yes Dad, I'm listening."

Wendy must sleep on the left side of the bed for the first two months, and every morning you need to massage the right side of her stomach."

"Dad, what are you talking about?"

"We want a little crabber - at least for the first one. I'll ask Chief Stanley how to make a girl for the next one."

"Dad, do you really believe he's a medicine man? He's not even a real Indian."

"He cured my indigestion with that powder he gave me."

"He's Latin, Dad, not Indian. You think everybody who is dark and old is Indian."

"Just try, Chance. Give an old man his wish, okay?"

"Okay Dad, I'll rub her left tummy every morning."

Dad screeched. "Right side, right side – pay attention son. You're killing me."

I laughed.

"Right tummy and left bed. Here's your mother."

Mom's sweet voice was a relief. "Chance, I'm just so proud of you. This baby will make you feel so complete, just the way you did us. I love you."

"I love you, too, Mom."

———————

I hung the phone up and went upstairs to check on Wendy. She was lying across the bed, sleeping like a baby herself. I quietly turned the fan on and crawled in beside her. Her shirt was rolled up just enough to expose the bottom of her tan belly. I placed my hand on it and prayed. She shifted when I touched her bare skin, so I helped her find a new position – on the left side of the bed.

Chapter 17

Week 20

Mr. Farlow slid a glass of brandy across the table before raising his glass in a toast. "I don't believe I've had a chance to properly congratulate you. What are you, half way there?"

"Around there," I said before downing the glass and enjoying the traveling burn through my chest.

"Big responsibilities," Farlow paused to also finish his glass, "being a father."

"I can't wait. Wendy and I have been as giddy as children waiting for the day."

"I just hope you continue the good work here. There's a lot of opportunity for a young man like you." Farlow eyed the bartender for another round.

"No more for me," I said.

"You still hanging in there with the Clayton account?"

"We're doing fine. I've been meeting with him once a week."

Farlow jiggled the ice in his glass. "That account means a lot to your baby, you know."

"I know."

"You keep Clayton happy and he'll see that kid through college one day."

I nodded my head. "He's been good for Wendy and me, at least in some ways. I don't know how much my liver appreciates him."

"That's part of the game - alcohol and gentlemen's clubs. You may have to sell your soul to the devil, but your bank account won't mind."

Farlow's words were sobering. Never could I have imagined myself selling out my values to earn a dollar. Yet there I was, working 70 hours a week, drinking large amounts of alcohol and hanging out in places that even the devil wouldn't go. It was all beginning to weigh on Wendy.

"Is the wife staying off your back?" Farlow asked.

"Pretty much, you know…"

"Giving you more headaches than the alcohol, isn't she? That's also part of the game."

"We're doing fine. She knows I work hard for our future."

Farlow downed another glass of brandy. "Son, haven't you learned yet? Don't kid a kidder. I know about wives. You learn a lot after the fourth one."

I looked down at my watch and felt a lump creep down my throat. "I've gotta run. I'm late for a meeting."

"Go on, I've got the bill," Farlow said while staring out the window.

"Thank you, sir."

I began walking toward the exit when Farlow's voice stopped me. "Remember, Chance. Take care of business first. Life will fit in fine afterwards. Keep Clayton happy and you'll be happy."

———————————

When I walked into the examination room ten minutes late, Dr. Morrison smiled brightly and shook my hand. Wendy's eyes weren't nearly as friendly.

"I was just reviewing with Wendy what changes were taking place," he said, bringing me up to speed. "As you well know by feeling it now, the baby is becoming more active. It's probably around 7 to 9 inches long, about half of its birth length."

"How much does it weigh?" Wendy asked, wondering how much of her weight gain was baby and how much was frozen pizzas.

"No more than a pound."

Wendy frowned playfully.

"The fetus can also make faces like that one." Wendy quickly changed to a smile. "Its ears are developed and it can actually recognize sounds now. And if it's a boy, it's starting to have changes we can soon see."

"We can tell what it is?"

"Soon."

I hugged Wendy, trying to picture the baby's thin shoulders covered with its pink skin. Wendy smelled the alcohol on my breath and gently pushed me away, hiding her displeasure from Dr. Morrison.

"I'll see you guys next time," Dr. Morrison said before also giving Wendy a hug.

"And I'll be on time," I added.

———————

As we walked through the parking lot to our cars, Wendy had a difficult time staying angry with me.

"I can't believe you showed up late again smelling like alcohol."

"I'm sorry, Wendy, I was having a meeting with my boss. I couldn't help it."

"You're sounding like a broken record, Chance."

I grabbed Wendy's arm and faced her to me. "I'm really sorry. Please don't let my stupidity ruin this wonderful day." Wendy looked down at the pavement, doing her best to remain angry. "Remember, our baby can hear us."

Wendy wrapped her arms around me. "I'm so happy, Chance. My dream is half way here."

"It's my dream, too. I'll do better, I promise. I'm going to be the best dad ever."

Wendy kept her head snuggled against my shoulder. "I'm so happy," she whispered again.

Chapter 18

Week 37...

The smoke was thick in the *Cheesecake Restaurant*, which happened to be Mr. Clayton's favorite place to eat in the upscale Buckhead community of Atlanta. I found it hard to believe that I was buying him dinner when he was the multi-millionaire, but that's business. My throat burned as I siphoned down the last few ounces of my rum and coke. The time was getting late and Mr. Clayton showed no signs of slowing down.

I pushed my chair away from the table and stretched my arms over my head. "I need to make a phone call," I said as I stood and looked through the fog-like smoke. "Maybe I'll take care of the check while I'm up."

"No need to hurry, Buddy, I've got a couple more left in me," Mr. Clayton said in his rough and intoxicated voice. "You're not a sissy boy, are you? I like to put my money in men who can handle their sauce." A volcanic laugh erupted from Mr. Clayton who became more amused at himself as the night wore on.

I longed to be home with my wife. The only thing that kept me from screaming was imagining myself washing the smoke out of my hair and lying next to Wendy, feeling those restless kicks inside her. I loved those times with her. The anticipation grew stronger each day.

Wendy picked up on the fourth ring. Knowing she would be upset I tried to act nonchalant. "Hey, baby, what took you so long? Is everything okay?" I heard the gush of breath as Wendy did her best to conceal her agitation.

"I'm fine. When will you be home?"

"I'm sorry. This guy will not let me go. If he wasn't such a big account, I'd leave him right now."

"Chance, it's eight o'clock. What if I go into labor tonight? And are you drinking again? Please tell me you're not drinking...again."

"Wendy, I've had a few, but I promise I'm okay. Really, you know I don't like doing this."

"Sometimes I wonder."

I sighed deeply, knowing Wendy was right. Maybe the money wasn't worth it.

"I guess this perfect job isn't so perfect." I waited for a reply as I poked at the alcohol induced numbness in my cheeks.

"Promise me that you'll change when the baby comes. I don't want it to know its daddy as the man who comes home late every night with alcohol on his breath."

"It won't, baby. You know I won't be like that. I'm going to be there."

Wendy became quiet for a few seconds. "I know you will, Chance. I know you'll be a wonderful dad."

I looked over at Mr. Clayton sitting at the table. His head bobbled around with a persistent smile glued to it. He noticed me looking and raised a fresh glass of Coke and rum up as he mouthed the word "yours." I didn't want the sound of my wife's voice to stop.

"Okay, baby, let me finish up with this guy and get home to you. I love you."

———————

It seemed much later than ten o'clock as I pulled slowly into the driveway of my house. What was once a hard rain was now just a drizzle that muddied up the driveway and stuck to me like a sweat soaked T-shirt. I decided against trying to maneuver the car into the close quarters of the garage, not sure if my slight dizziness was from smoke inhalation or the seven rum and Cokes I drank.

I sat in the car for a few more minutes chewing the life out of the last few pieces of gum that I had, hoping it would take the edge off the alcohol on my breath. It had gotten to the point that just the slight smell of alcohol on my breath would depress Wendy.

I was relieved as I opened the front door and saw no signs of activity in the living room. I looked upstairs and saw a strand of light escaping from the bottom of the bathroom door. A splash interrupted the silence in the house.

"Chance, is that you?"

"Hey baby, I'm gonna fix a snack and be right up."

I lost balance as I turned to make my way into the kitchen, knocking a picture frame to the floor. The adrenaline magnified my intoxication, causing my head to spin for a few seconds. I managed my way to the fridge and lunged at the freezer door. Inside was nothing but frozen vegetables and fish sticks that were as old as the house. I had planned to go grocery shopping the day before, but had been occupied with Mr. Clayton's account.

"Anything to soak up this alcohol," I mumbled to myself.

I filled a large pan with olive oil and began frying the frost-bit sticks. Placing my hands on the counter, I leaned my head down and rested my heavy eyes. The splatters of grease on my arms quickly brought me back to life and I briskly rubbed the burning oil off my forearms. There was no need for a plate; I forked the fried sticks one by one out of the pan and devoured them. The last one was stuck on the edge of the pan and remained partially frozen. I took a bite and threw it back into the smoking grease.

"Chance, can you please bring me a glass of water?" Wendy's voice again traveled down the stairway.

"I'll be right there."

Wendy was submerged in the tub of warm water. A candle flickered at the edge of the tub, shedding light on a discontinued book that had obviously lost out to the relaxation of humidity. I sat down on the edge of the tub and placed the glass beside me.

"Hey, Momma. I couldn't wait to get home to you," I said, keeping my distance.

"I can smell the alcohol on your breath, Chance. I can't believe you would drive home like that. What if you got pulled over?" Wendy said with disappointment filling her eyes.

"I'm fine, Wendy, please don't jump on my case first thing. It's been a long day already. I don't need you to make it longer." I stood up and looked through the fogged mirror. Wendy slid farther down into the bath water. All was quiet for a few awkward minutes.

The mirror showed the reflection of my red streaked eyes. Even my face had blotches of red that are typically reserved for veteran alcoholics. I didn't like what I saw in myself.

"I'm sorry, Wendy," I said as I walked away from the reflection and took my spot next to her on the tub's edge. "I'm sorry to put you through this. Never again – I promise."

I ran my fingers over Wendy's wet hair. She smiled and grabbed my hand.

"We just shook on it," she said.

We spent the next few minutes catching up on each other's day. The conversation continued along until Wendy noticed smoke rising from under the door.

"Chance, please tell me that's steam getting pushed back in here," Wendy said, quickly jumping out of the tub and placing a towel around her.

I moved swiftly towards the door, holding my breath until I was certain it was not smoke. As I reached out to grab the door handle, my hand sizzled and burned, sending an uncontrolled yelp from my mouth.

"Dear God, this can't be happening," I said as I cradled my hand. *The grease...did I leave it on?*

Smoke began to billow into the bathroom, slithering its way upward and into my hand-covered mouth. My lungs began to burn, causing a cough that seemed to release a dozen more. Wendy's eyes were filled with tears and horror. I knew I had to get her out before the air quality became any worse. She began to cough, prompting her to cover her mouth with a washrag.

I grabbed a rag and ran water over it before trying to open the door again. The rag hissed from the heat as a layer of flames shot through the small opening. More smoke poured in, causing a gag reflex as it burned into my chest. I managed to get the door closed but the fire was now raging out of control, engulfing the hallway around the bathroom, which was becoming nothing more than an oven with Wendy and me hopelessly trapped inside. The bathroom was fatally confined with one door and no windows. Flames began to push their way under the door and quickly spread up to the inside of it; the door began to glow with a bluish-orange hue.

The fire grew more vicious, causing my clothes to heat up like they were just taken out of a hot dryer. Wendy stood in the tub grasping at her towel with one hand and holding her stomach with the other. Tears were now flowing down her face and chest as she moaned in terror, unable to articulate with words. My eyes stung as the sweat from my forehead ran through them, causing me to squint as I searched furiously for some miracle to end the nightmare.

Under the sink I found an oxygen tank that Wendy's grandmother, who suffered terribly with emphysema, had left behind at her last visit. The smoke had become so dense that each half breath was followed by a series of coughs. My head was spinning from the lack of oxygen.

Wendy, meanwhile, was sitting on the edge of the tub rocking back and forth, her head down and arms crossed over her swollen stomach. She prayed a repetitive prayer: *God, please save my child.*

The lights flickered and died leaving only darkness and the hue of the hungry fire, which had spread to the ceiling and was now nearly complete in its effort to surround us. The heat was intolerable, causing my skin to turn red and dry. Wendy continued in her silence, her back moving up and down as she traded sobs for coughs.

Moving with pure adrenaline, I turned the cold water on in the tub and shifted Wendy into its coolness. I placed the oxygen mask over her wet face and held my hand on her back encouraging her to breathe. I slid in next to her, knowing the relief would be temporary until the fire finished its chore of engulfing us.

The sound of explosions filled the air. Some shifted the house and caused water to splash out of the tub. As the fire began its final path down the wall behind us and finished covering the carpet surrounding the tub, the house continued to scream with breaking wood and violent rocking.

I buried my head on Wendy's shoulder and slid us deeper in the water. We had not spoken in the few minutes that it took for the fire to close in around us;

shock and fear had paralyzed us. Not even a good-bye could be said. A final crash erupted from below us and we suddenly began to accelerate downward.

Everything went black.

Chapter 19

Mom screamed as she dropped the phone to the floor. She placed her head in her hands and knelt beside the sink where seconds earlier she was whistling and singing church hymns. She sobbed loudly which quickly brought Dad and Gramps away from their stargazing on the back deck.

Gramps somehow made it to Mom first and placed his hand on her back in an effort to absorb some of her grief. "What is it, child?" Gramps asked.

Before Mom could stutter out a word Dad picked up the dangling telephone. "Hello...who is this? What's going on?" He became quiet as he listened to the other line. He swallowed deeply and placed his head down as he continued to receive the information.

"But they're both still alive?" Dad's voice was broken and unsure. He gave the caller his cell phone number. "Thank you, nurse, we'll be there by morning, please call me if anything changes."

———————

Four hours later...

The pounding of my head rocked me back to a semi-conscious state where I found heavy gauze covering the left side of my face, leaving only my right eye to take in the surroundings. I blinked in an effort to focus my vision when a heavy-set woman appeared in front of me.

"Mr. Gordon, I'm nurse Kathy. You've had a terrible accident, but everything is going to be okay now."

I looked down at my arms and hands, which were attached to hanging fluids and a beeping regulator beside the bed. My arm was bandaged heavily; but with the exception of my head, I felt no significant pain. The memory of the evening rushed back into my consciousness.

"Where's my wife? Tell me where my wife is." I moaned as I quickly sat up.

Kathy quickly moved in and tried to push me back into a reclined position. "Mr. Gordon, you must keep your head down. Your wife is fine. You can see her later."

Panic filled my chest; there was no way I could lie there another second. I again forced myself up into a seated position. The room spun terribly and I choked down a vomiting impulse. Nurse Kathy again tried to force me down but I fought her back and climbed out of the bed and onto the cold tiled floor. I steadied myself and began walking to the door before being slowed by the jerking of my arm, reminding me of the leash that attached me to the bag of fluids.

My heart raced with my hysteria. I just wanted to see Wendy. I had to see her.

The nurse called for help as I pulled the tape covering the needle off my forearm. Without consideration of the pain it would cause, I pulled the needle from beneath my skin and covered the oozing blood with my gauzed hand.

Another nurse rushed in. "Sir, you must get back in your bed. You can see your wife after the doctor comes in to check you."

The words never had a chance to settle in my mind. I forced my way through the nurses half-hearted handle and walked out into the hallway.

"Where is she?" I screamed to anyone who would listen.

Nurse Mary's voice became more stern as she said, "Mr. Gordon, she is not gonna want to see you right now. She's with her family."

I looked back at the nurse, unsure of how to take what she said. I quickly turned my attention back to the hallway. The fight-or-flight response was in high gear, my visual acuity magnified as I peered down the barren right wing. I then looked over the nurse's station and into the left wing. I noticed the familiar faces of Wendy's sister and aunt who were leaning against the wall, lost in conversation.

Wendy's sister noticed me first and then tugged on her aunt who took her attention off the floor and turned it toward me. Their faces were cold and hateful as they scurried across the hall and disappeared into a room.

"Wendy," I said before beginning the longest walk of my life.

Chapter 20

My hands were tingling as I walked the path across the nurse's station and towards Wendy's room. My breathing was shallow and rapid as my heart beat with an increasingly panicked rhythm, sometimes releasing two breaths at once. Even the coldness of the tile floor didn't register in my head; I was completely numb to my surroundings.

As I got closer to the door, fear strangled me and wrenched my gut. I began to hear voices from the room, and although I couldn't hear what they were saying, the tone was clearly animated and intense. I took one more deep breath and walked inside.

I could only see Wendy's feet through the line of people surrounding her bed. Her mother sat the closest to her, at the head of the bed, running her hands across Wendy's forehead.

"Wendy," my voice was weak and nervous as the tears began to fill my eyes. My body trembled with remorse and my knees began to buckle. I wanted to fall to the floor and scream, but somehow I was able to stand. No other words came, only whimpering and cries made up my vocabulary. Wendy's mother bowed her head and joined in with my tearful outbreak. I couldn't move myself any closer than a few feet inside the door. My arms remained limp as I cried at the view of my wife, my life's love, lying in the hospital bed with her family surrounding her.

Mr. Summers stepped away from his position at the foot of the bed and moved toward me with an aggressive pace.

"Daddy, no," Wendy's voice sounded weak. Mr. Summers continued while the others kept their backs to me.

"Get out of here," he roared at me with an anger I had never heard from a man before.

Mr. Summers' hands met my chest and pushed me back against the unforgiving door. "You are never to see my daughter again."

I tried to look over his shoulder at Wendy. I saw her lips pucker and begin to quiver as she closed her eyes just a moment too late to stop the flood of tears from falling.

I tried to move past Mr. Summers, but his finger stopped me as it pierced into my chest again.

"Are you happy, Chance? Are you satisfied?"

I looked again at Wendy, her crying exacerbated by the commotion. "Wendy?" I mumbled again, unable to steady my voice to complete a sentence.

Mr. Summers' eyes glared through me, his head quivering with anger; and with his next words my life would be forever tortured by the memory of that day.

"You've killed your baby boy."

———————————

I screamed and covered my face with my hands as Mr. Summers finished shoving me into the hallway. I fell to my knees and laid my head against the cold floor. My opened mouth laid flush against the tile, as a temporary silence in

342

?:?.。/??。

Finding Life

my cry found its life again and echoed down the hallway. I had no strength to walk, and barely enough to breathe. I crawled away as the nurses and hospital security made their way to me.

"What do you mean, you don't know where he is?" Mom asked the administrative nurse.

"We told him that he couldn't leave, but he did anyway."

"Did he say where he was going?" Dad asked.

The nurse shook her head. "I'm sorry. He wasn't stable when he left. He had gone through a lot of emotional trauma just before he disappeared."

"More emotional trauma?" Mom and Gramps asked in unison.

The old Jeep was gone by the time Mom, Dad and Gramps arrived at what remained of the house. Any clothes and personal belongings that survived the fire and collapsed sections of the house were untouched.

Gramps noticed an old key ring shaped as a cross lying on the kitchen floor. The key was missing. He picked it up, scraped the dirt off the back and read the letters inscribed on it.

"I know where he is," Gramps said, "let's head back home."

121

Chapter 21

I'm really not sure how I made it back to Morehead City. I drove straight through the night in a cocoon of numbness. No thoughts or reasoning could enter the wall of despair that surrounded me. The crying was finished. There was no way a person could do what I did and have any fathom of a life left to live. Futility does bring some resolve, even when it's the epiphany that your life is finished. I had destroyed the two greatest things in the world to me. All the dreams of holding my new baby, of watching him grow, of teaching it life's lessons, were dead. The wounds of losing a child travel deep, and even deeper when your own hands are at fault.

I knew that Wendy's life would also be scarred forever, and that she would never leave the horror of that nightmare, a nightmare I created. My face would always remind her of it. I would always be a source of pain for her memory. Never would I be a source of peace or happiness for her, or anyone else.

Some suffering is worse than death. The agony consumes you, wraps you up in an airless tomb, permeates your body and oozes from the pores. For the first time in my life, I understood why some people chose death over life. There is no escape when you kill your child. Running back to Morehead City was not a search for peace; I knew such a place did not exist. My life began in that fishing community. I would end it there, too.

What was once a frenzied business with constant traffic from both boats and shipping trucks was now a desolate and lonely shack. After the governmental regulations made it too expensive to run a seafood factory, Gramps shut it down and returned to working the waters like everyone else in our little town. There were no complaints or ruefulness, which was typical of Gramps. He believed everything had a purpose in life, even when it didn't fit our agendas.

Gramps felt that losing the business was God's way of inducing him to concentrate on his ministry at the church. After forty years of preaching at the Shoreline Chapel, Gramps still considered himself an interim leader. But make no mistake about it, Gramps was a worthy and capable religious foreman. He accepted no praise, even in light of the packed sanctuary each Sunday. Gramps also accepted no money for his duties, instead preferring to use all the Church's earnings to help folks in the community who had fallen on hard times.

Within a year of closing down the business, Gramps had renovated the shack and made it into a lovely guesthouse. It was simple, but nice enough to accommodate the family members who came down from New Jersey each year. Gramps placed hardwood over the concrete floors and added wood siding to match. There were essentially two rooms, a bathroom and the other a large living quarters that was equipped with two sets of bunk beds, a kitchenette, and a reading area. The large fireplace was re-stoned and surrounded by two rocking chairs that sat upon the only rug in the shack. The outside was covered with cedar siding and a large eight-foot window was cut into the back wall, looking out at the river.

The marsh grass had grown tall around the shack, making it necessary to build wooden walkways around the property and out to the dirt roads that connected to the main highway. The closest house was a few hundred yards away, but not visible due to the patches of pines and spruces that hid the shack against the shoreline. It was once a peaceful place, but peace was not why I returned there.

––––––––––––––––––

I walked around to the concrete dock that Charlie and I sat upon so many times in our youth. I thought about how much I wanted my child to experience this place. I wanted him to see the fiddler crabs and throw shells as they scurried for cover. That would never happen. I looked over at the long wooden dock where only two years ago I had proposed to the most wonderful girl I would ever know. It had been a wonderful life, but it had come to a painful end. In one second it was wiped clean and replaced with tears and the fever of remorse.

As the shock of my baby's death and the agony on my wife's face began to fade, the pain grew more intense within me. The morphine of my daze was now gone and the true meaning of the events of the previous day were beginning to crush me. I picked up the .45 caliber pistol lying beside me and checked its chamber. I placed my head down and closed my eyes once more, wishing that I would just wake from the nightmare and roll over to find Wendy sleeping peacefully beside me. But that wouldn't happen. The sun was now fully risen, but the darkness remained for me. The wind picked up and blew an old plastic cup across the dock and into the water. The waves followed suit and began to increase their pace that ended abruptly against the concrete foundation.

I again picked up the gun and looked into its barrel. It was against everything I had been taught, but I couldn't stand another minute in that merciless world. I closed my eyes and placed the gun to my head.

My finger began squeezing tighter against the trigger when a rock came from somewhere behind me and landed in the water, causing a splash that brought my head back up. I recognized the footsteps and the voice that followed them.

"These decisions we make affect a lot more than just ourselves," Gramps said in his slow, yet sure, voice. "I've told the others to give you a couple of days before they come down here."

I placed my head back down on my knees, embarrassed by my weakness. I could see the ripples leaving the source of the splash and traveling away in all directions. It was an old lesson Gramps had taught Charlie and me many times as kids. Whenever we made poor decisions, he would throw that rock in the water and make us watch the ripples take off. He would tell us that they traveled forever. In much the same way, our decisions would travel out like ripples in the water and affect everyone in our lives, and that is why we must consider our actions before we take them.

Gramps slowly made his way down to sit beside me. His aged hips made it a lot more difficult to get down than in years earlier.

"Even the most tragic events have a way of working out."

"Not this one," I said.

"God knows your pain, Chance. Don't forget that, as easy as it may be right now."

125

"I don't need the God talk right now Gramps. My child is dead. What kind of a loving God allows that?" I responded with a broken voice.

Gramps began to say something but stopped himself. His chin protruded out a little farther than usual, which was the only way to tell that he was feeling pain. He patted me on the knee before saying, "I love you, child. As much as you're hurting right now, I'd hurt the same if I lost you." He held his hand out for the gun and I hesitantly gave it to him. He then rolled over on his hands and knees and used his good leg to push himself up. "I'll be back in a couple of days. If you want to talk, I'll be at the Church."

I had no doubts what Gramps would be doing the next two days. He was a big believer in doing things in forties, just like in the Bible. He would spend the next forty hours, to the minute, praying for me.

Chapter 22

I didn't sleep at all that first night. I paced back and forth across the wooden floor, taking a moment to pause and look out at the dark river. The rain started about two o'clock, just after a cover of clouds filtered out the moonlight. I kept the lights off, finding it better not to see my reflection in the mirrors and windows.

My mind wandered back to Wendy. My heart ached as I pictured her tortured face and helpless gaze. I pounded the wall until my hands swelled and throbbed. *If I could just go back in time...just a few minutes that I could change.*

The rain pounded against the roof causing a roar inside the house. I couldn't sit still; the rage and emotions consumed me. I hated myself, hated what I had done. I didn't deserve the air to breathe. My mind wandered through my life, through the good parts. I thought back to the day I first saw Wendy. Her innocence and laughter crushed me. I missed her terribly. I missed the way she would bury her head in my arms when I walked through the front door. It was all gone - my perfect life, my child, my wife – gone.

I continued pacing from one end of the open room to the other. The only light was provided by the occasional lightening flash. The complete darkness would have unnerved me before, but not now. If there was something lurking in the cover of night, I welcomed it - anything to end the misery that was driving me to the brink of insanity.

———————————

It was the next night that I decided to venture outside. The front after the rain left the night air cool and brisk. With the exception of the breeze through the marsh, all was quiet. I sat down on the dock and did my best not to think about Wendy, or my child, but it was a futile attempt. It was only two months previous that Wendy and I learned it was a boy. The doctor inadvertently let it slip out during a routine ultrasound. I immediately jumped up and gave the touchdown signal while playfully dancing around. That evening I called Charlie in Durham, where he was completing his residency, and told him the news. We talked about the names we liked for a boy and when Charlie said he always liked Dillon, I knew what it would be. Wendy said she needed more time to think about it, but the next morning she awoke me early and said, "Dillon's kicking hard this morning. I think he likes his name."

———————————

It was 5:30 am when I returned from a walk down the shoreline. I knew that nobody would be about that early on a Sunday morning. The sun was just beginning to rise over the calm river when I made it back to the house. I noticed a letter placed between the screen of the back door. It was Mom's handwriting, but Gramps' dirty fingers left the evidence that he was the messenger. It became clear that he had been watching me through the night. Somewhere hidden in the marsh was a chair where he sat, and watched, and prayed. When he saw me walk down the banks, he carefully placed the letter and left me in God's hands.

Dear Chance,
We have some business to attend to in Charlotte.
We'll see you tomorrow.

Love, Mom, Dad and Gramps

I knew what that business was – they were going to Dillon's memorial service. I threw the note in the water and watched it slowly succumb and sink out of sight.

Chapter 23

I hadn't eaten in four days. The hunger pains grew quiet, and with the exception of water, my body needed nothing. Darkness fell at 7:00 pm; I had not moved from the wooden chair since reading the letter. My mind did flip-flops, almost in a state of insanity as I sat there, head in my hands, and legs stagnant.

A soft knock echoed off the wood from the screen door.

"Chance, it's Mom. Are you in there?"

The darkness made it impossible to see inside the house, but I could see her silhouette from the moonlight.

I awoke from my trance. "I'm here, Mom."

The door screeched as she opened it and felt her way to my voice. She found my arched back and placed her hand on it. If only subtly, I felt the cessation of pain for a second. Mom's touch had a way of doing that, at least until reality came kicking back in.

"How is Wendy?" My voice was still weak and unsteady.

"It's still new for her, just like it is for you." Mom could never lie. Her hand began to smooth down my tangled hair.

"Did you see the baby?" I blurted out before my tears could stop me.

"Chance, that's not what you need to think about right now."

"Did you see the baby?" I asked again with more volume.

Mom began to cry along with me. "Yes."

My chest heaved up and down as I struggled for air. "Did it look like me?"

"Oh, Chance, don't do this."

"I need to know. I need to know or I'll just keep thinking about it."

Mom was wailing beside me, down on her knees, holding me like I was a child again. "Yes. He had your face."

I siphoned in a gasp of air. "He did? He had my face?"

The uncontrolled scream caused my lungs to burn. A quarter mile away, sitting next to his opened window with a Bible in hand, Gramps heard the faint screech travel in with the breeze. He dropped his head and whispered, "Dear Lord, give us strength. Help us not to question these days."

A tear dropped to the thin pages of the opened book and quickly soaked its way through.

Chapter 24

A month passed, leaving a predictable routine. I spent the majority of the daylight hours hiding in the house, curtains closed, catching catnaps when my mind would settle down enough to allow a transient slumber. With the exception of Mom and Dad, I saw no one during the daylight hours. Mom would come in around mid-morning with breakfast. She'd try to carry on a conversation without bringing up the obvious, but that was quite uncomfortable. I had let her down, and that was just another item on my list of transgressions. Of course, she would never tell me, but I knew it. Her eyes were sad and disappointed. Much of our conversation was dominated by my repetitive apologies, which she assured me were unnecessary.

I guess somewhere inside me I held hope that Wendy would make contact with me. Realistically, I didn't expect it, but through my dwindling and mostly neutered faith in miracles, I held some glimpse of hope that she would show up one day and say, "We'll work this out, Chance - you and I."

But that just couldn't happen. For Wendy, having a child was her ultimate goal in life. From the time she was a small child playing with dolls, she dreamed of taking care of her own baby one day. Her dreams never consisted of

Wall Streets, law firms, or delicate surgeries. She wanted to be surrounded by children and be that patient and nurturing mom that her mother was.

From the moment she walked out of our bathroom with those "glorious" two pink lines showing, her life was complete. Those were the happiest tears to ever leave a pair of eyes. And for nine months she lived a life that was exemplary of a pregnant woman. She had read all the books on the subject and searched every page on the web; she was a pregnancy expert. It was her dream and she would leave nothing undone that could undermine a perfect environment for a child to develop.

But there was one mistake she didn't count on – me.

Of course, this came as no surprise to her father. Although a virtuous man, he could never accept the fact that his daughter was marrying the son of a fisherman who sold power tools to construction companies. This was not his plan. She was supposed to marry a surgeon or some corporate attorney from Harvard, or maybe even a star baseball player. Any of these would do, but not me.

I didn't talk with the proper accent or wear the classical sweaters. My blue jeans and T-shirts were simply repulsive and embarrassing for a bank executive to showcase to his friends and clients. And I tried. I tried so hard to transform myself into a son-in-law that he would be proud of. When I began making the large sales and bringing home the million dollar contracts, I created a shell that I thought would disguise me enough to at least allow him to tolerate my persona. But much like those perfume and clothing impersonators, it really doesn't smell or fit the same. My life was formed in a small fishing village where status had nothing to do with money. There was nothing stuffy about me and regardless of how hard I tried to be more like Mr. Summers, it just didn't fit me as it did others. I found that

133

no matter how much you try to persuade yourself, if it isn't the true you, it won't last.

And thus was the case with me. I realized that I would never be that finely tuned socialite that Mr. Summers envisioned. Fighting this truth was like fighting a rip tide – no matter how hard you swim, it will carry you out as far as it sees fit. Fighting it too hard would only ensure a quicker drowning.

Although I knew Wendy would still love me, I would always be the face that took away the one thing that was more precious than our own love. Maybe if the death of our child occurred earlier in the pregnancy, it wouldn't be so insurmountable to rebuild our love. But as it was, the child was completely formed and simply awaiting the hour to make its grand entrance into our world. Wendy was days, perhaps even hours, from holding her baby boy. Nothing could be more catastrophic than traveling so far to bring life into this world, and then in a moment being told it was over.

It was a late afternoon when Mom came to the shore to let me know Wendy's fate. The wounds from the c-section had healed, but the damage to Wendy's reproductive organs was still quite severe. The trauma that took place in her body as it absorbed the force of the fall caused irreparable changes. In addition to the baby being taken away, it also removed any chance that she would carry another one in her lifetime. Wendy's one dream for her life was destroyed.

Mom had talked with Mrs. Summers, who was more understanding and willing to talk than any of the other Summers family members. She informed Mom that Wendy was severely depressed and would go home to Charlotte to undergo rehabilitation for her physical and mental injuries.

When Mrs. Summers asked about me, Mom informed her I was severely depressed at having destroyed my marriage and being responsible for my child's death. Mrs. Summers made no reply. It was already understood that Wendy was shattered and would never get over her loss. Some mistakes are not correctable, and this was certainly one of them.

Chapter 25

The sun had barely risen over the slumbering river when I heard Lobo's familiar gallop coming around the corner. Lobo was Gramp's dog, a beautiful midnight black mix breed of Siberian Husky and German Shepherd. I had been sitting on the edge of the dock for a few hours, tossing every available stone I could find in the water below. Time had lost its relevance, with night and day becoming generics of each other.

Lobo buried his sandy wet muzzle in my lap, which was his way of saying hello. As I figured, Gramps was not far behind. He came limping around the corner with two aluminum cups steaming with freshly brewed coffee.

"I figured you'd be up this early," Gramps said as he took a seat next to me.

"Guilt has a way of making sleep less of a commodity," I replied, continuing to throw stones in the water.

"I've been praying for you, son. It's going to be a long season of despair for you, but I'm going to be here for you, and so is God."

I sipped the cup of coffee and then looked up at the sky with its transgressions of daylight interrupting the darkness. "Gramps, I've had a lot of time to think. And I realize that I'm the one who caused this, but you have to wonder why a God that we consider gracious would allow such things to happen in the first place. I mean, what did my child do to deserve death? And what did my precious…" I stopped to compose myself, squeezing my nose to hold back the tears. "And what did my wife do to deserve the greatest loss a mother can have?" I looked Gramps in the eye for the first time since I'd returned home. The look of complete desolation in my eyes suddenly had a new ingredient of anger. "How am I supposed to have any faith in that God? I mean, He has the power to do everything. Why didn't He just let me die?"

Gramps looked down as he wrapped both of his hands around the coffee cup. "I admit it seems easy to argue against a loving God when we see all the evil and pain in this world, but I tell you, Chance, I believe God is crying over your loss just as you are."

"But he's supposed to be all powerful. It doesn't make sense. And don't tell me about sin entering the world and allowing bad things to happen. That's an overused excuse when things go wrong."

"I don't have all the answers, Chance, just like I don't understand why your Grandmother had to suffer with her cancer. You couldn't find a better woman than her, and she died a horribly painful death."

"And yet you still choose to have faith?" I asked rhetorically.

Gramps rolled onto his right hip and rested his arm behind him. He took another sip of coffee before speaking. "Shortly after grandma died, I went out fishing, just me and old Lobo. I wasn't looking to catch anything. I just wanted to get away by myself and talk to her." Gramps' deep voice cracked, but he quickly composed himself. "So there we were, just me and Lobo, and wouldn't you know it, that dog got into my tackle box and got a hook stuck right through his nose."

Gramps took a moment to pat Lobo on the head before finishing his story. "So this dog was justa squalling from the pain. But when I went to get him he cowered away, afraid that I was going to hurt him more, but you see, I was just there to help him. So I finally get down to him and I have to hold his head down against the bottom of the boat, because he certainly wouldn't allow me to touch the nose you see. And I tell you, this dog was a screaming. But I knew I had to get that hook out. So Old Lobo here thinks I'm trying to hurt him, you know, with the pain and all. And he really thought I was trying to hurt him when I had to push that hook deeper into his nose to get it unlocked. By that time, he was growling and showing his teeth because you see, Chance, he couldn't understand that I was trying to help him. He couldn't understand because Lobo is a dog. He's not human. But in his mind, he would have sworn that I was trying to hurt him. But I wasn't. I was trying to help him, because I love him."

The story was beginning to make some sense to me and Gramps paused to let it sink in a little further.

"Chance, there is no way that poor Lobo here could have understood that the pain I was causing him was to help him. There's simply no way he could know that. And I believe that there is no way that you and I can understand why you are feeling the pain you have. But I believe it has a purpose, somewhere. I have to believe that there is a reason this all happened."

I put my head down as I deciphered the story. Gramps put his hand on my back and began talking again.

"And you know what old Lobo did after I yanked that hook out of his nose? You know what he did after I caused him so much pain? He came right back to me and laid his head in my lap. He had so much faith in me that he did that. And that got me thinking. That got me thinking about your grandmother's situation. She had lived a full life.

We were both in our eighties and we can't live forever." Gramps took a moment to recollect his thoughts before continuing, "I loved your grandma so much..." Gramps again paused as tears began to fill his eyes. "I loved her so much that there was no way I could have let go of her. The only thing that could allow me to let her go was the suffering. I wanted her to move on. But only suffering could make me want her to do that. And I believe that was the only thing that could allow her to let go of this earth, her children, and me - the pain that wore her down day by day. You may think that sounds silly right now, but one day I hope it makes sense to you. One day you will have faith that God knew what to do with this situation."

My head remained tucked away in my hands. I knew Gramps was right. There was only one reason the tragedy happened, and that reason was me. His stories always seemed so timely. They were never forceful or hurried. Gramps just had a way of soothing your soul.

I found myself breathing a little easier while listening to Gramps talk. For the first time, I was not asking so many questions. But as Gramps pushed himself up off the concrete dock, I felt the gush of depression as it strangled my heart and wrenched what little peace he had given me.

Chapter 26

It was four o'clock in the afternoon when my eyes opened from what I thought was going to be the most wonderful dream. I was sitting on the floor in the nursery at our house. It was painted sky blue with streaks of clouds filling the open walls. Butterflies were littered throughout the scene in addition to a few fluttering from the light fixture above. Wendy was in the glider with baby Dillon, feeding him before a mid-day nap. She smiled as his innocent stare looked right into her eyes, as if trying to memorize every detail of her face.

Wendy crunched up her nose and made little giggles. Her long hair fell across his face and he, too, began to giggle. Everything was so perfect. Even the rays of sun that squeezed through the plantation blinds, showcasing the usually invisible dust particles, seemed to add life to the carpet below. One of the light beams caught Dillon's attention and he reached out as if to catch it. He leaned a little farther from Wendy's lap and, without warning, fell suddenly to the ground.

The fall seemed benign enough so we both began laughing, which was our way to keep him from crying, but Dillon didn't move. His lifeless body just laid there as Wendy screamed for help.

Before I could move my seemingly frozen body, Mr. Summers broke through the door and began screaming, "What have you done, Chance? What did you do to this baby now?"

I awoke in a panic with sweat running down my face. The horrid reality that I found myself in was not much better than the dream. These crazy dreams were happening more, to the point that I dreaded falling to sleep, knowing that my guilty mind would take me back to that horrible night. I never imagined myself so weak and dreadful. There were no reprieves, not a moment that I didn't hate breathing.

A knock came from the screened door, which rattled me out of my semi-consciousness. I leaned forward in the rocking chair, waiting to hear who would announce themselves. The knocking continued with no identification. I knew it couldn't be Gramps or my parents.

"Who is it?" my slumbering voice called out.

"It's Scotty Foreman. I heard you were hiding out here."

I was certainly in no mood for Scotty's persistent jovialness. "It's not a good time, Scotty. I don't want any visitors."

Scotty leaned his head against the door. "Yeah, I know, Chance. Charlie told me to leave you alone for a while; but I never listen to him. Look, I won't tell anyone that you're down here. I promise. And I won't bother you anymore, but if you need anything, anything at all, you know where to reach me."

"I appreciate the offer, Scotty."

James Graham

I made my way over to the door and watched Scotty disappear down the path of oyster shells and behind the cluster of trees. At the foot of the door, I noticed a paper bag from the Red and White grocery store. Inside were bags of snacks that we used to eat as kids: Cheetos, Doritos, Pringles and others. I opened the door and brought the bag inside. As I emptied its contents, I noticed a letter inside. It was from Charlie.

———————————

Dear Chance,

I hope you don't mind that I gave Scotty your whereabouts. I've been keeping up with you through Gramps. He says you are going to tough this out. I knew you would. I understand you don't want to see anybody right now, and I will certainly make sure that Scotty doesn't tell anyone where you are staying.

I'm doing well. I miss talking to you. I miss talking to everyone. My residency is doing as well as can be expected.

Chance, I hope you know that if you need anything, I'll be right there. Gramps insists that you don't need my company at this time, and I will trust his assessment. I just want you to know that I'm thinking about you.

Charlie

Chapter 27

The sun had yet to show the genesis of its glow as I waited with my usual trepidation of new days. Drops of dew fell from the eaves of the house and glistened on the marsh grass that surrounded me. Mornings on the coast seemed to always be wet, no matter how little rain we had.

From a distance I heard crackling in the marsh, which changed pace every few seconds. I had a strong suspicion of the source...

Lobo came crashing through the marsh, his wet coat proof of his refusal to not use the wooden walkways to the house. He preferred to snake his way through the jungle of marsh grass in search of some poor creature that decided to take refuge in the seemingly safe haven of the wetland. On that day the poor creature was me.

Lobo quickly encircled me as I sat perilously on the loading dock, leaving the smell of his wet coat fresh on my clothes and face. Before I could get my hand up to defend myself, he left a slobbering lick on my cheek as well.

"Thought we'd find you up," Gramps said as he sat a cup of coffee next to me.

"Don't you ever sleep, Gramps?" I replied.

"When you get as old as I am you try to squeeze every second that you can from this orange," Gramps chuckled.

I took a moment to enjoy the aroma of the coffee before placing it against my lips. It was perfect, just the right amount of cream and sugar. Gramps pulled a bag out and placed it next to me. "You still like donuts, don't you? I've had all I want, and besides, I hear they're bad for you. I wouldn't want to risk it."

I looked over at Gramps as he humored himself. His age was showing over the last few years. It dawned on me that I was stealing the joy from the final chapter of his life. I tried not to stare but continued to glance at his frail body, his hands shaking without control. Lobo laid down beside the old man and placed his head on Gramps lap, nudging him for a rub.

I placed my coffee down and watched a seagull drift effortlessly to a river stake before ruffling his feathers and settling in for a rest. "I'm sorry, Gramps. Here you are at the end of your road and I've done this."

"Chance..." Gramps tried to interject, but I wouldn't allow him.

"It's true, Gramps. I always wanted to make you proud, but now I'm just hurting you. You've had enough heartbreak. I didn't need to add to it."

Gramps placed a hand on my shoulder. "Don't sell me out so early, son. I just read about a woman on some island that claims to be one hundred and twenty-six years old. There might be two or three chapters left in me."

Gramps humor missed me. "I'm serious, Gramps. I'm sorry."

"You're a good boy who made a mistake. It's going to take some time to forgive yourself, but one day you will. In the time being, I'm here for you." Gramps patted me on the back. "That's what grandpas do."

Gramps performed his customary roll before pushing himself to a standing position. "When's the last time you caught a clam?"

I huffed at his question. "I guess you're trying to tell me to get to work."

Gramps carefully rolled his pants legs up before saying, "A man can't eat donuts forever."

The wet sand along the river banks mortared its way between my toes as Gramps and I walked along the shore in search of a place to start digging. The eastern shore of the river was sandwiched with clean sand that provided a great home for small, tasty clams. Unlike the oyster infested banks along the western shoreline, it was safe to walk barefooted on the east side. Lobo ran ahead of us chasing the occasional crab that found itself like a deer frozen in headlights. Of course he never completed his intimidating assault, having learned the frailty of a protruding nose in the personal space of a claw-yielding crustacean. Gramps had pulled more than one crab off Lobo's sniffer.

As Lobo aggressively circled his doubled-sworded assailant, Gramps and I walked quietly down the banks. The sun began to shed full light on our world. The constant singing of the night crooning whip-poor-wills was replaced by the sounds of seagulls, geese, and marsh hens. It had been years since I took the time to go clamming with Gramps. Clamming had always just been for fun until Grandma became ill. Together they had worked hard and saved a sizable nest egg to comfort them in their retirement. But when Grandma's insurance denied coverage for home care, and instead insisted that she go to a facility, Gramps took every penny he had saved to keep her at home. "The best money I ever spent," he would say later. Three years after Grandma died, Gramps found himself needing to pick up a few clams and oysters to make ends meet. But this was something Gramps loved to do.

Gramps squinted his eyes as he followed a faint line along the sand. "I'm onto one." He found the end of the line, which represented the path of a traveling clam, and reached blindly in the sand and pulled out a perfect, inch wide clam.

"Final chapter nothing," Gramps said under his breath. "Old men can't see like me."

Whereas Gramps had the gift to see clam paths, I did not, and instead used my feet to feel the defined oval and rough texture of the shell.

When Charlie and I were kids there was nothing quite as exciting as a walk down the banks with Gramps. For years Gramps would toy with us as he seemed to mysteriously grab clams from the sandy bottom. He would often stop along our walks and say, "Do you boys see that clam there?" And no matter how close Charlie and I looked we could only see sand. Gramps would insist, "It's right there boys, just open your eyes a little farther." Still, Charlie and I could see nothing. As planned, Gramps would have us step aside and then he would reach down and pull a clam out of the clear water. We'd giggle forever after he performed such miracles.

Charlie eventually figured out Gramps' little trick of locating the squiggly lines in the sand, and knowing that the clam would bury itself at the end of this path. It was a lot like tracking an animal. Charlie didn't let on that he was privy to Gramps little secret, instead deciding to walk along the shoreline with a branch, drawing lines that mimicked clam trails. He made hundreds of these lines, knowing that Gramps was taking us on an expedition that afternoon.

After a few dozen times of reaching in the sand and coming up empty handed, Gramps began scratching his head. It didn't take him long to figure out our great heist, especially with Charlie and me belly laughing every time Gramps would repeat with a fading confidence: "Okay, then, and do you boys see that one there..." Gramps had been had, and he loved every minute of it. He loved us boys and looked forward to our expeditions as much as we did.

Walking behind Gramps as a youngster, eager to hear his next story, I could have never imagined the current state of my life. Although I loved Gramps' company, I also felt ashamed when he would look at me. Nothing I had ever accomplished in life felt better than making Gramps proud of me. Just the same, not much felt worse than letting him down.

Gramps put another clam in his pocket before taking a moment to stretch his lower back. He looked out across the river and inhaled the morning air, savoring its salty aftertaste. "Have you thought about calling Wendy? It's been over a month now. She might be more willing to talk now that she has had some time."

I shook my head, adding a pessimistic smirk. "I don't think so Gramps. She hates me."

"Come on, child, she doesn't hate you. I remember the sparkle in that young lady's eye when we talked at the church. You can't just erase that. Maybe you should pick up the phone and call her."

We continued our walk, both our heads down pretending to search for clams. "You don't understand, Gramps. She begged me to stop drinking so much with my clients. She despised the smell of alcohol on my breath. And I just kept promising her that I would stop, but I never did. That last night when I was out with a client, a big drinker, when I talked to her on the phone and heard the disappointment in her voice," I paused to shake my head in disgust. "I promised myself that I was done letting her down."

My eyes began to swell with tears, something I had grown accustomed to over the past month. I was never one to shed tears. Instead I held a strong disdain towards those I thought were weak and let them go too often. But I had underestimated the power of real pain; undeniable pain that took my breath away, like a solid punch to the gut. There was no pride left inside and therefore no way to dam off the faucets of emotion. I despised everything about myself. Walking beside Gramps, like a child again, I could only think that I was just beginning my slide downward to a state of unimaginable gloom.

Gramps made no initial effort at a reply and instead closed his eyes to digest my words. After a few moments of silence he said, "I still think you should at least try to call her. See if you guys can maybe talk about things a little. It couldn't hurt."

Chapter 28

It took me all afternoon to work up the courage to pick up the old rotary phone. And once I did work up the courage, I felt the need to spend almost an hour cleaning the dust off the headpiece. Gramps' words kept echoing inside my head. *What could it hurt?*

Mrs. Summer's gentle and inviting voice surprised me when she picked up on the first ring. I swallowed hard before speaking. "Mrs. Summers," I didn't dare ask how she was doing. "This is Chance. I know I probably shouldn't be calling, but I just wanted to see if I could talk with Wendy. That is, if she wants to talk to me."

It took what seemed an eternity for Mrs. Summers to answer. I was surprised by the absolute kindness and congeniality in her voice. "Sure, Chance, let me see if she will answer the door."

After some obvious persistence by Mrs. Summers, I could hear the rustling of the phone as it switched hands. Wendy's voice was indifferent and without temperament as she said hello. I felt as if I were talking to a stranger, as if I had never known the voice before. For the past two years I rarely used Wendy's name, instead feeling suffice to call her "Sweetie" or "Baby." But that was not the case as I again quaffed down the butterflies in my stomach to make space for my words.

"Wendy, it's Chance. How are...," I stopped myself before completing the rhetorical question. "I'm not even sure what to say."

I could hear Wendy's breath through the phone and imagined her with her eyes shut, ready to quickly end the conversation. She said nothing. The moment was awkward and painful.

"I'm so sorry, Wendy. I just can't believe this has happened. I just can't stand the thought of you hurting. And I know you hate me. I can't stand me either."

"I don't hate you, Chance," Wendy's voice finally returned. "I just don't have a lot of words to offer anyone right now. It was an accident. You should just move on and get over it."

"I can't, Wendy, not without you. I want us to be us again. And I know..."

"That's not going to happen, Chance," Wendy quickly cut me off. "There's just no way I can put this behind me. It's going to always be there, reminding me that..." Wendy's tears overcame her momentarily. She composed herself and fought to say the words that would cut at her very being. "Reminding me that I will never be a woman who can comfort her child."

The flood of emotions overcame Wendy and she wailed like a child. There is no description to surrender the true feelings I felt as she sobbed for what seemed an eternity. "Why, Chance, why?" she managed between her sobs.

Her plea for some palliative answer traveled sharply through my spine. Again I found myself filled with tears of disgust and rage. I could only repeat "I'm sorry" over and over through the phone, hoping that just one would find itself as a seed in Wendy's heart, able to grow once the environment was more fertile. I knew not when or if that day would come.

Wendy's sobbing quieted to a whimper and she effectively placed the last brick in the wall between us. "I will always love you, Chance. I will always. But I am never going to be any good to anybody again. My face is full of scars and my womb will be forever empty. As much as I loved our time together I would gladly trade it in to just have my baby back. I'd trade every moment we ever shared to just have a chance to have another one. But that won't happen."

"Wendy please, I'll do anything, anything at all..."

She again cut me off before I could finish. "There's nothing left of us, Chance. Let's not make this any harder than it already is. Daddy will be flying in next week to have you sign some papers. I hate this as much as you do."

I sat frozen in the chair, holding the phone to my ear until the beeping of the dial tone forced me to lay it down. I couldn't help but think that I had just finished the last conversation I would ever have with Wendy.

Gramps once said that there are folks who say hell may not be a place of torture by fire. After all, would a place described as utter darkness also be filled with fire? And since fire is used figuratively throughout the Bible, who's to say that it's not used the same to describe the pits of hell. Maybe it's the closest way to describe to us the pain of not being with God. Gramps never suggested that he bought this theory, but as he would say, "It's an interesting idea."

Maybe true hell is the acknowledgement that we will be forever separated from the greatest love of all – the love of God. It's been said that we will one day truly know that there is a love greater than that for a child, parent or spouse. Feeling the pain of not ever having Wendy in my life was as much hell as I could imagine. Being separated from a love greater than what I had for her was surely the worst torture that could be created.

Chapter 29

I awaited Mr. Summers' arrival like the deadly plagues of the Middle Ages. Mom had already prepared me for his agenda. His visit would be cold and swift. There would be no small talk or apologies; it would be purely business. His chief concern was dismissing Wendy from the financial quagmire that I produced after burning the house down and leaving everything behind in Atlanta. The bills would be astronomical. Between the hospital, missed mortgages and the plethora of other bills that were left unmanaged, things had quickly spiraled out of control. My new position at Delwood was understandably terminated. Clams were selling for eleven cents a piece, which would not even come close to handling the debt I had acquired. I was buried and there was no way out.

There was not much I agreed on with Mr. Summers, but keeping Wendy out of this mess was one area we would see eye to eye.

I was not expecting Mr. Summers to be in until the afternoon, which left me speechless when his knocking at the front door disrupted me from cleaning off my catch of clams from the morning. Realizing that I was covered in sun-dried mud, I quickly rinsed my legs and feet off. I patted a few grains of dirt off my cut-off jeans, which had become my work uniform, and proceeded to the front door. My bare feet left a path of prints across the hard wood floor. Mr. Summers covered his eyes from the sun as he peered through the screened door. He was professionally dressed as usual, with a neatly starched shirt and perfectly bowed tie.

"Good morning, Mr. Summers. I'm sorry to be so dirty but I wasn't expecting you until the afternoon," I said, embarrassed by my appearance.

"Nonetheless, Chance, let's take care of this so I can get going," Mr. Summers replied, obviously not in the mood for apologies.

"Yes, sir. I understand why you're here. I'll sign whatever you need."

Mr. Summers smiled sarcastically and pushed himself by me, putting his briefcase on the small table. He looked around the shack and then sat down. "Nice place. I hope it's fire proof."

His words didn't phase me. I stared blankly at him. "What do we need to do, sir?"

"Well, Chance, it looks like your wonderful insurance is only going to pay half of Wendy's medical." He considered stopping there, but decided to go farther. "And none of her psychological bills." He emphasized psychological for my benefit.

"What can I do to alleviate this? I'm afraid I don't have any money right now."

Mr. Summers laughed. "Yeah, right now. Here's what we are doing. We're basically going to have you take responsibility for these bills since you caused it. I guess essentially we're suing you to make these go in your name."

I shook my head in agreement. Nothing mattered to me; he could have given me the national debt and I wouldn't have blinked.

"What's left of the house will be sold and will have a significant loss," he continued. "You will also be responsible for repaying that. I'll take care of the selling part and won't charge you for my time." He placed the papers on the table in front of me along with his designer pen. I immediately recognized that Wendy's signature was forged. She obviously would have no part in this. She was the exact opposite of her father, always kind and gracious.

Mr. Summers had me sign a few other release forms and proceeded to stash the documents in his briefcase. When I had signed the last one in the pile, I placed the pen down in front of him. "I guess we're done here," I said.

"Not quite son." He reached into the back fold of the briefcase and pulled out another thin stack of forms. "These are the most important in my opinion."

He placed the divorce papers in front of me and re-clicked his pen. I went to the last page and studied the signatures. This time they were authentic. I leaned back in the chair and took a deep breath.

"There's no need to contemplate, Chance. This ride is over for you. Sign the bloody papers and let's get this done with."

I placed the pen to the paper but couldn't move it any further.

"Sign it, Chance. You're wasting my time."

My blood pressure boiled and my eyes began to sting. "Why do you hate me, Mr. Summers?" I asked with a petulant voice.

"Why do I hate you, Chance? Why? You kill my grandchild and destroy my daughter's life and you wonder why I hate you? Any father worth his salt would hate you."

I signed the papers as anger contracted my lips. I slammed the pen down and then stood up and walked to the door. "You've always hated me, sir. You never gave me a chance."

Mr. Summers also stood and straightened his tie. He cleared his voice and said, "I guess I just always knew you would end up hurting my girl - somehow." He walked through the door and stopped. "Looks like I was right. Wouldn't you say?"

I continued staring at him, detest on my face. The anger fumed through my eyes.

"You're free to destroy someone else's life now, Chance," he said through the window of his car before leaving a trail of dust up the hill and disappearing behind the cover of trees.

———————

The afternoon sun toasted the back of my shoulders as I sat on the dock that was once a monument of my happiness. It was there that Wendy said yes, and my life became complete. The world seemed to know when she smiled, and it always smiled back. The birds sang with more passion and the dolphins played a little longer; even the crabs seemed to bite softer. But without her it was hollow and stale.

There was indeed a fate worst than death, and I was living it.

Chapter 30

Gramps startled me awake as I cleared my eyes and wondered where the sunshine had gone. I had drifted away during some point of my reminiscence. Sleep was the only peace I had, at least when no dreams haunted my slumber.

"We were worried about you," Gramps said. "Been looking for you for a couple of hours. Why don't you slip back to the house and I'll meet you in a few minutes. We'll have a little cookout."

"I don't want a pity party, Gramps. I just want to be alone tonight."

"Let me find your mom and dad and I'll be back in a few to at least say goodnight. I'll be alone."

Once Gramps informed everyone that I was fine he hurried back to the house. True to his word, he came alone. "Tough day with the in-laws, I take it."

"Ex-in-laws," I replied.

"I see." Gramps put his head down and was quiet for a few minutes. I was certain that he was saying some sort of prayer. "Probably not a good time to bring this up, but

I guess you'll hear it anyway. Charlie ran off to Vegas and got married to Jessica."

"That's wonderful, Gramps. I'm happy for him," I replied without emotion.

"With everything going on, he didn't want to have a big to-do."

"Looks like I just help everyone out, doesn't it?"

"He said he'll redo the vows when you're doing better; when you can stand beside him and all. Besides, she didn't particularly want her parents together that long."

"Sure, Gramps."

———————

The evening calm brought an influx of mosquitoes to the dock, causing Gramps to fill the metal drums with wood and start the fires blazing. The smoke quickly subdued the nuisances while Gramps used the warmth to cook some hotdogs he brought with him. We stayed up most of the night, Gramps listening to me as I opened my shell and talked about Wendy. Even he opened up and talked about how much he missed Grandma. Life had trained him well. Gramps always had so much to teach me. But only a divine miracle could remove the iron despair that controlled my life.

Part Two

Four years later....

Chapter 31

There are defining moments in life, events that nick an indelible mark in the timeline of our days. We often talk of our lives as a measure of the years before and after these events. Until our final hours, as we rest in our retiring bodies, we think back to those events and retrace the new path our lives took because of them.

It was a cold, winter's morning in January when time gave birth to a new defining moment in my life. Early, as usual, I awaited Gramps' arrival with the steaming coffee, breakfast in hand, and conversation to pacify me through another day. Nearly every morning for the past four years that I lived in that renovated oyster shack, he came to me, smile first, without judgment, to see me into another day. But on that fresh dawn, as the frost concealed any sense of life, Lobo came alone, more slowly than usual. He kissed me less aggressively and chose my lap as a substitute to cushion his head, since Gramps' was absent that morning. I needed no further proof, no additional news, to know Gramps' fate. At some point during the night, as he lay covered with the hand-sewn blankets Grandma made for him, he slipped out of my life and into her arms again. I had loved him long enough, used up my time, and she waited no longer.

The short walk to Gramps' house that morning, with Lobo at my side, seemed to take an eternity. I thought back to the day he saved me, as my finger gripped the trigger of death, and taught me the value of life, even in the midst of unimaginable disaster.

Gramps dedicated his last days to me. From the moment I returned home, every breath he took and move he made had my fate as its purpose. I could never count the hours amassed when he sat by my side and watched the boats troll their way out to sea. Sometimes our conversations were exact replicas of the day before, but we still drank daily from each other's company, not fully recognizing the enjoyment our simple time together provided us. I had always loved the ground Gramps walked upon, but during those dark years I grew to appreciate the full character of his spirit and the superiority of his heart.

The screened door remained open from where Lobo had pushed his way out after failing to awaken his slumbering master. Even so, it was warm and cozy inside, a stark contrast to the bitter cold outside. The old music box played Gramps' favorite Christian channel, sitting where it had for decades near the gas stove where he made my coffee each morning. The smell of mothballs filled the living room, where pictures hung of the Last Supper and Jesus holding a child in his lap. Not much had changed from the time I could crawl up and down those hallways.

The house was still and peaceful, which was how I found Gramps lying in his little bed, the covers pulled up to his head. The coldness of his face didn't deter me from kissing his forehead before I pulled the covers closer to his face. I sat beside him for a few minutes, with Lobo mourning at my feet, and talked to him like I did every morning, knowing this would be our last. Somehow I thought he could still hear me. I told him how much I loved him and how I missed him already. I assured him that I would carry on and never forget what he did for me and how he touched my life. I was stronger than I thought I would be, up until I promised to take care of Lobo, just as I knew he would be taking care of Dillon. The tears fell from my face and moistened his covers.

Gramps always told me that those in heaven couldn't see us, because they could no longer see sin. But I had to believe there was no sin at that moment, and that my love for him was as pure as that in heaven. I believed he could hear my voice. And if he could not see me, I could certainly see him. He was holding Dillon in his lap, his knee with a steady rock, telling him the story of how Charlie and I shared a kidney when we were small boys.

———————————

During the four years that I sentenced myself to the oyster house, I had never made the trip up the hill to Mom and Dad's house. Not even on Christmas or other holidays. I shut myself in, worked in the early mornings with Gramps, and awaited Mom and Dad's visits to me in the afternoons. That was my life each day. It never changed, not one bit. It was for this reason that Mom knew something terrible had happened when I awoke her that morning. As Dad slept soundly she followed me to the kitchen where I told her about Gramps. She covered her mouth and walked back to the bedroom to tell Dad.

———————————

In twenty-eight years I had heard my dad cry once - the day Grandma passed away. As he found himself at Gramps side that morning, he only shed a few tears. Dad ran his hand over Gramps lifeless face as he stared deeply at him, obviously allowing his mind to take him on a nostalgic ride of their days together. An occasional grin would appear on Dad's face, only to be quickly replaced by a heavy frown. His memories were filled with a rollercoaster of emotions, some making him laugh out loud, others causing tears to streak down the cheeks of his face.

Mr. Robinson arrived shortly after Dad and together the two men held each other, an occasional slap on the back interrupting the silence. When people from around the community began to show up with food and condolences, the two men closed the bedroom door and spent the remainder of the morning alone with Gramps. I too, slipped away before too many folks saw me and walked quickly back to my recluse, honoring Gramps' memory my own way.

The world seemed to stop that day as I loaded up the metal drums with wood and started a fire. The river was empty as I looked across its vastness. Once news got out that Gramps was gone, no fisherman would start his engine, an honor to the greatest fisher of men that our community would ever know.

I was allowing my hands to warm against the red glow of charcoaled wood when I felt the gentle nudge of Lobo at my legs. I shifted back to Gramps' usual spot on the concrete dock and allowed Lobo to nestle his head in my lap. "It's just you and me now, Lobo." He sighed and closed his eyes.

Chapter 32

Over the next three days the small fishing village that stored our family heritage became filled with travelers from all over. Not even when the festivals came to town would you see so many license plates from other counties and states. The news of Gramps' death spread quickly to the many souls his life and sermons had touched, and each of them felt the need to say their last goodbyes. His popularity was a testament to the power of humbleness and purity. Gramps would never seek glory and was adamant about keeping pride far from his heart. He accomplished that as no person could. Never did I hear him say a demeaning word about another person. For Gramps these traits were not something he had to work at; it was simply the way he was. So after more than nine decades of life, there was no shortage of people who had come to love the man that led by quiet example and modest opinions.

At the edge of the road, a hundred yards up the hill from my house, was a gathering of live oak trees with a blanket of densely packed marsh grass. It was there that I sat most of the morning, hidden from the influx of cars that drove back and forth, waiting for the official time to pay their respects. I wanted no one to see me, mostly out of respect for Gramps. Not many people would have noticed if they did come face to face with me. The internal changes from the past four years had now fully formed my outer appearance. A low maintenance beard adorned my face and dirtied my neck. My clothes were for work purposes only, mainly mud stained flannels and overalls. A pair of short, yellow boots made up my choice of shoes. Appearance simply had no priority in my life. I had become hardened and emotionally impotent.

As kids, we could sense these people who had been beaten down by life, and at some point drained of every ounce of compassion or regard in their souls. They scared us. Their eyes were as deep as the cold, dark ocean. We wondered if they just walked out of their mother's womb that way. There were no highs and lows as experienced by most people, just a steady existence with emotions buried deep beyond some impenetrable tundra that disaster, disappointment, and loss had effectively formed.

As I sat there that morning, hidden from the world in my little fortress of trees, that's exactly how I found myself. I was an outcast to society, a terror to the innocence of children and completely at odds with peace. I represented everything Gramps did not. I was a hardened recluse, a murderer of a child, and a sinful diversion of the life Gramps lived. I would do him the honor of not showing my face at his final celebration.

I fumbled my way out of the evergreen camouflage and quickly made my way back to the house. As I rounded the back corner, I found the door had been left opened. I knew Mom and Dad were with visitors, so it couldn't be them.

"Scotty, is that you?" I called out.

"Lord, don't put that on me." Charlie came walking out of the house, his tie hanging loosely around his neck.

A mixture of embarrassment and excitement hit me. "I've become quite the overachiever haven't I?"

Charlie's smile quickly subsided from his face as he gave me an awkward hug. "Chance, my God, you look horrible." Realizing what he had said Charlie shook his head and hands to ineffectively erase the comment. "I didn't mean it that way, Chance."

I was unaffected by the slip. "It's okay. I guess most people don't expect to find their old friends like this."

"Gramps never told me you were living like this." Charlie began to stumble again, "I mean, you're living fine, but I didn't know you had walled yourself off like this. Dad said you never leave this place. He never sees you."

"Well, there's just not a lot to be seen for. Besides, I'm doing okay down here. A lot of people prefer to live alone. Maybe it just fits me best," I replied.

Charlie squatted down on the dock. He now had the distinguished look of a fine doctor. His wire glasses hung lightly on his nose and his neatly shaved head suggested that a significant amount of knowledge was stored within it. Time and genetics had evidently caught up with Charlie, causing his hair to recede much like his father's. Never one to be defeated, he evidently shaved it all off before nature beat him to it.

"Man, we had some times out here." He looked out across the river and took a deep breath of the salty air. "I tell you, Chance, I could see why you would want to live out here. There's nothing like it."

"Well, I just wish I had better reasons for hiding here," I confessed.

"It's been four years. Don't you think its time to forgive yourself? It was an accident."

I shrugged my shoulders. "You only get one chance at what I had. I lost it. That's just how it is. What I want I can't have. And I'm not looking for pity or compassion or anything else. I just want to be left alone and live the way I'm living."

Charlie shook his head as if he would try to understand my position. "Does Scotty leave you alone out here?" Charlie asked after a short period of silence.

"Of course not. Sometimes he catches me, but most of the time I crawl into the attic and watch him through the vents. He still makes himself at home, especially to my bathroom."

Charlie laughed. "Old Scotty. Man, I've missed you guys." Charlie stood back up and tightened his tie. "Are you going to change?" he asked.

"I'm not going. I'll go to the gravesite later and pay my respects."

Charlie started to convince me otherwise, but quickly realized the futility of the conversation. He patted me on the back. "I need my friend back. I'm sorry I haven't been home for all this time. There's really no excuse, but believe me when I tell you that I have good reasons."

"Trust me when I tell you there's been nothing to come home for," I replied.

"There's a lot to come home for here. I know that more than ever." Charlie put his hands in his pockets and started to walk away. "Look, Chance, I'm not flying out until tomorrow. What do you say I meet you back here tonight? Maybe catch up a little."

"That would be nice, but you'll be doing most of the talking," I said.

"Whatever, I just want to talk to my best friend again."

Chapter 33

It was six hours later when I heard the clapping of Charlie's flip-flops coming down the old oyster shell road. I had spent most of the afternoon cleaning the house, hoping it would make Charlie feel a little better about my living arrangements.

Charlie carried a bag under his arm, filled with food he had more than likely taken from his mother's fridge. A borrowed toboggan provided coverage for his head. "I noticed Gramps' little grill was down here. Thought we could cook some burgers."

"I didn't know doctors ate burgers."

Charlie looked around with a sarcastic posture. "I don't think anyone will find out."

"So, how did everything go?"

"If Gramps' dead body wasn't laying in front of me, I would have thought it was a party. The man lived ninety years, died in his sleep, didn't suffer - what more could you ask for? The church was filled with people I have never seen. There were tents all over the grounds, also filled with people. It was something to see."

"Sounds like the perfect funeral."

Charlie stared up at the sky. "Nothing less for Gramps."

I nodded my head in agreement. "Yep, who knows where I would be without him?"

Charlie returned his attention to me. "You guys got pretty close after the accident, I take it."

"Oh, yeah. Gramps was here every morning, except when he was out of town visiting you," I said as I gave Lobo a pat. "Gramps and Lobo, sometimes as early as four in the morning. I didn't sleep much for the first few months, lots of nightmares."

"I heard. Gramps and I talked often about you," Charlie informed me as he opened the bag of charcoal and began filling the grill. "I bet you guys did a lot of cooking out, too."

"All the time."

The trite sun hid sheepishly behind the distant tree line, seemingly in pursuit of a more inviting environment. It left a subtle incandescence that defined the treetops from the bitter sky. Charlie and I surrounded the burning drums and allowed our hands to absorb the heat. We traded stories about our fondest memories with Gramps, taking time to reflect on our disappointments with his last years; mine for allowing Gramps to see such failure, and Charlie for not seeing him as much over the last four years. Medical residencies are consuming, but Charlie obviously had other reasons for not coming home.

"So why haven't you been home?" I inquired.

"Well," Charlie hesitated, "really for a lot of reasons. Residency was beyond busy. I'd spend days trapped in the hospital and when I had a day off, I'd study and sleep. It was crazy. Then I got an opportunity to go to Johns Hopkins, and I couldn't pass it up." Charlie collected his thoughts again, obviously leaving something out of his explanations. He tried to reason with himself. "Gramps did make it up a few times, and saw the...," Charlie caught himself before completing his sentence, "the schedule I kept."

The breeze from the quiet night air pushed the occasional spray of frigid water harshly against my skin. My teeth chattered with each attack. Charlie and I sat in our old places, feet hanging off the concrete loading dock, talking like old times. It was getting late and the unforgiving cold began to slur our speech. I knew Charlie would need to get some rest before leaving the next morning. We had been avoiding the subject of Wendy, and I was curious if Jessica kept in touch with her. I didn't want to sound too obvious.

"So how is Jessica doing?" I asked nonchalantly.

"Don't know."

"What does that mean?" I asked.

"I haven't seen or heard from Jessica in three years."

"Three years," I repeated. "What happened?"

"We just got married for all the wrong reasons. I thought I liked having someone to come home to and she thought marrying a doctor would make her happy. We were both wrong."

"I'm sorry Charlie. Gramps never told me." An awkward minute passed without words. "Look at us, a couple of twenty-eight year old divorcees."

"It's okay. I got some good things out of it," Charlie said.

"Like what?"

"Ah, you'll see Chance...later."

"And what does that mean?" I asked. Charlie had been away for four years, and I didn't expect that he would be back anytime soon.

"I gave my six month notice to Johns Hopkins."

"You what?" I said. "You get a residency at the best hospital in the country and then get a position on their staff and now you're walking away? That doesn't make any sense, Charlie. Why would you do that?"

Charlie shrugged his shoulders and didn't offer an answer immediately.

"What's going on?" I asked again.

"Sometimes you just need home."

"Look around, Charlie. There's nothing here but depressing has-beens like me."

Charlie puckered his lips and extended his head, a position he often took when thinking. "There's more here than you know Chance," Charlie said before standing up and wiping himself off.

"You won't make half the money that you do up there," I shot back.

"Money feeds you, maybe places a roof over your head. That's it, Chance. It doesn't buy you the precious things in life."

"I think Gramps has possessed you. Maybe we should call an exorcist."

Charlie laughed. "I'll see you here in six months. It'll be like old times. Well, almost. It may be a little different. Regardless, I need you to get this guilt and depression under control between now and then."

"I'm not the same person you used to know Charlie."

"Yes you are. You're just buried under a bunch of regret right now." Charlie smiled and said goodbye with a strong hug.

Chapter 34

It was a few days later when I heard the squealing engine of Scotty's S-10 Chevy rambling down the road. I immediately climbed up the wooden ladder to the attic and took my place in hiding. Scotty knocked on the screen door once and ceremoniously let himself in.

"Chance, you in here," he yelled.

I, of course, didn't answer.

Scotty made his way through the house and began opening the drawers of my desk. He found a stash of twenties that I had saved over the last few years from the clams and oysters I sold. It represented the little bit of money I managed to save each month after paying the insurmountable mountain of bills I had agreed to through the bankruptcy arrangements.

Scotty hastily shoved a bundle of the cash in his pockets and then picked up the phone. He dialed the numbers and then waited nervously for the person to answer. "Yeah, this is Scotty Foreman. I've got the rest of the money. My boss should be walking out of the office in 30 minutes. Make sure you say 'Scotty Foreman sent me' before you shoot."

My jaw dropped as I began to comprehend the enormity of the moment. Scotty was hiring a hit man to take out his boss. He had often talked about his dissatisfaction with Ralph, especially since he had blocked Scotty's promotion over the last few years, but I never imagined it could go this far. Part of me wanted to speak out immediately, but I reserved my thoughts until I could figure out a better plan.

Scotty hung the phone up and kept his hand on it while he bowed his head. "Lord, please forgive me. I need that promotion and Ralph must go. Please understand." He then turned to walk away but stopped and opened the drawer again. He looked inside at the few bills left behind. "I'm hungry," he said before pilfering the remainder of the money into his pocket.

I couldn't believe it. I knew Scotty my entire life and had never seen him even the slightest dishonest, much less a murderer. This, of course, is not including the Jack Armstrong incident.

I waited until I heard Scotty's truck drive away and then hurried down the ladder. I could still hear the uncoordinated rattling of the engine in the distance. He was having second thoughts. Through the front window I could see his truck halfway up the shell road, idling while he obviously thought about what he was doing. I knew I had one opportunity.

As I ran out the back door in pursuit of his truck, I was met with the harsh sensation of freezing water over my head. Scotty sat tucked outside the door with an empty five-gallon bucket of Lobo's water in his hands. He had emptied it over my head.

"What are you doing?" I screamed as water shot out of my mouth.

"Hey, Chance, I was just changing your dog's water and you ran right into it. What are the chances of that happening?" Scotty replied with a strong sense of excitement in his voice. I stood shivering as water made its way through my clothes and down my leg. "Did you know there was green stuff floating in it?" Scotty continued as he picked a particle off my beard. I was silent with anger. "I guess you do now, eh buddy?" Scotty went back to cleaning the bucket before going farther. "I'm surprised you couldn't see how dirty this water was from up in that attic."

It quickly became evident that this was no accident. I had been scammed by the most unlikely of characters.

"Charlie told you, didn't he?" I asked.

"Yep, right nice of him. Don't you think?" Scotty was really enjoying his discovery.

"It's forty degrees out and you're throwing frozen, crud infested water on my head? This is why I hide from you Scotty."

"Oh, come on, honey, it was just a little joke. Besides, you shouldn't be hiding from me. I'm sensitive."

"Right," I rolled my eyes. "Sensitive." I turned to walk back inside the house.

"So, old Charlie's coming home. That's nice, isn't it?" Scotty said as he blocked the door before it could lock and followed me inside.

"There's nothing here for a guy like Charlie. He's giving up a great position to come back to a dried up fishing community. Just not a good move if you ask me."

"I didn't," Scotty replied. "Hey, do you ever talk to that pretty girl anymore?"

The question caught me off guard. Only Gramps mentioned Wendy to me over the last few years. It was a subject my parents knew to avoid. Just hearing her name fall from someone's lips caused my heart to struggle. I still loved her deeply. I always would.

"No, Scotty, never," I said nothing more.

———————

James Graham

Dear Wendy,

It's been a long time. I hope this letter finds you with some peace in your heart. I still live the nightmare, every day that I live. Gramps passed away and, without him to talk with, my mind has no reprieve from thoughts of you. I only hope that your life has found more meaning than mine. They say you sometimes have to lose everything to find yourself. I'm now convinced that what made me a person was you. And so without you I have found only emptiness. I'm sorry if my words bother you. I just wanted to say one more time that I love you. I always will.

Yours

Chapter 35

There had already been four days and nights of hard rain as I sat and listened to the clattering against the windowpane. The gales of hard wind forced the rain down at a strong angle, which magnified the commotion against the glass. An occasional flash of lightening illuminated the marshland and fully revealed the ominous black clouds that filled the dreary sky. It was early May, with the official start of summer still a few weeks away. The heat was already breaking through the mid-nineties causing an earlier than usual warming of the ocean. The forecasters were calling for one of the more active hurricane seasons in years with a prediction that twelve to fourteen storms would be named with three or four hitting land. The local forecasters had always told us not to worry too much about the early hurricanes, for these didn't typically have a lot of warm water to energize them. That rule of thumb quickly died when Andrew and Bertha devoured the Florida and North Carolina coastline a few years earlier. Dade County was still rebuilding its shipyards.

This current torrent was no hurricane, just a good drenching thunderstorm system that was finally moving off shore. A cool front had moved in behind the wet, sweltering heat, causing instability in the atmosphere, a perfect recipe for destructive thunder squalls.

Heavy rains were especially not welcomed by the fishermen. Too much fresh water falling in the salty river caused run off from sewers, creating a state of pollution for the shellfish. This would force the authorities to close down the river for a few days, or even weeks.

———————————

Ray "Diesel" Stephenson got a job with the Marine Authorities a few years earlier, courtesy of some family connections. State jobs were not easy to come across, so having inside help was necessary to get a chance at this lap of luxury. After a certain number of years with the authorities, a company truck was issued with bright orange letters to notify others of your position around town. Even better were the siren and flashing lights that were certainly necessary for those emergencies when a clam or oyster needed immediate attention.

Diesel had not been "on" long enough to earn one of these glorious chariots, which was quite disheartening to him. After two years of watching his colleagues speed past his 1980 Chevy short-bed truck with their lights in full glory, Diesel simply had to make the next step on his own. He felt his reasoning was sound; even the volunteer firemen had lights on their cars, so why not him? He was, after all, a uniformed authority in the county. This was a disgrace. No wonder more women didn't fall for his splendid uniform and "husky" appearance (Diesel weighed a tad over three hundred and fifty pounds). It had to be the lights.

It was nothing less than fate the day Diesel ran across an old siren and light set at a junkyard he visited while on vacation in the Blue Ridge Mountains. The excitement was so strong that he came home three days early so he could attach the lady-magnets to his wheels. For two weeks he sat in a chair under the old pecan tree in his parent's back yard and watched those lights dance. He couldn't help but gloat when he called his mom out to hear the different screams of the siren. Socks, their pet cat of fifteen years, couldn't take it anymore and abruptly left after the third day.

When the rain subsided, Diesel received his first "post-siren" emergency call. A lump entered his throat, mostly from the burrito he decided to swallow before answering the phone. His time had arrived. He was needed to do a water check at the river and deliver the sample to the lab immediately.

I, unfortunately, was picking up a few clams at the shoreline when Diesel's truck came racing down the shell drive, his light and siren in full force. My initial thought was that an ambulance was coming, but once the mud and dirt settled, I saw the leaning pickup just a few yards in front of me.

Diesel's voice was preceded by a loud click that escaped from the speakers. "This – is – the – Marine – Authorities. Please – place – the – clams – on – the – ground – beside – you." Diesel smiled with anticipation as he changed the pace of the lights and made another siren noise before getting out of the truck. Once his weight was completely out of the vehicle, it bounced back and forth, nearly causing the tires to leave the ground. I dropped the bag of clams and started to put my hands up. Diesel walked to the shoreline and gave me a good looking over.

"Well, I'll be a jumping mullet, it's Chance Gordon."

"Hey, Diesel, I see you got some lights on your truck."

Diesel gave me a smug look and then proudly turned to gaze at his trophies. "That's right, partner. It's surprising what some of us accomplish after high school." Diesel stuck his chest out a little farther, competing with the clearance of his stomach. "Hard to believe, ain't it?"

"You've done well. I'm sure your parents are proud."

"Well, I haven't killed anybody, either. That helps. Speaking of which, I hear you've been hiding out down here the last few years since you killed...I mean, had that accident. Nobody ever sees you except Scotty and your parents. Isn't that right?"

I took Diesel's comments in stride. "I don't get around much. Scotty keeps me updated on everyone."

Diesel's eyes lit up. "Old Scotty better watch himself. He put a rotten fish head in my glove department last week. He's lucky that I didn't arrest him for it."

"I think you should," I said. Diesel nodded his head like he would give it a second thought.

"So what's the deal? You just gonna hide out here the rest of your life like some hermit?"

"Probably. Is that against the law?" I asked.

"You just watch yourself, Chance Gordon. I know how you weirdos turn out. First, you hide out in the woods for ten years. Then you change your name to Unabomber or start suicide cults. I'm trained in these things." Diesel pointed his finger at me. "Don't you forget that, mister."

Diesel walked down to the water and pulled out an empty vial. He inspected the container for a few moments, taking time to ensure that I saw the expertise needed to collect water. From the corner of his eye he glanced at me and then turned his attention to the water in the vial. He assured himself that I had seen his skillful technique. I watched, more out of sympathy than interest, as Diesel sniffed the water then tried to calculate if it smelled polluted or not. In truth, the only test for water pollution was in a laboratory. A well-behaved monkey could collect the water and deliver it to the lab.

But the Marine Fisheries had Diesel, and like most things, he made the routine seem like much more than it really was. He again allowed his eyes to look my way, and when he saw me continuing to watch him a smile broke across his wide face. He held the vial up again, swirled the water around a few times and then sipped a good amount of the muddy concoction.

Now Diesel really had my attention. He swished the water between his teeth and began gargling until bubbles oozed from his mouth. After spitting the water out, with most of it landing on his belly, he savored the aftertaste and then began shaking his head as if the answer was now clear to him.

"Yep, yep, just as I expected. You'll need to leave them-there clams in the water. I've never been wrong before," Diesel said, very impressed with his quick analysis. I'm not sure he understood the definition of polluted – a combination of sewage run off, fecal material, bacteria and all sorts of nasty organisms. By no means should this be siphoned through the human mouth.

Diesel licked his teeth before getting back into his truck. The shocks and suspension crunched under his weight. He astutely changed the light sequence and sounded off the siren once more. "I'll be watching you, Chance. And tell your buddy Scotty that old George Reubans at the prison is looking for a new boyfriend. If he plays another childish prank on me, I'll be playing cupid with his sorry butt."

"You bet, Diesel. Good job out there today," I replied. "And I'll tell Scotty what you said."

———————————————

It turned out that Diesel was right on the money. The very next day the Marine Authorities closed down the river for a week. I saw Scotty three times and told him nothing of Diesel's warning. I could only hope that he would play another prank on Officer Ray "Diesel" Stephenson.

Chapter 36

As advertised, June began as a scorcher. Temperatures hit triple digits three times during the first two weeks. The other days were much cooler, somewhere in the high nineties with a suffocating humidity. Lobo and I decided to find clams in the waist deep water in an effort to keep cool. This of course, did little to keep my face and neck from baking in the sun.

For reasons unknown by the local researchers, clam season was quite profitable that year. It was not uncommon to haul in four or five hundred clams in a four-hour romp down the shoreline. Lobo would easily corner a dozen different crabs in that time. He unfortunately ran into a streak of bad luck and was bitten twice in a four-day period. I wasn't nearly as quick as Gramps at dislodging his nose from the crab's grip. Lobo's disappointment in my ineptness was apparent in his sad eyes, as I struggled to dismantle the crab's hold without becoming a victim myself.

During his days off, Scotty would bring a folding chair to the dock and sit with me. I provided the sweetened iced tea and he, of course, provided most of the conversation. I had to admit, with Gramps gone, it was nice to have someone to talk to – or in Scotty's case, listen to.

———————————

There wasn't a cloud in the sky the day Scotty came running down to the house in a panic. With no breath to spare, he managed to say the word "Diesel" before climbing up the ladder and hiding in my attic.

"Scotty, what's going on?" It was a rhetorical question.

"Diesel's going to arrest me."

"He can't arrest you," I said matter-of-factly.

Scotty was not convinced. "I've seen his hand cuffs."

"He got them from Wal-Mart," I argued.

"Whatever, he has them, he weighs three-times more than me, and he's surprisingly fast. I'm sure he could arrest me."

I was in no mood to play games, and even less enthusiastic when I heard Diesel's siren in front of the house. The loud click of the speaker again preceded Diesel's intimidating voice. "This – is – the – poli…" Diesel decided not to impersonate a police officer. Another click. "This – is – the – authorities. Scotty – Foreman – come – out – with – your – hands – up."

Scotty screeched in terror. I allowed a smile to enter my face for the first time in four and a half years. Diesel began counting down like a chastising mother. Click. "One – Two – Three." There was a long moment of silence. I heard the shocks on Diesel's truck celebrate as he stepped out of the vehicle.

"I'm coming in," he screamed, this time with no speaker.

Even I was a little nervous for Scotty as Diesel's simple white T-shirt exposed his massiveness. "Scotty, you're dead," I said with a not so calming voice.

Diesel walked through the back door uninvited. His plastic handcuffs were twirling around his finger. "Where's he at, Gordon?"

"Who?" I asked, my voice cracking like a pubescent boy.

Diesel's face gnarled and twisted. His voice became suddenly more sinister. "You know who I'm talking about. This time I caught him red handed. I was at the EZ-Check and saw him throw an oyster toad in my front seat."

Oyster toads are by far the most repulsive of fish in the river. Favoring a horn toad with shark teeth, they are inedible and known for their ability to cause extensive damage to the unlucky finger that crosses their path. People usually cut the line to rid themselves of the little monsters. Scotty decided on a different fate for his catch.

I exhaled loudly. I allowed my right index finger to point up at the attic while saying, "I don't know that I've seen him today."

Diesel proved to be smarter than I thought and immediately caught on to my sell-out. He walked to the ladder and evaluated its stability. He thought better of climbing it. "Get down here, Scotty, before I call back-up."

"You can call all the back-up you want, I'm not coming down," Scotty screeched.

Diesel huffed loudly. "One – Two."

"You probably can't count any higher than three, and even if you could, I'm not coming down."

Diesel's face turned red. Scotty had gone too far this time. Diesel placed one foot on the bottom step and tested it under his weight. He then climbed to the second step and again hesitated. The creaking of the wood alerted Scotty that something unnatural was occurring. He slid to the opening and surveyed the scene below.

Scotty looked back at me with terror and question in his eyes. "You're dead," I mouthed.

Diesel surprisingly ascended the ladder, his eyes fixed on the suffering steps. Scotty was trapped. I could tell that he was eyeballing the width of Diesel's shoulders compared to the attic opening. It would be close, and Scotty was taking no chances. Diesel's head was now just a couple of feet from the top. Without warning Scotty slid his torso farther out and placed both of his hands on the top of Diesel's head, attempting to halt his ascent.

The combination of Scotty's pressure and Diesel's determination to push his way up the ladder proved to be disastrous. Scotty was now placing most of his weight on Diesel's head. Diesel, on the other hand, allowed one arm to leave the ladder and swing at Scotty. It was during one of these swings that things took a turn for the worse. Under the massive weight, the step cracked a little louder and suddenly broke loose, hurling Diesel to the floor, flat on his back.

I groaned at the impact. Before I could even ask if he was alive, Scotty lost his balance without Diesel's head to hold him, and also plummeted to the ground. He landed squarely on Diesel's stomach, which provided as much cushioning as an airplane could have needed. In a blink of an eye, Scotty bounded off Diesel, who was surprisingly conscious enough to grab his prey. A heinous scream erupted from Scotty, sounding like a stuck pig, which seemed to energize his legs. With Diesel's finger barely grasped to his buckle, Scotty spun around in three or four circles before finally breaking lose from the hold. Scotty's scream quickly changed to a mimicking laugh as he bolted out the back door. Diesel, now up in a seated position, began rubbing his head and checking for open fractures.

I couldn't imagine an individual being more furious until Diesel heard the sound of his truck door open. A loud click then preceded the sound of Scotty's voice on the speaker. "Diesel – Stephenson. Please – get – off – your – butt – and – stop – causing – earthquakes." This, of course, was followed by a series of giggles.

Knowing he was cheating death, Scotty jumped back out of the truck and ran up the shell road, disappearing behind the coverage of trees. He would make it home in record time.

Diesel slowly stood up and continued checking himself for injuries. He was amazingly unscathed from the fall.

"You okay, Diesel?" I asked with a feigned concern.

"Not a word to anyone, you hear?"

"It's not like I talk to many folks to begin with," I said convincingly. "Why in the world is Scotty throwing dead fish in your truck?"

Diesel continued wiping himself off. "We had a disagreement about our churches. He called us a bunch of hypocritical Pharisees because we don't believe other churches worship God properly."

That was a conversation I didn't want to get involved in. "Sounds heated," I replied.

"It's not over yet. I'm going to give Scotty a reason to run around his church hooting and hollering."

"So you believe only your church will go to heaven?" I had to ask.

"Yep, and other churches like it. We serve God the right way."

I gave his comment some thought. "So you don't think my Grandfather is in heaven?" Gramps' church was non-denominational.

"Now, I can't say that. Your Granddad was a righteous man. And I believe he's in heaven. But I also believe he was one of us. He just preached in a different church."

I didn't think it would be healthy to argue with Diesel. Besides, he surely knew a lot more about the Bible than

I did. I let the conversation die. "Well, I'm sorry things didn't work out with Scotty today. I would have grabbed him but I was too concerned about you."

"Whatever, Gordon." Diesel stomped out of the house. His siren broke the peaceful quiet of an afternoon lull as he began another pursuit of the great Scotty Foreman.

———————————

Dear Wendy,

It's been a suffocating summer thus far. It's hard to believe that almost five years have passed since I last saw you. I don't need pictures to remember you. You're always there in the back of my mind, reminding me of our times together. I miss them with a pain I could never begin to describe. I miss what could have been, what should have been. I now accept it as my past and as my permanent scar. I will never get over it, but I hope to someday travel farther through it, and find some semblance of peace. I only hope you can remember the way I used to be.

I love you,

Yours

Chapter 37

It was late June on a Sunday afternoon that I found myself alone on the back dock. There was a welcomed reprieve from the humidity, which made the dry heat much more pleasant to bake in. The sunset was full of kaleidoscopic changes that left me marveling at its unfathomable creator.

Things would have been relatively peaceful had it not been for a neurotic bee that insisted on buzzing by my head every time I got comfortable. I had enough, after its fourth flyby, and began chasing it around the corner of the house, my complete attention focused upon the retreating nuisance. It was for this reason that I did not notice the small child who unfortunately awaited me on the other side. He landed flat on his back as our unfairly matched bodies collided. The first thing I noticed was his curly blonde locks, which I was certain I had seen somewhere before.

"Are you okay, little fella?" I asked. His eyes were the size of grapefruits as he lay frozen on his back, grasping a Pepsi in one hand and a bag of peanuts in the other. He kept his elbows locked at ninety degrees, which allowed the cola to continue pouring out onto his shirt. I picked him back up and began wiping the grass off his face and shirt.

"Who are you?" I asked, not expecting his state of shock to allow an answer.

His eyes remained stoic and magnified through the thin pair of spectacles that adorned his pale face. He continued to stare blankly at me.

I shook him lightly. "Buddy, can you please tell me where you came from?"

Tears began to flow down his dirty cheeks. "I'm Dillon Robinson. My phone number is..." he stopped and took a big breath. "My phone number used to be 352-1876. I live..." he stopped again. "I used to live on 154 Drury Rd. My dad's name is Charlie Robbins."

He was without question an offspring of Charlie Robbins. His big blue eyes studied me through the round-framed glasses. His eyes drooped like a sad puppy, much the same as his dad's did many years before.

My shock began to thaw as I took in the reality of what I was seeing. Charlie had a son, a spitting image of himself.

"What did you say your name was?" I asked as I tried to shake the cobwebs out of my head.

"My name is Dillon Robbins. My phone number..."

"I know the rest," I said cutting him off.

"Did that bee sting you?" he asked.

"What? Oh, yeah, I mean, no. No, it did not sting me."

Pepsi continued dripping down the young boy's face. "It must have been a boy bee. Daddy says they can't sting. Only the girls can. He says that's true most always, even with people."

"How old are you?" I asked, amazed at how well this small child conversed.

"He's four," Charlie's voice came from behind us.

The boy ran behind Charlie and peered out at me. "Daddy, he ran over me," he said with a pout. "He was chasing a boy bee."

"I hit him pretty hard. I didn't see him," I confessed.

"That's okay, he's a tough little man. Right, Doodles?" Charlie patted him on the back.

"My name is Dillon," he shot back.

"Nice name, Charlie. Couldn't leave that one alone could you?"

"This isn't the only Dillon you'll run across in your life," Charlie replied.

"Trust me, I could have done without the honor," I said.

"I didn't figure you'd be impressed at first," Charlie replied. "But you can call him Doodles."

Dillon peeked back out from behind the cover of Charlie. "No, you can't. I'm Dillon."

The young child placed a hand over his mouth and began whispering to Charlie. Like most children's whisper, it was audible fifty yards away. "Daddy, why does he have hair on his face?"

Charlie smiled at me before answering, "He's part gorilla."

Dillon playfully hit Charlie in frustration. "No, he's not, Daddy. You're picking."

"You mind if I use your bathroom to clean him up?" Charlie asked.

"Not at all. Help yourself."

Charlie lifted the thin child, obviously small for his age. Dillon laid his head on Charlie's shoulder and placed his hand over his face so I couldn't see him. "Your Uncle Chance was just teaching you how to play football," Charlie joked.

"Football hurts," Dillon moaned. "Is he really my uncle?"

Charlie kissed him on his dirty forehead before answering, "Yep."

"What are uncles again?" Dillon asked as the two disappeared into the house.

While Charlie and Dillon were inside I allowed my mind to wonder. I thought about how different my life would be had it not been for that God-forsaken night. I saw the love that Charlie and Dillon had for each other, and as pure as it was, it made me nauseous. One second in time denied me from experiencing that kind of love. It denied me the dream of having a loving wife, as Wendy was, and sharing the miracle of our passion. The simple things, such as us both holding our child's hand while crossing a parking lot, seemed like the ultimate lottery to me. I had lost out in life.

Like the sensation of a cold shower erupting across my body, all the feelings from five years earlier returned as the wounds, which were poorly healed to begin with, reopened and oozed throughout me. My head began to pulsate. Flashes of Wendy's horrified face as she grasped her stomach flipped through my head. Her horrible screams as the house crashed to the ground echoed in my ears, followed by the sudden darkness that quieted her and stole the life from within her. Any healing that I had experienced over the last five years was quickly erased; the pain was back. It reminded me of why I lived the kind of life I did, secluded from the world.

Charlie came back outside with Dillon continuing to hide behind him. I studied what I could of his face. "He looks just like you," I said.

"Yep, he's my buddy," Charlie glowed as he looked down at the cowering child.

"Four years. You had him shortly after you were married," I calculated.

192

"Yep, a trip to Charleston with Jessica right after we got married. It was a seminar - pretty boring. We found other things to do."

I allowed my mind to turn. "And Gramps saw him?"

"Twice," Charlie replied. "We decided not to tell you."

I looked down at the ground and kicked at some pebbles. Dillon continued hiding behind Charlie, not sure what to think about me. Charlie reached behind and pulled the boy in front of him. Like Charlie as a child, he was lacking size and eyesight. He was obviously intelligent and significantly advanced for four years of age. He was also a little shy, something his dad quickly grew out of. All in all, he looked vulnerable and yet adorable. His hair was full of slight feathers and curls. He was the kind of child that strange women would attack with kisses and hugs in public places, much to his chagrin.

"Dillon and I wanted to invite you to our house tonight for dinner, right buddy?" Charlie gave Dillon a gentle shake.

"Yes," Dillon replied with a severe lack of enthusiasm.

"Thanks, guys," I replied, "but I'd rather not."

"Come on, Chance, I want to show you the new place. I built a house across the road from deadman's curve. I even left an oak tree in the back yard, next to the house. Dillon will be climbing down from his window in no time. Right, buddy?"

Dillon nodded his head with a newfound enthusiasm.

"Look Charlie, it's really good to see you but it's not like it used to be. You couldn't understand."

"It's only a half mile away. I'm not asking you to go to Wal-Mart," Charlie continued to coax.

"I don't leave here," I said with some unintentional agitation.

"Okay, Chance, it's okay." Charlie quickly soothed the tension.

"I'm sorry," I said. "I'm sorry you have to see me this way. I'm sorry..." I paused before saying the name again. "I'm sorry Dillon has to meet me this way. I'm sure your house is beautiful. Maybe you guys can sit out on the oak tree and talk, like we used to." My voice became unsteady, prompting me to stop talking.

Charlie walked over and squeezed my shoulder. "Time to say goodbye Dillon," Charlie said while motioning for the child to join us.

Dillon walked over, his head flexed strongly to the ground. Without looking up at me he put his hand out. I shook it. "Goodnight, Mr. Dillon."

"Goodnight, Mr. Chance."

"Uncle Chance," Charlie corrected him.

"Goodnight, Uncle Chance."

I watched as Charlie and Dillon walked away. They held hands as Dillon became obviously more animated without my presence. Charlie pointed out at the river, obviously trying to show Dillon something. A pelican dove hard to the water and resurfaced with a fish hanging from its beak. Young Dillon jumped up and down as he pointed at the scene with excitement. Charlie continued teaching him as they disappeared down the shoreline.

Dear Wendy,

Today I went back to the night we lost our Dillon. All the scars reopened and I felt the pain all over again. I know this probably happens to you sometimes, if not all the time. I became acutely aware of how much I've lost. I will never stop being angry with myself. I would sell my soul to erase the pain I caused you. Charlie has moved back. He built a house close to where I stay. He also has a son. His name is Dillon. I can't tell you how much it hurt to see him. He is precious, just like our Dillon would have been.

Yours

Chapter 38

Not even an hour had passed when Charlie and Dillon returned to my house with a basket full of food. Dillon continued his demurring ways as he kept shelter behind Charlie.

"We got bored. Decided to come back and bother you."

"Not much better here I assure you," I replied from my sitting spot.

"Yeah it is. My furniture hasn't arrived yet. It's pretty depressing sitting on a floor to eat. Besides, you've got the grill."

Dillon moved away from Charlie and sat at the edge of the dock. The afternoon brought with it a low tide, which exposed thousands of tiny sandfiddler crabs.

"What are those, Daddy?" he asked.

Charlie peeked over at the mud. "Those are little crabs called sandfiddlers. They don't bite hard like the big ones do."

Dillon became quiet and puckered his lips out, identical to the way Charlie would think about things. "Can I keep one for a pet?" he asked.

"A pet crab?" Charlie repeated.

"It can sleep with me."

Charlie chuckled. "I tell you what, big guy, you can have one for a pet but we'll just let it stay here with Uncle Chance."

Dillon wasn't convinced of Charlie's sincerity. "No Daddy, I'll lose it out here."

"No, you won't. Your Uncle Chance takes care of all these little crabs. He'll make sure to check on yours every morning. Right, Uncle Chance?"

My mind, of course, was elsewhere. "Yeah, sure, whatever you want me to do," I replied coldly.

My mind was thinking about Wendy's fear of crabs when I felt a tug on my shirt. I looked down to find Dillon staring up at me. His face was somber. "Do you promise, Uncle Chance? Do you promise to take care of my crab?" he asked.

The way he said "Uncle Chance" made my heart feel a little less heavy. I was actually pleased that he didn't feel the need to hide from me. "I promise," I said and gave him a smile. He returned one twice as big.

"One more thing, Uncle Chance."

"What's that?"

"Your beard scares my crab. He wants you to shave it off," he said with his best sales pitch.

"Your crab is scared of my beard?"

"Yes."

"How do you know?"

"He's hiding in his hole."

"Crabs like going in their holes."

"Not mine. He's scared of your beard."

I smiled down at him again. "I'll see what I can do."

Dillon frowned. "What's wrong?" I asked.

"That's what Daddy says when he really means no but doesn't want to talk about it anymore."

I knelt down and looked in Dillon's eyes. "I promise that I'll shave my beard so your little crab will be happy."

Dillon stuck his hand out. "Shake on it, mister."

———————————

While Dillon sat at the edge of the dock and talked to his new pet, Charlie and I stood around the grill watching the hotdogs begin to blacken.

"Hard to believe he's only four," I said.

"He's my world."

"Wished I knew what that was like."

Charlie squeezed my shoulder. "I hope you can be a part of his life, in spite of everything that's happened."

I took a sip of my drink and looked over at Dillon. "So, what does he know about his mom?"

"Not much. He doesn't ask."

"He never had a chance to know her?"

Charlie bit his bottom lip as he thought of a good way to explain the situation. "It became very obvious early in the pregnancy that Jessica wasn't healthy. Mentally, I mean. She began acting weird, wouldn't talk to any of her family or friends. She wouldn't talk to me half the time. Being a mom was not what she had planned for her life. Like I said before, being married to a doctor was not the easy life she had hoped for."

"Did she go crazy?" I asked.

"No, not crazy. She just wasn't happy with life. She wasn't happy with me as her husband and she definitely wasn't happy being fat with Dillon. We both knew it wouldn't last. We didn't have to say anything."

"Didn't she get attached to the baby?"

"No, she didn't let herself. She went through the motions, made all the doctor appointments, but never bought into the mother thing."

"That's hard to understand," I said. "I mean, I remember she was always a little different, maybe self absorbed, but a baby would change that."

"Like I said, she wasn't healthy mentally. Jessica had issues that she needed to take care of. She had her things packed up a week before the due date. When the nurse handed her the baby she looked at it and gave it straight to me."

"Unbelievable. How about her parents? Didn't they want to see it?"

Chance sputtered his lips. "I don't even know if they knew. Her parents got divorced a few years earlier when both were caught having affairs. They remarried and forgot about each other and the family. Jessica never heard from them, nor did she seem to care. Neither of them would take time from their social world to acknowledge it. Besides, they always told Jessica to never have kids."

"Sounds like a tough time. I guess that's why your mom stayed for a month."

"Yeah, she helped a lot, but she's not as young as she used to be and her diabetes always had me worrying that she would pass out while watching Dillon. When Mom started showing the strain, I decided to hire an extra nurse so I could bring Dillon to the office with me."

"You really had your hands full."

"But it was worth it; he's been great. He started reading some a few months ago - unheard of for his age. He's just like a sponge. Now he's even scribbling his name."

Charlie was obviously proud of Dillon. His eyes lit up whenever he said the name.

As Charlie and I sat devouring our hotdogs, Diesel came strutting down the road.

"Here comes the river authority."

"Who?" Charlie asked.

"Diesel Stephenson," I answered. "He comes down every afternoon and checks the water. Really makes a spectacle of it."

When Diesel noticed more than one body on the dock he made an aggressive turn towards us. After realizing that the extra body was not Scotty he tapered his pace and carried on to the shoreline. Charlie noticed this sudden change in direction.

"What was that about?" he asked.

"He must have thought you were Scotty," I answered.

"What's going on with them?"

"It's a grudge match. Scotty has supposedly been placing rotten fish heads in Diesel's truck. He's been running from Diesel ever since."

"Not that I'm surprised, but why would Scotty put dead fish in his truck?" Charlie inquired.

"They had a heated disagreement about their churches."

"Arguing over churches. I'm sure that makes God happy."

Diesel finished his collection and strutted his way towards us. When he got close enough to the edge of the dock he placed a foot up on it and rested his elbows on his thighs. His stomach stretched down and escaped from the bottom of his T-shirt.

"Where's the truck and new lights, Diesel?" I asked.

Diesel stared at us with a look of disgust. He abused the toothpick in his mouth as he slid it back and forth. He spit a lump of tobacco on the ground and then wiped his mouth with the back of his hand. "Why do you care, Gordon? I know you boys make fun of it. I'm sure the big time doctor gets his licks in, also."

I acted innocent, but said nothing to defend myself.

"I think it's great you got lights on your truck, Diesel," Charlie quickly separated himself from the friction.

Dillon's ears perked up at the sound of lights. He walked over to Diesel and tugged on his shirt.

"What do you want, kid?" Diesel snarled down at him.

"Are you a policeman?"

Diesel shifted his eyes toward us before answering. "Kind of."

"Wow," he said with one long syllable. "And you have lights and a horn?"

Diesel obviously liked the respect, even from a four-year old. "That's right, kid, lights and a siren." He looked back at us before continuing in a softer voice. "Maybe I'll show it to you sometime."

Dillon jumped up and down while clapping his hands. "Can I see it now?"

"Soon, partner. I'll bring it by tomorrow, how's that sound?' Diesel spoke with a surprising gentleness.

"Okay, mister," Dillon agreed. "Let's shake on it."

As Diesel shook Dillon's hand, the familiar sound of Scotty's truck came rumbling down the shell road. Diesel's eyes squinted as he cocked his head to the side in an effort to identify the familiar noise.

"Scotty Foreman," Diesel grunted. "And he doesn't see my truck here. I'm gonna kill'em."

Dillon's eyes filled with terror. Diesel saw the reaction and quickly relieved him. "Not really kill him, just beat him up a little bit." Diesel made his way into the house and hid just inside the door. "Not a whisper, or I'll make your life miserable."

"That'll be a change," I whispered to myself.

Scotty came hopping around the corner and stopped suddenly when he saw Dillon. "Who is this little chipmunk?"

"I'm not a chipmunk. I'm Dillon Robbins. My daddy's name is Dr. Charl...."

"I know who your old ugly dad is," Scotty interrupted Dillon.

"My dad's pretty," Dillon said as defensively as a four-year old could.

Scotty grabbed his stomach and pretended to double over with laughter. He straightened back up and made his way over to us, right in front of the door. Diesel slid farther back to conceal himself.

Scotty looked at Charlie and said, "Pretty like the south end of a north bound mule. Now what's the chipmunk's name again?" Scotty asked as he slapped Dillon on the butt.

Dillon spun around and gave him a nasty look.

"Yikes, big man. You're not going to stomp my pretty little toes are you?"

Diesel slid out from his place of hiding and steadied himself behind Scotty.

"Just give me a name, Chipmunk."

Diesel caught Dillon's attention and motioned for him to move aside.

"What's – the – name?" Scotty repeated slowly.

Dillon stepped aside before shouting "Diesel."

"Who?" Scotty asked.

Diesel had a running start by the time Scotty turned around to see him. The momentum behind Diesel's weight made him no less dangerous than a loaded train. Scotty had no time to move - except to duck down, which is exactly what he did. Diesel's massive arms barely missed their target, his knees instead making the only contact against Scotty's cowering body. As large as Diesel's upper body was, his legs were surprisingly lacking. This anatomical disproportion produced a weakness that was instantly apparent – Diesel was top heavy. His momentum carried him right off the end of the dock, the weight imbalance creating a centripetal somersault that lacked any element of grace. Scotty remained cowered down on the dock, his arms still protecting the back of his head, as Charlie, Dillon, and I watched Diesel finally end his flight with a crash landing in four feet of raunchy, thick mud. The mud sputtered around him and between his legs, along with every other crevice of his body, like a can of busted biscuits.

Diesel didn't move. Scotty slowly removed his arms from his head and peeked over at the horrific scene. Dillon ran to the edge of the concrete dock and covered his face in terror.

"He's okay, buddy. That's like falling in a pool of pudding," Charlie said with a comforting voice.

Dillon shook his head "no" as small tears began to glass over his eyes. "My crab."

"Oh, your crab. I'm sure he's fine too."

Dillon continued shaking his head. "There's no way, Daddy. He's dead."

Diesel did his best to push himself out of the sinking mud, experiencing numerous falls during his attempts. Scotty, although dazed by his brush with death, began to comprehend the enormity of the moment. His belly laughing nearly made him soil himself as he crossed his legs and began hollering at his would-be attacker.

"If that river wasn't polluted before, it sure as heck is now," he cried.

When Charlie threw a rope out to help Diesel back in, Scotty made an abrupt exit to safer grounds. "That would have killed off the dinosaurs again," he said as he ran through the house. His laughing was audible even above the clanking of his truck engine.

Although embarrassed, Diesel's anger was more evident. "I'm gonna kill 'em I tell ya. Kill 'em."

Diesel left a trail of muddy footprints on the dock as he walked back home, humility trailing his every step.

Charlie looked at me and smiled. "I hate to laugh, but that was something to see," he said.

There was no laughter on my part. My mind was far away, lost in another moment in time when Wendy fell off the dock and landed in the shallow water and mud. She made it seem so cute, so graceful. I wished I could laugh like that again. I loved all her reactions and memorized them all. They still played in my head, all of them.

"What's wrong, Chance?"

"Nothing. If you guys don't mind I want to be left alone right now. There's somewhere else I need to be."

I had never seen such disappointment on Charlie's face. A frown was something that rarely found Charlie, but at that moment it found him in a big way. I had nothing to say.

Charlie grabbed Dillon's hand and led him off the dock. Dillon pulled away and looked back at me. "Uncle Chance, if you see my crab, will you save him?"

I closed my eyes. "Sure, kid."

And they were gone.

Chapter 39

I kept the doors locked for the next three days, denying access to everyone who happened by. This was easy when Mr. Robbins wanted to use my bathroom during a break from catching oysters. It was not so easy when little Dillon came knocking, with Charlie, of course, and called for "Uncle Chance." But it was better that he not see me as I was.

Some bouts of depression were worse than others, and with him around to remind me of my loss, I found myself sinking deeper in a vicious despair. I spent most of those few days sleeping or at least lying on the sofa. I covered myself with blankets and prayed to God that I would close my eyes and not wake back up. I slept quite a bit; and when I did, I had the opportunity to see Wendy. Even the nightmares became welcomed, just to see her face.

On the fourth morning, I felt the first signs of hunger, which inspired me to venture out to catch a few clams. I ate what I found.

I continued to distance myself from Dillon. As much as I wanted to see Charlie, the side effects were too strong. I knew there was no way I could ever accept a child named Dillon in my life; it represented too much pain.

Over the next month, Charlie continued his desperate and futile attempts to get me away from the old oyster shack, which I considered my permanent home. He offered me medications, which I had no interest in trying. I knew what my problem was, and no drug could fix it. Nothing could.

Charlie's invitations ranged from boat rides to dinner at his house, even a trip to Costa Rica for a few days. I firmly denied his repetitive requests until finally he stopped asking. He continued to bring Dillon around, although the visits were brief. Charlie saw the difficulties I was having with it. As for Dillon, none of this seemed to bother him as long as he had his dad's leg to hold onto. He was, however, pleased that his crab miraculously survived its Hiroshima-like attack from Diesel.

———————————

It was a typical Saturday afternoon in the midst of another smoldering summer. Sweat beads ran down my forehead and assaulted my eyes, calling tears to soothe the pain. I was just before retiring to the dark coolness of the house when Charlie approached the dock in his skiff. He pulled close enough to reach out and grab a docking pole. "Want to go for a ride?" he asked with no hesitation.

I thought he had grasped the futility of his invitations, but Charlie seemed to relapse into a state of forgetfulness. I said nothing and instead waited for him to realize the error of his question.

"Well?" he said. "It's a great afternoon."

"No Charlie," I said before turning back to the house.

"Chance," Charlie screamed out. I stopped and looked at the sky before turning back and staring at him.

Charlie's face showed a plead that would usually be reserved for children. "Come on, buddy, just you and me. Nobody's out today. It's too hot to fish. Mom and Dad have Dillon for a couple of hours." There was a short silence before Charlie spoke again. "This is the last time I ask you to do anything away from this house. I promise."

"We go out for a few minutes and you will stop asking me to do things? Right?"

"You got it. Last time."

Charlie zipped the boat around and headed across the river to the Morehead City port. The large phosphate domes quickly filled the skyline and I immediately thought back to the night I first kissed Wendy. Charlie steered to the middle of the ship channel and cut the engine. It was a calm afternoon, the glassy appearance of the water looking more like a lake than a river. Charlie leaned back against the side of the boat and looked around, following the puffy white clouds for a few minutes.

"I bet I know what you're thinking about," he finally said.

"I'm sure you do."

"You kissed her here. I've heard that story a thousand times since then."

"You won't hear it anymore."

"Nope, I don't suspect I will."

"How long will Dillon stay with your parents?" I asked, trying to get an idea of how much time Charlie planned for us.

"Only a couple of hours. They can't do much more than that. Mom's been having some bad days with her diabetes and Dad can't take care of both of them. Multi-tasking is not his thing."

"I'm sorry your mom is not doing well," I said.

"Well, at least I'm close now," Charlie responded.

"Mom says she's been really down over the last few weeks. Some kind of depression, I guess."

Charlie was obviously not satisfied with the direction of our conversation. "Yeah, some kind of depression," he quickly retorted before changing the subject. "So, what's it going to take to get you out of this funk? It's been a long time, Chance. You've got to wake up and get on with the years. Nobody's promising you tomorrow."

"Is this why you brought me out here, Charlie? So you can feed me this self-pity story without me walking away? I'll swim to shore. I swear I'll do it."

Charlie was determined to say what he had planned. "I'm not saying to just sweep it under the rug. I just wish you could at least learn to live with a past that you understandably regret. Just turn the next page. Take what you have left and make the most of it."

"I've got nothing left, Charlie. Why can't you just accept that?"

"Because it's not true. You have plenty left. You have me and your parents and…"

"And what, Charlie?" I stood up and screamed. "Why don't you consider this: just imagine yourself taking too many of those pills you prescribe to your patients. Imagine that you like taking those pills, even though everyone is telling you not to. Then imagine that while in one of your sloppy highs you burn your house down and kill Dillon along the way. And then add to that a person whom you love more than anything else on earth - and you rip her heart out." I stopped just long enough to catch my breath. "Guess what you'd be doing, Charlie?" His face saddened with defeat. "You'd be me."

Charlie looked away and said nothing. I sat down with my back towards him, drying the tears from my eyes. The engine started and we headed back to shore. Not a word was spoken when I climbed out of the boat and disappeared into the house. Charlie pulled away from the dock. I didn't expect to see him for a while.

There was a time in my life when I couldn't fathom causing someone pain like I did for Charlie. But I was used to it. The hardness of my heart wouldn't allow one ounce of remorse to penetrate even a layer of skin. I didn't give his pain a second thought. As the sound of the engine disappeared, I easily settled back into my life.

———————————

Dear Wendy,

When love was new it was the most exciting time of my life. I remember lying awake half the night thinking of what I would say if or when I saw you again. I remember the shallow breaths that overcame me when I did see you, and the misery when I didn't run across your beautiful smile. And then the first time we kissed — nothing will ever move me the same. Love is beautiful; it is completeness. It gave me unknown strength and feelings I never knew I had. Love is wonderful — and then it's gone.

I love you always.

Me

Chapter 40

I didn't expect Charlie to soon forget my hostile outburst, but somehow it seemed he did. When he showed up at the dock two days later he made no mention of the event. I thought about apologizing but decided otherwise in an effort to keep the point grounded.

Dillon, as usual, hurriedly made his way to the edge of the concrete foundation to search for his pet crab. "I see him, Daddy, right there. He's looking at us." Dillon pointed to a cluster of scattering crabs.

"He certainly is," Charlie played along.

Charlie's eyes were puffy, obviously from some extra hours at work. Without asking if I was hungry, he fired up the grill and placed four sizzling steaks on it. I was starving.

"Putting in some long hours?" I asked to break the silence.

Charlie sat down a few feet away from the grill. "Yeah, it's getting better though. I just took on a partner, G. Lewis Evans. We worked together at Hopkins."

"I take it you're doing well already."

"Just making room for growth," he humbly replied.

The sun sank into the dark river as Charlie and I finished off our steaks and settled down for an evening conversation. Charlie's mood was different, seemingly restless and out of character. I assumed it was related to our last meeting; Charlie and I had never argued so vehemently.

"I'm sorry about the other night," Charlie finally broached the subject. "I just thought I could change things when I moved back here."

"I tried to warn you, Charlie; I died with my child. It's not in your hands."

"I understand," Charlie said after a huff and then allowed the subject to pass on.

———————————

It was well after midnight when the convulsions first erupted inside me. The bed was soaked with sweat. I tried to lift my head but quickly laid it back down when the room began to spin. The salivation in my mouth hinted that things would quickly become worse - which they did. Unable to raise my head, I allowed it to hang off the side of the bed as a violent stream of vomit shot against the floor making a loud thud when it hit. I had never felt so sick in my life. I tried again to lift my head but was met with a storm of dizziness, which caused another explosion of vomit, followed by a series of dry hacks. I considered calling Charlie but decided not to. I couldn't make it to the phone anyway. *"Maybe I'll die,"* I thought as I turned to my back and pushed the covers to the floor. I passed out and slept the remainder of the night.

My eyes opened the next morning with the amazing discovery that the dizziness and vomiting were gone. I sat up in bed and assessed the damage - the floor and bed were covered with vomit. It wasn't a dream. Fatigue weighed on my body as I walked to the bathroom and washed my face. "What was that about?" I said to myself.

Dad and Mr. Robbins stopped by the house at around nine o'clock to see if I would join them for a floundering trip at the intracoastal waterway. They found me lying on the couch with a wet towel around my head. Dad immediately began looking around for signs of alcohol. "What's wrong, son, have you been drinking again?" he asked with an interrogative voice.

"No, Dad, I'm just sick, a virus or something. I'll be fine."

Mr. Robbins sat on the side of the couch and pulled his glasses down to the tip of his nose. "Let the doc take a look at you," he said. He inspected my face while letting out a perfectly timed "Aha" every few seconds. I did my best to ignore him by pulling the covers off the floor and hiding my face. He was not deterred by this maneuver.

"Stop, I'm really sick," I moaned when he began examining my toes. I kicked his hand away.

Mr. Robbins stood back up and placed his hand on Dad's shoulder. "I've got some bad news," he began. "It's one of two things, and neither one is very good." Mr. Robbins paused and looked down at the floor. He exhaled loudly. "It's either malaria or hammer toe."

"Oh, please, let it be malaria," Dad joked.

Not lacking all signs of sensitivity, Mr. Robbins fixed me a glass of water while Dad got a fresh towel and checked my temperature. When they were satisfied that I didn't have a fever, they packed up and headed for the boat.

"Does malaria cause fever?" Dad asked as they left through the back door.

"I don't know. Does hammer toe?" Mr. Robbins asked back.

———————————

Dillon came running through the back door shortly after five o'clock with rope in his hands. I could hear him shouting "Uncle Chance" from a hundred yards away.

"Uncle Chance, look what Grampy showed me," he said excitedly.

Charlie, along with Dillon, typically visited his parents in the afternoon before his cursory stop at my house. Dillon rarely stayed alone with his grandparents due to Mrs. Robbins' chronic illness and Mr. Robbins' difficulty managing the ups and downs of her severe diabetes. Over the last couple of years, the disease had destroyed much of the covering of the nerves in Mrs. Robbins' legs and feet, making it impossible to walk even short distances on bad days. Even worse were the ravaging affects that the disease had on her eyes. After multiple surgeries by the best surgeons at Duke, they finally conceded that blindness was inevitable. She took it all in stride, accepting that her life would not reach the average age for a woman. This reality made Dillon's visits even more special.

Mr. Robbins also loved the diversion that occurred when young Dillon made his short visits. Caring for a sickly wife had a way of making any change welcomed. Every day when Mom came to visit Mrs. Robbins and take over her care, Mr. Robbins was given the opportunity to disappear in the river, catching clams, fishing, or just sitting out on Cross Rock enjoying the solitude. He knew the best years of the relationship were behind, yet he loved his wife even more in her sickness. The earnestness of that love made it necessary to have breaks from seeing her accelerated decay.

Dillon was his new diversion, and much like he did with Charlie and me as kids, he taught him everything he could. This was even more of a joy with Dillon, who was an amazingly quick learner. Tying knots with a rope was one of the most important skills a man of the water could have. There were dozens of different knots to fit thousands of situations in a typical river day. Grampy, as Dillon had come to call him, taught the young student two on that fateful day – a stress knot to tie a boat to the dock and a hard knot to attach an anchor. Dillon quickly mastered the ties and was itching to show someone else his new skill.

———————

"Look, Uncle Chance," Dillon said when he found me semi-reclined on the couch. "I can tie a knot."

My head was clearing, but still fragile when standing too quickly. With the temperature cooler, I decided to take in some fresh air and watch Dillon as he excitedly tied knots to everything he could find. Charlie sat at the edge of the dock throwing shells into the shallow water.

"What's up, Doc?" I said rubbing the light from my eyes.

"Just another day," Charlie responded. "I hear you were a little sick last night?"

"I thought I was going to hack a spleen out," I admitted.

"Maybe I should check you out?"

"I'm better now. It was just a little virus."

"Don't see many viruses in this weather. Tell me what it felt like."

"It was just some nausea, nothing more."

The rattling of Scotty's truck made Dillon stop tying knots and hide behind Charlie.

"Here comes mean Scotty," he said with great disappointment.

Scotty skipped around the house with his usual affable flare. "Hello, ladies, what's happening here at the Melrose strip?"

Before anyone could answer he turned his attention to Dillon. "Chipmunk, how's about you and I do some wrestling?"

Dillon ducked farther behind Charlie.

"Why don't you show Scotty what Grampy taught you today," Charlie said as he tried to find Dillon behind him.

Still excited about his new skill, Dillon reluctantly came out of hiding and fetched his ropes.

"Whatcha gonna do with them ropes?" Scotty asked.

Dillon continued hanging his head as he replied, "I'm a fisherman now. Grampy taught me how to tie knots."

"Oh really? I think you're too young to be a fisherman."

"Nu-uh. I can tie a boat knot," Dillon defended himself.

"I tell you what, Fisherman Chipmunk, I'll bet that you couldn't tie me to this chair. And if you can, I'll call you Captain Dillon from now on."

"You sit down," Dillon barked. "I'm a fisherman." Scotty sat down in the folding lawn chair and made himself comfortable. In true child fashion, Dillon laid down the ground rules. "You can't move until I say so."

It took less than a minute for Dillon to wrap a maze of rope around Scotty's wrist, ending the barrage with a quick yank which firmed the knot enough to make Scotty's eyes blink with surprise.

"I gotta admit Chipmunk, that felt a little snug."

"You don't move," Dillon reminded him.

With the same know-how, Dillon wrapped the other rope between Scotty's legs and feet, again ending it with a yank and the familiar sound of a grunt that Mr. Robbins let out at the end of his ties.

Scotty seemed mildly impressed. He looked down at the extra piece of rope. "Maybe you should reinforce with that extra piece," he said sarcastically.

Dillon shook his head no. "I don't need to."

"Oh really?"

"Tie one around his waist, like a seatbelt," Charlie suggested.

Dillon agreed and forced the air out of Scotty's stomach when he made his finishing touches to the knot.

"Okay, all done." Dillon stepped away and gloated in his work. Scotty smiled as he examined the knots, acknowledging a job well done.

"It looks good, Chipmunk, but to tie a fisherman's knot you need muscle. And you don't have that yet." With that Scotty tried to burst through the ropes with a dramatic show of strength.

Nothing budged. Charlie laughed out loud; I, too, was amused.

Scotty showed no signs of concern as he began wriggling his arms and legs in an effort to loosen the well-functioning knots.

Again, nothing moved.

Charlie walked over and reviewed the job. "I gotta tell you, Scotty, those look like they're only getting tighter." Scotty's face turned red with exertion as he continued fighting the knots. Charlie looked closer at the knots. "We might need to cut those off."

Dillon began laughing and jumping up and down. He applauded himself as he scampered around the dock repeating: "I'm a fisherman. I'm a fisherman."

Charlie looked over at me and gave a wink. "Hey, Chance, do you have anything to cut through this rope." Scotty hung his head in defeat.

"Nope."

Charlie looked down at his watch. "No worry, I'm sure Diesel will have something in his truck. He's due any time now, isn't he?"

Scotty lifted his head and exposed his bulging eyes. Sweat immediately beaded on his forehead. "Oh, come on, guys. Get me out of this chair. Diesel will kill me."

No one moved.

"Please," Scotty pleaded. "Chipmunk, I mean Captain Dillon, let me loose buddy. We're friends now, you and I. We're fellow fishermen. We take care of each other."

Dillon stepped back and nodded his head. "You're not a fisherman. I haven't seen you tie any knots."

"He's got a point, Scotty," Charlie added.

"Let me out of here," Scotty said with significantly more fervor.

"Nope," Dillon quickly answered.

The three of us moved back to the edge of the dock, ignoring Scotty's threats. It took about ten minutes before the glorious sound of Diesel's truck came crunching down the shell drive. Scotty's anxiety level caused mild concern from Charlie, but certainly not enough to release him to safety.

Diesel initially ignored us as he walked down to the water's edge. This was surprising, given that Scotty's truck was plainly parked out front. Dillon made a point not to be ignored. He began waving his hands and shouting, "Mr. Diesel, I have a surprise for you. Hurry up and see."

Diesel looked over and squinted his eyes when he noticed Scotty struggling with the chair. A big grin filled his face. "Well, I'll be a lucky man. Looka here what I have." He almost skipped to us, an impressive feat in itself for a man of his size. When he arrived at the edge of the concrete dock, he took a moment to cherish the gift in front of him.

"I tied him up myself," Dillon bragged.

"Well, little buddy, I sure do appreciate it. That's gonna earn you a ride in the truck and you get control of the siren."

Dillon again jumped with joy. Diesel walked slowly, like a western gunfighter, and knelt in front of a terrified Scotty who was trying to flex his knees to cover his stomach. He couldn't budge them.

Diesel placed a hand on Scotty's knee and tried to relax him, which of course was impossible with his state of panic.

"Don't kill me, Diesel, please, I beg you. I was just defending myself. It was an accident," Scotty squealed.

I was flabbergasted at Diesel's lack of aggressiveness. He again tried to calm Scotty by shushing him as he placed a finger across his lips. Scotty's eyes widened and his mouth stopped moving when Diesel put more pressure against his quivering lips.

"Take it easy, Scotty. I just want to talk for a second." Everyone became quiet as Diesel collected his thoughts. "I want to tell you a little story," he began. "After I fell in the mud, I cut my foot on an oyster shell and it got infected." Scotty's eyes cut down toward Diesel's feet. His lips quivered harder. "Anyhow, I had to go see Dr. Robbins over here and we talked. It turns out Charlie really is a pretty smart guy." Diesel hesitated, obviously enjoying the undivided attention he was getting. He continued, "You know, us fighting over which church is right isn't helping God at all. God made us all different and therefore we will all worship him different. We forget that the second greatest commandment is to love each other."

"So you're not going to kill me then?"

"No, but I am supposed to love you. And because I have to love you I want to make sure you understand that it's not right to throw rotten fish heads in other people's vehicles."

Scotty gulped.

Diesel grabbed the chair, with Scotty in it, and tossed it over his shoulder. "This is going to hurt me worse...who am I kidding? This is going to definitely hurt you more than me."

Scotty began hurling ear-piercing screams at us. Diesel stepped off the dock and motioned for Dillon to follow. "Let's go for a little ride buddy. We'll put old Scotty in the back."

The next two hours would be some of the longest of Scotty's life. The anticipation, however, was much worse than the punishment. Diesel dressed Scotty in an old, moth-ball smelling dress, applied ample make-up to bring out his features, and drove to El's drive-in for shrimp burgers and milk shakes.

Scotty, of course, was left tied to the chair in the back of the truck.

When they were satisfied with their night out, Diesel and Dillon began the slow ride home. Diesel laughed at Dillon's milkshake-covered face, not knowing that he was wearing the same amount on his ample cheeks. The siren remained on, with the occasional announcement: "Scotty Foreman, the hottest momma in town." Dillon laughed uncontrollably every time Diesel said it.

It was Diesel's finest moment. It was also the most fun Dillon could ever remember having.

Chapter 41

It was shortly after Charlie and Dillon left that the sensations returned. The nausea came quickly, barely giving me time to reach the toilet. I hurled what little dinner I had eaten and laid my forehead on the edge of the commode. It was every bit as severe as the previous night's episode. I managed to wet a towel and wiped my face and mouth clean. "I can't take this again," I said to myself.

After two more blowouts things calmed down, allowing me to crawl back to the bed and fall into a deep sleep.

For two weeks these vomiting spells continued, happening only at night, leaving me weak and lightheaded throughout most of the next day. I was losing weight, which Charlie caught on to quite early. He insisted that I stop by his office, but I had no intentions of showing my face in Morehead City.

"You've got to do something," Charlie said when he learned of the spells. "This could be serious, Chance. You look like you're already dehydrated."

With my eyes half closed from weakness, I turned to Charlie and said, "Good, maybe I'll die soon. Put me out of my misery."

"That's nice," Charlie responded with frustration. "Look, at least let me draw some blood and check for bacteria."

It was a struggle to even talk, but I managed to agree before falling off to sleep again. When I awoke there was a band-aid over the crease of my elbow and a supply of Ensure next to the bed. My head was throbbing. I tried to stand, but stumbled into the wall. I fell to the floor and gave no effort to pick myself up.

I awoke the next morning with Lobo licking my face and the phone ringing. When I finally picked it up, Charlie's voice was serious and lacked all sense of gaiety.

"Chance, we need to talk," he paused, "it's very important. I need you in my office this morning."

"Can you make me stop puking?" I said in defeat.

"If you get here I can."

"I'll call Mom."

"No," Charlie said. "I'll have Dr. Evans swing by and get you."

Dr. G. Lewis Evans arrived a few minutes after Charlie hung up. He cautiously knocked on the door before letting himself in.

I laid face down on the bed, still unable to move without severe nausea. I put my hand out without looking up. "I'm Chance."

Dr. Evans shook my hand and began a general exam. He began by auscultating my lungs and noting my vitals. He then unwrapped a syringe and siphoned a clear fluid in it. "This is phenergan. It will help with the nausea." I felt a slight pinch and then the pressure of a bandage over my arm.

The doctor then placed his hand on my shoulder and guided me up. Once in the car I could already feel the effects of the medication.

"Thank you, doctor," I said.

"You can call me Lewis, and you're welcome."

"I can't believe how sick I've been."

"I've heard." There was an uncomfortable silence while Dr. Evans concentrated on the winding roads through the Mill Pond. "Charlie thinks highly of you. He's a good friend."

"He is," I agreed.

"Better than you know."

I wasn't sure how to take the comment. "So why am I going to your office?"

"You're not. We're going to the hospital for a MR scan."

"A what? Why am I doing a scan? I've just got an unset stomach."

Dr. Evans continued facing straight ahead. "It looks like a lot more than an upset stomach," he replied matter-of-factly. The conversation went cold, leaving us both quiet until we arrived at the hospital.

Once inside I was placed in a sterile room and given a gown to wear. I was then led to the scan room and spent the next thirty minutes in a tunnel surrounded by clicking and banging noises. When it finished, I could hear Charlie's voice in the hallway. "Did you get a good shot of the stem?"

"Got it all for you, Charlie," another doctor replied.

"Great, I'll take those films to my office when you're finished."

Charlie walked into the room. He was rubbing his bare head, trying to think of a way to explain everything to me. I was at a complete loss. *Why was I going through all these tests when all I had was a sick stomach?*

"I guess you're wondering why I have you here?" Charlie began with the obvious question.

"I've heard of preventative care, but this is ridiculous. I just have a stomach virus."

Charlie looked up at the ceiling. "I'm not so sure about that."

"What are you talking about? Is this some trick to get me out of the house?"

"This is serious, Chance. Some things showed up that we need to evaluate."

"I'm not staying here another minute, Charlie. Take me home."

Charlie sat on the edge of the scan bed. "I will. Just let me get your films and I'll give you more information this afternoon."

There's a peace in futility that happens when you give up on life. As I awaited Charlie's news at home, I had no worries. Whatever was wrong with me would be just fine in the scheme of things. I didn't care what the future held; being lost makes you feel that way.

Dear Wendy,

I miss you terribly today. I've been sick over the last two weeks. Charlie seems to think something is really wrong with me. I miss being sick around you. I remember the way you cared for me, when you loved me. The softness of your face against my warm forehead was worth any sickness I could come down with. The cold rag against my chest and the silent kiss

you left me with – there's no better medicine on earth.
I wish you were with me now.

Love,

Me

Chapter 42

The sun was just beginning its southerly descent when Charlie arrived alone. I was studying the different colors of the afternoon sky, amazed at the plethora of shades created between the tie-dyed clouds. The seagulls seemed to cry a longer note, somewhere hidden in the great escape of the dusk.

Charlie sat down beside me and removed his glasses. He rubbed his eyes for a few moments before giving me the news. "You've got cancer."

The words didn't fully soak in. "What kind?"

"Glioblastoma Multiforme."

"Is that a fancy term for stomach virus?"

Charlie shook his head and began wiping tears from his eyes, barely able to speak. "It's brain cancer, Chance. Bad, bad cancer."

My thoughts froze. *Cancer?* Part of me actually felt relief.

"How bad is it?" I asked without emotion.

"Three months without treatment – max. With chemo, radiation, and surgery you might last a year."

I continued to feel no emotions as I let Charlie's news soak in. "So I'm really dying?" I said, amazed at how well I felt at that moment.

"The nausea comes from brain swelling. I can control it with medication. You won't feel any pain throughout the ordeal. But there is definitely not a lot of time left." I took a deep breath and almost smiled at the news. Charlie continued crying.

"It's okay," I said. "I've been dead for a long time."

"No, you've wasted five years," Charlie said. "Don't waste the next three months."

For the first time, I agreed. Knowing I was dying made everything else in my life seem small and temporary. I would soon see my child for the first time; I would see Gramps and leave behind the burdens that controlled my every breath.

"The only thing I don't look forward to is telling Mom and Dad," I thought out loud.

"Let me take care of that. You stay here and I'll be back with Dillon later. He wants to see you."

I smiled a genuine smile. "I want to see him, too," I said. Charlie cried like I had never seen him cry before. He hugged me quickly and walked away.

———————————

Charlie called and asked Mom and Dad to meet at his parents' house. They all gathered in the living room as Charlie sat on the coffee table and began telling a long story. There was complete silence as everyone stared disbelievingly at him. "It's cancer," he finally said. "At most, we're looking at three months."

Mom placed her hands over her mouth and began to sob. Dad sat speechless beside her, unable to comprehend the horrible news. Mrs. Robinson screamed and fell to the floor, while Mr. Robinson pounded the couch and then walked into the kitchen to be alone. Charlie tried to fight back the tears as he rocked back and forth.

"I'm sorry to tell you like this."

226

Chapter 43

I took a long walk down the shoreline as the moon overcame the sun and the creatures of the day took refuge in the darkness. My feet felt light and giddy. I savored the sounds of the waves as they marched to the silent flute of the moon. I would miss this. I would miss the water and the sand. I would miss the birdsongs and the predictable breeze that came to visit me each night. Being alone for so long allowed me to make friends with these wonders. I talked to the river and I felt at times it talked back. I awaited the breezes to awaken the chimes of nature as I lay awake in bed. I called them my dark friends – for they came in dark times.

The evening visitors brought with them the books of my life. I never knew which one they would open, but they usually sought the ones of pleasure. My life, after all, was good up until that night when I strangled away any chance of happiness in my world. I wondered if I would take those memories with me – the good ones, or would they stay behind, unwritten and transient? With no one to tell them to, they would fade and soon disappear. Yes, I would miss those memories.

I thought about things I would change. I would have never hurt my mother's feelings. I would have acted more interested in Dad's lessons. But mostly, I would have cherished Wendy more. I would never have fallen prey to the poison of alcohol. This thought made me sad. *What if?* I could have enjoyed five years of holding my baby and loving my wife. *What a waste,* I thought. Five years of waste - Charlie was right.

I began to cry, though I'm not sure why. I wasn't sad that I was leaving, but I was sad in how I was leaving. "Sleep will be nice," I told myself. Eternal rest, that's what they call it.

The tide moved in quickly and the water began to surround my feet. It was warm and inviting. I looked out into the dark vastness of the river. "My friend," I said again. I took off my clothes and walked until I could no longer touch bottom. I felt free, and I knew it was only a taste of the freedom I would soon have. I began to swim with no target in sight. I was never a strong swimmer, but it didn't matter that night. The salty water carried me where I wished. When I was satisfied, it carried me back to shore where I got dressed and walked back to the house.

———————————

The lights were on and Dad's truck was parked out front when I returned. I knew I had to face them at some point. This would be more painful for them than it would me.

Mom was unable to talk when I went inside. Dad acted even stranger as he avoided eye contact and stared mostly at the floor. I, ironically, felt strong and alive. "I'm fine, guys," I said. Inside, I just wanted to get this part over so I could get back to soaking in what life was left. It was a selfish thought.

"I love you so much, Chance," Mom said as she hugged me tight. Dad walked behind us and patted me on the back, keeping his head down.

"If it helps any at all, this is what I want," I said with Mom holding me tightly. "My life has been a chore for so long. I'm tired of the nightmares and smells that take me back. I'm tired of the memories and the dread of every new morning. I'm tired of hurting you guys. I'm tired of it all."

I was walking around in a euphoric state when Charlie and Dillon arrived shortly after Mom and Dad left. The feeling was one of nervous excitement, a lot like moving to a new town. I would miss some things, but mostly I looked forward to ending the cancer, the one that had become my life.

Charlie held Dillon in his arms as he sat down in the chair. "How are you doing?" he asked cautiously.

"Surprisingly well," I responded. "It's funny. Now that I'm dying, I feel more alive than I ever have."

"I understand," Charlie said. "There's a story of a man being chased around a mountain by a vicious tiger. Just before it pounces on the poor guy, he jumps off the edge of a cliff and is able to grab a vine. As the guy is hanging there, he looked down at the jagged rocks a hundred feet below. He then looked up at the hungry tiger ready to eat him should he try to climb up. Either way he knew he was dead. The vine began to break, but before it does the man notices a sweet berry growing from it. He reaches up to it and savors its sweet juices just before falling to his death."

"Are you trying to bore me to death?" I asked.

Charlie laughed. "No. It's just a parable about enjoying what you have left."

I nodded my head. "I'm gonna try." I smiled at Charlie. "I really am."

"Good," said Charlie. "Tomorrow I want the old Chance, my best friend in the world, to take care of my boy."

"I've got three months to live and you want me to baby sit?"

"He'll be here tomorrow morning."

"Are you sure this is a good idea?" I volleyed.

"It's a great idea. See you in the morning."

Charlie lifted the slumbering Dillon and began walking home. After a few steps he stopped. "Hey, Chance," he yelled. "I know you're not going to sleep tonight so make a list of what you want to do before you..." He was unable to finish the sentence.

"Die," I said.

"Make a list."

Chapter 44

The house looked more like a prison as I stood in the doorway and took in the scene. The bed was unmade with the covers scattered across the floor, leading to the couch. For the first time I didn't want to be there, alone and hidden from the world while it moved on without me. I walked outside and stared at the moon. I wanted to live, at least for the moment. I had been caged as a criminal for too long; I needed to run, and so I did. I sprinted down to the shoreline, kicking sand behind me as I chased the life I had lost. I focused my eyes and continued sprinting into the dark night until I had no air left in my lungs.

When I stopped, I looked back at the boats tied to the river stakes. Charlie's old skiff looked as lonely as I was. I waded out to it and climbed aboard. I felt freedom at my fingertips; I wanted to taste more of it. The engine cranked on the third try and I sped away into the dark abyss. When I crossed into the deep water, the waves fell flat and the boat seemed to set up and fly across the calm slick. I locked the gas at full throttle and stood in the middle of the boat, my eyes closed again, the wind whipping across my face. I wondered if that was what it would feel like. Would I feel myself fly out of my body and ski across the heavens? I spread my arms apart and began to fly, just like I did long ago on the old phosphate domes. I was alive.

Along the shoreline, Charlie ducked behind the marsh grass and watched me surf his boat across the river. He laughed and cheered me on, knowing I was too far away to hear him. When I disappeared behind the tree lines, he traced back to the house, praising God with every step.

It took less than ten minutes to reach the Atlantic Beach Causeway. I tied the boat to a rented dock and climbed out, ready to see some of the world that had left me so far behind. I headed straight to the Circle, where hundreds of tourists were gathered, enjoying the activities of the fun park. The Ferris Wheel was full of laughing children whose parents admired them from below. Cotton candy hid most of the faces I passed. I recognized no one.

The bungee jump was empty, with the exception of a small crowd that waited around it to see who would brave the make-shift attraction. I handed the guy a wet five-dollar bill and together we embarked on a slow climb to the top of the temporary crane that held the platform. A large crowd quickly gathered around to see the lost soul who would trust a couple of glassy-eyed twenty-year olds to lift them a hundred and fifty feet in the air, tie their legs to a rubber band, and then jump into the thin air. I was that person. Never before would I have considered doing it; I thought my life was too valuable. Now, I thought my life was too valuable not to do it. I jumped from the ledge and cheated gravity for what seemed an eternity. The voices muffled below me as I bounced through the night air. I had no fear. I was living.

I drove home slowly, taking in the gentle ways of the river at night. I stopped the engine a half-mile from the shore and anchored the boat. It was the same location where Wendy and I shared one of our most memorable heart-to-hearts. Our love was exciting and brand new.

We talked about the deepest and most heart-felt dreams for our lives. Without saying it too soon in the relationship, we both knew our greatest dream was to have each other, forever. As I sat there thinking back to that night, listening to the light clapping of the bow with each passing wave, it almost humored me that I no longer had her and would soon no longer have my life.

Chapter 45

I was surprised when Mom and Dad didn't bring breakfast on that Monday morning. Given the short time I had left, I thought they would want to see me as much as possible. But maybe that would just rub salt in their wounds.

I paced back and forth across the loading dock waiting for nothing in particular. I just couldn't sit down. That would be wasteful. My planning ended when I heard Charlie drive up. It still eluded me how he could ask me to baby-sit with so much going on in my life.

When Charlie walked around and opened the door for Dillon, he didn't budge from his seat.

"Come on, Dillon, I need to get going," Charlie said with a gentle voice.

"I don't want to stay here Daddy. I want to go with you," Dillon cried.

"You can't. I need you to stay here with Uncle Chance."

"No, Daddy, please," Dillon cried harder.

"Yes, let's go." Charlie tried to hide the irritation in his voice, but it was obvious he was not going to lose this battle. "Now," Charlie said again with more power.

Dillon placed his hands over his face and sobbed loudly as he waddled to the house. He stopped halfway there and looked back at Charlie whose eyes were becoming moist and red. Charlie looked away before yelling, "Now, Dillon. I'm not going to ask you again."

Dillon walked into the house, dropped his little lunch box to the floor and sat down Indian-style. He crossed his arms and hid his face while a steady whimper escaped his quivering lips.

My heavy heart reached a new low when I walked in and found him shivering with emotions. He looked up at me with tears rolling down his cheeks and then put his head back down to hide his embarrassment.

"Hey, little buddy, what's wrong?" I asked.

"My daddy's mad at me," Dillon said, continuing to hide his head.

"Why do you think that?"

"Because I didn't want him to leave me."

"Nah, your daddy's not mad. He just wants you to spend some time with me before I have to go away."

He lifted his head, "Where are you going?"

I considered a few ways to answer the question. "I'm going to visit some old friends I've been missing."

"So, my daddy's not mad then?"

"Absolutely not. Your daddy loves you too much to be mad."

"My daddy does love me."

"He sure does."

"We tell each other all the time," Dillon said, drying the tears with his hands.

"Hey, you know what?"

"What?"

"I've been teaching your pet crab some tricks."

Dillon stood up, beaming with excitement. "Really, Uncle Chance? What did you teach him?"

"I taught him to run to his hole when I throw a shell in the mud."

Dillon smiled while he thought about the trick. "Wouldn't he do that anyway?"

"Oh, no," I said. "I had to teach him to run to a certain hole. And do you want to hear something really neat?"

"Yes."

"That smart crab of yours taught all his friends how to do the same thing."

"Wow," Dillon said in disbelief. "Show me, Uncle Chance." Dillon was jumping with excitement.

"I tell you what. You sit here for a few minutes and I'm going to take care of some business in the bathroom."

Dillon agreed and tried his best to hide his excitement. "Uncle Chance?" he said before I could make it to the bathroom.

"Yes?"

"Use the fan. Daddy says it's good manners."

I laughed. "Not that kind of business."

After five minutes, I reappeared rubbing my smooth face. I hadn't shaved in almost four years, my lack of practice evidenced by the multiple cuts on my neck. Even with the nicks, I felt fresh and clean.

Dillon smiled and gave me a thumbs-up. "You look handsome like my daddy."

"How do you know what handsome means?" I asked.

"I get called that a lot."

When we got outside, I threw a shell in the mud, which as predicted, made the crabs scurry in all directions, heading to the safety of the nearest hole. Dillon clapped with approval. "I have a good crab," he said with pride.

We spent the remainder of the morning exploring the shoreline and tracking the path of his remarkable crab. I forgot all about the cancer, instead finding myself lost in the enjoyment of caring for a child. "This is what it would be like," I told myself.

After lunch I took Dillon clamming, amazing him with Gramps' old trick of the invisible clam. Dillon rolled his little Levi's up to his knees and began running his perfect little toes through the sand and mud in search of the hidden crustaceans. His innocence and severe honesty entertained me.

Naptime came at two-thirty, Dillon reminded me, as he crawled onto the couch and quickly drifted away. I watched him sleep with his fragile little chest rising and falling in perfect harmony. I found myself staring at him a half hour later, lost in thoughts of what it would have been like to be a father. Dillon could make anybody want to be a father.

While the house was quiet, I pulled out a writing pad and began my daily routine.

———————

Dear Wendy,

I decided to write you earlier than usual today. I'm taking care of Dillon and I have to tell you how wonderful it is to have him around. It's the greatest love in the world – that which we have for an innocent and helpless child. I'm watching him as he sleeps, his eyes fluttering as he dreams of playful summer afternoons and seashore expeditions. I can't help but envision you lying beside him...

———————

"What are you doing, Uncle Chance?" Dillon's voice startled me away from my letter.

"Hey buddy, did you have a good nap?" I asked while shoving the letter in a shoebox.

Dillon pointed to the overstuffed box. "What are those? Are they stories?"

"Kind of," I replied.

"What kind of stories?"

"These are stories that I write to someone I care about."

"Like a girlfriend?"

"More like an ex-girlfriend."

"What's that?"

I stared at Dillon, trying to figure out a way to change the subject. His obvious fascination with the letters made it clear that this would be no small task. I gave in. "An ex-girlfriend is someone who used to love you."

Dillon got off the couch and sat next to me at the table. "Why don't she love you anymore?"

"Because I hurt her very badly. It was an accident."

Dillon thought about things for a moment before continuing his interrogation. "So you didn't mean to hurt her?"

"Right, but I did and some things can't be fixed."

Dillon frowned. "What was her name?"

"Wendy," I managed to say.

"Do you write her everyday?" Dillon continued his questions.

"Everyday."

"Does she write you back?"

"No."

"Is it because she's really mad?"

"It's mostly because I don't send them. I write her letters because it's the closest I can come to really talking to her. I pretend that she's here." Dillon stared at me with a look of confusion. "It's kind of like a make believe friend. Don't you have one of those?" I asked, hoping it would change the conversation.

Dillon ignored the question. "You just keep them in a shoebox and never send them?" he clarified.

"Yep."

Dillon became quiet and sunk his skinny shoulders down. "You love her a whole lot, don't you, Uncle Chance?"

I looked down at his squinting eyes, lost without their glasses. I chuckled at his comment. "What do you know about love?"

"I know a lot," he replied bluntly.

"Okay, then, you tell me what love is."

Dillon again sunk down in his thinking posture. "Love is when you go out to eat and you give the other person most of your ice cream and don't make them give you any of theirs."

I laughed. "How do you know that?"

"Because Daddy was in love when we lived at our other home."

His comment caught me by surprise. "Are you sure your Daddy loved somebody else?"

"I'm pretty sure because he gave her his ice cream and he usually would give it to me."

"What was her name?"

"Miss Susan. She was a nurse."

I was enthralled, my cancer far away from my mind. "What happened to Miss Susan?"

"Daddy just stopped letting her come over and then we moved here. She was nice. I even let her have some of my ice cream."

"That's interesting. But giving someone your ice cream doesn't mean you love them."

Dillon seemed disappointed in his error. "Then what is it?"

"It's," I considered my answers. "It's when you..." I again tried to think of a good way to describe it. "I can't explain it. It's just something you feel."

Dillon looked down at the ground, his wheels turning. "That doesn't help."

———————————

When Charlie came to get Dillon, I found myself missing him almost immediately. My mind drifted back to the cancer, something it rarely did while he was around. *This is what you wanted, Chance.* My head started to pound. I squeezed my temples and sat down on the couch. Before long I was lost in a movie of memories, watching the events of my life cross sequentially through my head.

Chapter 46

Wendy floated across Independence Boulevard, her thick hair bouncing with every step. When she reached the other side, she took a moment to study her reflection in window of Barnes and Nobles. She pulled her skirt down, straightened her blouse and proceeded through the front door.

"I've got to start dating again, eventually," she whispered.

Her deliberate walk hid any signs of nervousness, but it was there. She recognized him immediately, mainly by the way he was obviously looking for someone. He had a boyish face with curly black hair. The gentle dimples on his face gave him a look of trustfulness and sincerity. His blue polo shirt was neatly pressed and matched nicely with his khaki pants.

"I'm Scott," he said extending his hand.

"Wendy Summers. It's nice to meet you." As much as she didn't want to admit it, she liked his smile and his voice.

Scott Sanders was from Kansas City and recently moved to Charlotte to begin his career with The Sanders Group, an architectural firm owned by his uncle, who also happened to be the Summers' neighbor. He never dated much in school, mostly due to his diligence in the classroom. He was a nice kid, Mr. Sanders kept telling her; voted most likely to succeed in high school and class favorite, two awards you would never hear about from him. Like Wendy, Scott was apprehensive about a blind date, especially considering he may run into her when visiting his uncle. But, in the end, his aunt convinced him to give it a try. He needed to meet new friends anyway.

They stood there for what seemed an eternity, shaking each other's hand and forcing uncomfortable smiles upon their faces. Scott broke down first and laughed. "This is every bit as awkward as I thought it would be," he said.

Wendy liked his smile. There was a freshness about him, like the first signs of Autumn. Wendy began laughing also. This wouldn't be so bad after all.

———————————

Mom and Dad stopped in for an afternoon visit. Having each other's support made it easier for them. We talked around the subject for an hour, doing our best not to mention the word cancer or anything that may lead to it. When Charlie arrived with Dillon, they quickly said their goodbyes and headed home. There was an awkward, yet surreal, feeling in the air. Talking to a dying person has a way of doing that.

Dillon jumped up in my lap and gave me a big hug. I returned it without hesitation.

"I missed you, Uncle Chance," he said as he laid his head on my chest.

"I missed you, too. And, by the way, your pet crab and Lobo are starting to get along better now."

Dillon smiled approvingly. "I knew they would work it out."

"How's the medication doing?" Charlie asked.

"Two nights without vomiting. I guess it's doing well."

"Good," Charlie said. "If you get anymore headaches, let me know and I'll get you something for them."

"I hope that's not necessary."

Everything was quiet for awhile, except Dillon who pretended to catch up with Henry, the most current name for his crab. The afternoon air was dry and the sun was still warm. A light wind kept most of the insects away.

"It's hard to believe," I interrupted the silence.

"What's that?"

"I just can't believe I'm dying. It's just not soaking in completely."

"I guess the only justice is that it's happening to someone who welcomes it."

"Right," I said. Another long moment of silence followed. "Are you sure it's only three months?"

Charlie sat up straight and looked at me. "Are you sure you're dealing with this okay?"

"Sure," I replied, though not very convincingly.

"Three months max," Charlie answered the question.

I thought about this for some time. "So by October I'll be gone." Charlie nodded his head. "Any possibility that someone will find a cure anytime soon?"

Charlie fixed his eyes on Dillon. "There's been no improvement in the treatment of this cancer in twenty-five years. Nothing."

I accepted his answer and stood up to walk around. My head and body felt strange, almost numb and unattached.

"Should we leave?" Charlie asked when he saw my discomfort.

"No, no. I'm fine. I'd like for you guys to stay."

Charlie closed his eyes and whispered, "Thank you."

I thought I was hallucinating when Scotty and Diesel came walking around the corner of the house together.

They were talking like old friends until their eyes met mine, causing a pause in the conversation.

Diesel walked up first and patted me on the back. "I'm sorry to hear about it, Chance. I'm praying for you."

Scotty, always one to be more emotional and softhearted in these situations, tried to follow with his own words but kept choking up. After three or four failed attempts to find his voice, he finally threw his arms around me and managed the words, "Miss you."

"I'll miss you too, Scotty." And I meant it.

Dillon studied the commotion from a distance, his curiosity getting the best of him. He left his pet crab and pushed his way through Diesel and Scotty to get to me. He tugged on my shirt. "Aren't you going to come back, Uncle Chance?"

I looked to Charlie for help, but even he didn't seem to have a good answer. Everybody fell silent as Dillon's questioning eyes remained fixed on me. I knelt down and placed both hands on his shoulder. "You know I couldn't leave my little buddy for too long?"

Dillon smiled. "You have to come back and take care of me when Daddy's at work."

Charlie rubbed his head, a habit of his when he became emotional or upset. Scotty began crying again and found support on Diesel's massive shoulders.

"And your crab," I said.

"That's right, my crab, too. So you can't stay gone for long."

I sat back down in my chair and studied the sunset. I loved the sound of the seagulls crying and the early orchestra of crickets in the afternoon. It represented a culmination for the day; it epitomized my fading life.

Dillon crawled in my lap and soon fell asleep. I ran my hands through his hair as his breathing quieted and his arms became limp. The other guys gathered closer after Charlie started a fire and we talked about old times.

"What would you change?" Scotty asked, referring to the events of my life.

"Just one thing stands out," I said, "and you know what it is already."

Scotty looked down at the concrete dock, realizing how rhetorical the question was.

"Would it be better to have never known her?" Diesel followed.

I thought about the question for awhile before answering. "I still believe she was placed in my life for a reason."

Charlie flexed his head to the side, surprised at my answer.

"You believe God intended her to be in your life?" Diesel asked.

I shrugged my shoulders and shifted Dillon to a more comfortable position.

"Even with the pain that came from it?" Charlie chimed in.

"Maybe," I answered.

"I don't think God would place you in a situation knowing it would harm so many people," Diesel added.

"I've been thinking a lot about it. I'm the one who messed things up, not God."

Charlie listened intently to my words. "Are you saying that you have peace with everything?"

"Not everything. But, I look at it differently now that my life is ending. It's making me understand things better."

Charlie got out of his chair and walked to me. He kissed Dillon on the head and then stared out across the river. I could tell he had a question, but was unsure if he should ask it.

"Do you understand why your child died?" Everything seemed to pause with the question, at least Diesel and Scotty did. Charlie continued, "Do you not wonder why God wouldn't save an innocent child, even if it was your fault."

"I've thought about that," I answered without hesitation. "And it will always be a question in my head. Well, maybe not always." I thought about the approaching sunset of my life. "Before Gramps died, we talked about this. Nothing could get through my head at that time, but I'm thinking clearer now."

"I'm curious," Charlie said.

"There have to be tragedies. I think its part of having freewill."

"But why you?" Charlie pushed me farther into my thoughts.

"If God decided to interfere with everything and stop some tragedies, where would he mark a line in the sand? Would he stop at murder? Or how about child abuse? Or maybe he would just stop all pain and suffering. What kind of world would that be? That wouldn't require any faith."

"So at some point we'd be a bunch of robots," Charlie injected.

"Yes, love wouldn't mean anything. And that's the greatest thing we have."

Scotty and Diesel shook their heads in approval.

"So, to answer your question, even with the darkness that I have seen and the pain that I have felt, having the opportunity to love someone like Wendy once in my life is worth it all."

Charlie smiled at me. "That means more to me than you could imagine."

The next two hours disappeared and the guys began to say their goodbyes. I had come to hate goodbyes. "You guys will be here tomorrow night?"

"I'll bring the food," Diesel said.

"Like there'll be any left by the time you get here," Scotty joked.

"Goodnight, guys." I kissed Dillon goodbye. In his stupor he raised his hand and ran it down my face. "I'll see you in the morning, little buddy."

I walked down the long dirt road to the highway and then made the short trip to Mom and Dad's house. Mom was up reading when I got there. We talked until late and I fell asleep on the couch. She covered me with a handmade blanket and kissed my forehead.

Chapter 47

One Week Later...

Scott pulled in front of the Summers' house and gave a quick look in the rear-view mirror. He hated the feeling in his stomach. He tried to convince himself that this was no big deal. *She's just another girl*, he told himself. It wasn't working. His palms became moist and his throat felt like it would close at any moment. He knew there was something special about this girl.

Mrs. Summers spotted Scott's car in the front and yelled for Wendy to hurry up. Scott took one last look in the mirror and said, "Here goes nothing."

When Wendy opened the door Scott nearly lost his breath; she looked radiant. Her tan skin perfectly framed her soft blue eyes. She smiled and invited him in. Mrs. Summers offered hot tea, which he accepted without giving it much thought. He couldn't take his eyes off Wendy. She sat across from him and crossed her legs, making sure her cotton dress didn't expose above her knees; that wasn't her style.

After a few minutes of small talk and no improvement in Scott's nerves, Wendy was out the door to begin her first real date in almost five years.

Mrs. Summers sat back down on the couch and sipped her tea. Her heart was particularly heavy at that moment. At any other time she would have been thrilled that her baby girl was starting to live her life again. She had watched Wendy suffer in her dark room for years, her eyes always showing the turmoil that came with being a childless mother. She had been waiting so long to see her smile again...and now this. She pulled the envelope out of her pocket and unfolded the letter. She read it for the third time, and like the first two, she was unable to control the tears from falling. She placed the letter against her chest and embraced it. She cried for a few minutes and then went back to the kitchen for another cup of tea.

I was just finishing my second cup of coffee while reading through Gramps old Bible. I loved to read the parts he underlined; it made me feel like he was still talking to me.

"Not much longer, Gramps," I said, "and I'll be with you again."

I heard the screen door slam behind me. Dillon came running in and headed straight for my knees. He gave me a big hug, his head only reaching the midpoint of my thigh.

"Good morning, Uncle Chance. Did you miss me?"

I picked him up and gave him a kiss on the cheek. "I couldn't wait to see you this morning."

I cut my eyes and saw Charlie silently watching through the front door. He gave a subtle smile and waved goodbye without saying a word. Everyday for the past week he dropped Dillon off, and then watched us for a few minutes before disappearing for another day.

I pulled the miniature coffee cups out of the cupboard and gave Dillon his usual - chocolate milk. We walked out to the dock and watched the sun complete its assent into a cloudless blue sky.

Dillon chugged the last of his milk and then wiped the excess from his mouth. "I've been thinking, Uncle Chance."

"Oh really? About what?"

"I know what it is."

"Know what?"

"I know what love is," he said confidently.

I couldn't wait to hear his answer. "I'm ready."

Dillon stood in front of me and placed his hands up to add emphasis to his words. "Love is when a girl puts on her perfume, and the boy puts aftershave on his face, and they go out and smell each other."

I laughed at his enthusiasm. "Were you watching television last night?"

"Yep. Me and Daddy watched a show and I figured it out." Dillon watched my reaction, looking for signs of my approval. "Is that what it is, Uncle Chance? Is that what you and Ms. Wendy did?"

"I don't think that's completely it, buddy." I picked him up and placed him on my knee. "But it may be the best description I have ever heard."

Dillon wasn't satisfied. "I'll keep thinking."

When the tide finished rising, we walked to the end of the wooden dock. Charlie's boat was tied at the end of it.

"You want to go for a boat ride?" I asked.

Dillon screeched with excitement. He crawled down and immediately manned the front of the boat. After getting his life preserver on, we slowly bounced across the white-capped waves. "Where are we going, Uncle Chance?"

"Somewhere special."

The phosphate domes dominated the sky after we cleared the tree-lined outlet. Dillon was fascinated by the large structures.

"What are those?" he asked while stretching his arm towards them.

"Those are storage domes. And you know what else they hold?"

"What?"

"One of the greatest memories I have."

"What was it?" Dillon asked without looking back at me.

"Ms. Wendy and I climbed to the top of that highest one."

"Really?" Dillon was amazed. "What was it like up there?"

"Well, it was raining and thundering."

Dillon turned around. "That's neat, Uncle Chance."

"You know what's even more neat than that?"

"What?"

"That's the first time I kissed her."

Dillon scrunched his nose in disgust. "That's not so neat." He turned around and stared at the domes for a moment longer. "Maybe that's what it is."

"What?" I asked.

"Maybe love is when you kiss a girl and it doesn't make you sick."

I acted like I was considering his answer. "Nope. It's not that either."

In the distance a couple of dolphins jumped from the water. Dillon jumped up and down until the boat splashed water over the sides. We watched them continue to jump out to sea, finally disappearing in the blinding sun.

As we rode back to the shoreline, I began thinking about the cancer. Another day was ending and I was getting closer to the end. I could feel the pressure building in my head.

I watched Dillon's curly locks blow in the wind. When he looked back at me and smiled, I realized the change – I didn't want to die so soon.

Chapter 48

Dear Wendy,

I find it quite amazing really. We go through life and meet thousands of people. What is it that makes us fall in love with one? They say it takes a minute to find that special person, an hour to become interested in them, a day to fall in love with them, but then a lifetime to forget them. I've lived under the assumption that nothing could make me forget you. I recently found out I was wrong. I have cancer.

Chance

I read the note back to myself, suddenly inoculated by its reality. If it wasn't for the nausea and headaches, I wouldn't have believed I was closing in on death. I thought about researching the cancer but then decided I didn't want to know how it would end. Charlie made it sound fairly peaceful. He said there would be no suffering. Once the swelling increased, the brain would become compressed and things would move along quickly from there. All I could do was wait for the inevitable.

I spent most of Saturday with Mom and Dad. As usual we strayed away from the conversation of death. I was pleased they were taking things as well as they were. Even so, the conversations were strangely uncomfortable.

Charlie and Dillon arrived that afternoon and we took advantage of the low humidity by going for a walk along the shore. Charlie brought a pitcher of sun tea; I savored its sweet southern taste. The jingle of the ice against the glass played like a sacred instrument of summer.

Dillon walked between us and held each of our hands. We swung him until he was parallel to the sand, but he never lost his trust in us.

"Did you write your letter today, Uncle Chance?" he asked me.

"I did."

"When you go away can I take care of your letters?"

"Why would you want to do that?"

"They're nice letters."

"You've only read one of them. The others may not be so nice."

"I'm sure they are," he said with his special air of confidence.

"We'll see."

"You know I don't like that," Dillon snapped.

"Like what?"

"We'll see. It's an easy way to say no."

I swung him a little higher. "We'll see."

Charlie didn't have much to say during the walk. He seemed more pre-occupied with Dillon, holding his hand a little more firmly than needed during our walk. Charlie adored his son; just spending a few minutes together with them left no doubt. I knew I would have acted the same way with my son.

Diesel and Scotty were waiting on the back dock when we returned. As had become the routine over the last two weeks, they each greeted me with a quick hug and the usual condolences. A cool front brought a refreshing sea breeze with it, dropping the temperature quickly as the sun sizzled out into the river. We refilled our glasses with tea and sat back in the chairs, letting our hair tangle in the breeze.

Diesel became a little too comfortable and let out a ground shattering belch. He covered his mouth and excused himself, although the apology was not very convincing.

"You're a very attractive man, Diesel," Scotty said sarcastically.

Diesel slid back down in the chair and leaned his head back, rediscovering his position of comfort. "I gave up on being attractive many years ago," he said with his eyes closed.

"It's just as well," Scotty said, also closing his eyes.

"You guys couldn't understand what it's like to grow up the fat kid. Your skin becomes thick early in life. All your jokes, they don't affect me anymore."

I looked over at Diesel and tried to remember if I ever said anything ugly to his face. Charlie was obviously doing the same thing. "Have I ever hurt you, Diesel?" he asked.

Diesel flattened his lips and thought back through his life. "Not on purpose."

"But I have in other ways?"

"It's not your fault, Charlie, it's just reality. I would have liked you to invite me to a party in high school or ask me to hang out after a football game, but I was the fat kid. Nobody invites the fat boy."

Charlie was obviously hurt by the comment. "I'm sorry, Diesel. If I had of known..."

"Don't worry, Charlie. I know you wouldn't do it on purpose like some people." Diesel punched Scotty in the arm, jarring him awake.

"I'm sorry if I ever did anything..." I began to say before Diesel interrupted me.

"You're my friend, Chance. You don't need to worry about anything in the past. If anything ever did happen, you're forgiven."

"Thanks, Diesel, that means a lot to me."

Diesel stood up and swallowed down the last of his tea. He walked to the edge of the dock and looked down into the water. "I'd change everything."

"What?" I asked, thinking I had missed something.

"You would change how things went wrong with Wendy and your boy. If I could change anything about my life I would change everything about me. I would have lost weight when I was younger. I would have fit in with the other kids. I'd be somebody." Diesel stopped and looked back at me. "At least you had some good years. You have something good to remember."

"I'm sure you have something positive to look back on," Charlie added.

"Don't think so. I've always been a miserable failure. Always been the outcast. The best days of my life have been hanging out with you guys the last couple of weeks. And I know this won't last much longer with Chance being sick."

Diesel inhaled deeply and blew out. He turned back toward us and placed his hand on my shoulder. "Anyhow, I'm being selfish," he said. "These days are about Chance."

I grabbed Diesel's hand. "You've been a good friend, and you're a good guy. Your day is coming." Diesel's wide face filled with a smile. I squeezed his hand. "I just wish I could be here to see it happen."

"I wish you could, too."

Charlie stood up quickly and began rubbing his head. "Robbie Seffers."

"What?" Scotty and I said in unison.

"Chance and I need to find Robbie Seffers. We owe him an apology."

"We do?" I said.

"We need to make some things right."

"I'm not sure I know what you're talking about, Charlie."

"When we were younger we used to let the older kids pressure us into calling him 'retard'."

"I guess I did. I can remember you doing it more than me."

"Regardless, don't you want to make it right?"

"I guess," I said, not sure if Robbie would even remember me.

"The Brintwood house in Pollocksville," Diesel said. "It's a loony barn."

"What about it," Charlie said.

"That's where they keep him. He's been crazy as a bat since his momma died."

Chapter 49

We arrived in Pollocksville at noon the next day. Charlie drove his new black truck, which was somewhat of a surprise considering his favorite color was green.

"Why did you get a black truck?" I asked. "You've never driven a black vehicle."

"Just wanted a change. Do you like it?"

"Of course. I love black trucks."

"I thought you would," he said with a smile.

We pulled up to the home and saw people gathered around the front porch. We both noticed Robbie immediately. He was sitting at the far left of the porch, leaning against the railings. The other residents seemed to hang in small groups of three to four. Robbie was alone.

The closing of the door drew everyone's attention, including Robbie. He looked up and stared for a moment, making sure he wasn't mistaken. When he realized who we were, he walked quickly behind the house.

"Are you sure this is necessary?" I asked Charlie.

"We've got to make things right before..."

"I know."

When we walked back, we found Robbie hiding between the corner of the house and an air conditioning unit. We walked slowly toward him.

"Robbie," Charlie said softly, "do you know who we are?"

Robbie kept his face hidden and nodded his head.

"How are you doing here?"

"Okay," Robbie responded with a soft voice.

"Do you get many visitors?" I asked.

"Not many."

There was an awkward moment of silence before Robbie spoke again. "Mommy died."

Charlie and I looked at each other. It had been nearly ten years since Robbie's mother, his only caretaker, died in her sleep of a heart attack. Nobody ever visited the house. It was over a week later that the mailman decided to bring the mail to the front door since the box was overflowing. When Robbie opened the door babbling, "Mommy won't wake up," the bitter smell alerted the mailman. The police arrived a few minutes later and found Ms. Seffers on the bed, covered with cold oatmeal and raw fish that Robbie had been trying to feed her. The investigators found ten inches of food stuffed down her throat and took Robbie in for suspected homicide. It was only after they cuffed and placed him in a cell that the coroner report showed she had died of a massive heart attack. By that time, Robbie had completely lost control, screaming for his Mom for two days straight. What had been a mild case of mental retardation suddenly became severe. With no family left to care for him, Robbie was sent to a halfway house in Newport. It closed down some years later and he was subsequently shipped off to Pollocksville.

Charlie walked closer to Robbie, who continued hiding his face in the corner. "I'm sorry to hear that Robbie. She was a good woman."

"Good momma," Robbie repeated.

"She loved you very much. And you know she's waiting for you in heaven."

"She can see me?"

"She's watching over you."

Robbie turned around and looked at us. He looked the same as when we were kids.

"Can we go for a walk?" I asked.

Robbie nodded his head. "We can walk."

We walked farther around the house and discovered a garden maze, which was maintained by the residents. "Do you like it here?" I asked as we crossed onto a brick pathway surrounded by holly bushes.

"No. I want to go home." Robbie answered quickly.

"Maybe one day you can," I said.

"Nobody wants me."

"Sure they do," Charlie said.

"I don't even want toys at Christmas. I just want to go home."

I could tell the conversation was bothering Charlie as much as it was me. Robbie was a child of our village. We had all forgotten him; after all, who could care for a forty-five year old child?

Charlie put his arm around Robbie's neck, while I walked in front of him. "Robbie, I owe you an apology," I began. "When I was a child I called you names that I didn't mean. I'm sorry. I hope you can forgive me."

Before Robbie could answer, Charlie jumped in and also apologized. His voice was unsteady and he swallowed frequently during his apology. When finished, we both put our arms around his shoulders.

"Charlie and Chance are my friends," Robbie said as tears ran down his cheeks.

After proving he was a doctor, Charlie was able to talk the social worker into allowing us to take Robbie for an hour leave. We found an old- fashioned hotdog stand, just out of town, and enjoyed catching up with Robbie. At the end of the day, we dropped him off at the house, and said our goodbyes. Robbie grabbed us both and pulled our heads into his chest. "Will you come back to see me?" he asked.

We studied each other before Charlie answered, "One of us will be back to see you again soon. I promise."

Robbie smiled walked back to the far end of the porch, again taking his position isolated from the others.

Chapter 50

Scott was determined to make the third date special. He made reservations at The City Bistro, arguably one of the finest dining experiences in the state. When Wendy answered the door at six forty-five, Scott greeted her with an armful of Cala Lilies.

Wendy, of course, was as beautiful as ever. She wore an evening gown that cut low across her back, showing the slight curves of her shoulder blades. Her skin was smooth and not overburdened by the sun. The slight scent of her perfume filled Scott's nose as he took a moment to appreciate her subtle beauty.

Scott's eyes beamed as he studied the perfect grace Wendy walked with. He opened the door and held her hand as she slid into the car.

"The flowers are beautiful," she said. "Those are my Mom's favorite."

"I know," Scott said with a sheepish smile.

Scott continued to look over at Wendy, amazed that someone of her beauty was still available. "I just cannot comprehend how a girl like you has stayed single all these years."

Wendy swallowed and looked out the window. "I guess your aunt and uncle didn't tell you."

"Tell me what?" he replied.

"I used to be Wendy Gordon. My ex-husband's name was Chance."

Scott drove in silence for a few minutes. "Is he still around?"

"No, he lives out on the coast somewhere."

Another long moment of silence followed. "It's really none of my business, but do you still have feelings for him?"

"Yes," she hesitated. "But we're done, haven't seen or heard from each other in five years."

Scott accepted the answer for its honesty. "Do you want to talk about him?"

"No. I'd rather just talk about us."

Scott smiled. "Sounds fine to me."

———————

Dillon arrived earlier than usual that next morning. I was sipping my coffee while looking over a calendar. It was just over three weeks since I learned of the cancer. Time had never passed so fast.

Dillon came running up and hugged me tightly before making his way to the small coffee cup I hung on the wall near mine. I watched him as he carefully pulled the milk out of the fridge and poured the cup full. He then grabbed the chocolate syrup and mixed it to his satisfaction. We both sat down on the couch as Dillon sipped loudly, mimicking the way I drank coffee.

"I wrote a letter," he said between sips.

"To whom?" I asked.

"Ms. Wendy. Daddy's been teaching me to spell the names."

"Let's take a look." I unfolded the chocolate stained note.

———————

Dear Ms. Wendy,

Uncle Chance is a good uncle. He loves me and I love him. He loves you a lot too. I hope you still love him and that you will love me too.

Dillon Robbins

———————————

Dillon's eyes stared at me, longing for my approval.

"That's a nice letter," I finally said.

His smile covered his face. "Good."

Dillon jumped off the couch and walked to the bed. He lifted the covers and got down on his hands and knees.

"Hey, what are you doing?" I said, before he pulled the box containing Wendy's letters out and opened it.

"Mine goes in here, too."

I smiled at his innocence. "I've got to watch you snooping around here."

When he finished, Dillon climbed back on the couch and resumed sipping his milk. He snuggled in as close as he could to me.

"Uncle Chance," he began, "do you think that you'll ever love someone else?"

I looked down at him and said, "Even if I had time, no."

"Why?"

I placed my arm around him. "Let me tell you something. When you become a big boy and someone really, really special comes into your life, she will take up all the love in your heart. That's how you will know if it's real love. There won't be room for anyone else."

Dillon thought about what I said for a few moments. "That's not true, Uncle Chance."

"What?"

"That's not true because I love my Daddy and I love you."

I laughed and squeezed him against me. "I meant to say the love that you have for someone who's not your family."

Dillon thought a little longer. "Still don't think so."

"You're just like your daddy," I said.

Dillon looked up at me and gave a toothy smile. "Thank you."

Chapter 51

The days continued to fly by and before I knew it another two weeks were behind me. The nausea and headache spells were less frequent and seemed to respond well to the medications Charlie kept me on. "When they start getting worse, I'll give you more," he assured me.

The routine was essentially unchanged. I spent the morning with Dillon and in the afternoon the three of us would do the things we had never taken time to do before. We spent one day parasailing, which was even more entertaining when a strong gust threatened to blow Charlie's shorts off. Dillon laughed heartedly at that.

I tried to keep my mind off the cancer, but it was difficult when everyone went home for the night. The one thing that kept me going was the time spent with Dillon. He had an amazing way of making me forget about everything else in the world.

On Saturday afternoon, the three of us took Charlie's boat out for a sunset ride. It was early September and I knew it would likely be the last time I watched the sun fade while floating in the river.

For a long time we sat looking out at nature's canvas, absorbing the pure reverence of the marshland. There's a place for everything, I thought. The cranes find their comfort hidden in the tall marsh grass while the seagulls prefer the wide-open spaces of salty water. The fish travel in schools, somewhere in their liquid tranquility. I, too, would soon return to this genesis of life. Gramps always said that the same elements that made up the human body also made up the surfaces of the earth. We should have no doubts that our body of clay will soon become one with the dirt that fills the soles of our shoes. God takes life away from each person, some sooner than others. It is not for me to understand.

"Does it scare you?" Charlie asked while helping Dillon bait his fishing line.

"It's beginning to," I answered honestly.

"It shouldn't."

"I didn't think it would. I never thought I would feel this way."

"My last year at Hopkins, I spent a lot of time with people who were dying. I also met some people who had died, but were revived." Charlie tossed the fishing line out and handed the rod to Dillon. "Mostly cardiac patients."

"This one patient, Edward Macon, coded for a few minutes before we got him back. When he awoke, he talked about lights and tunnels and peaceful surroundings. He claimed to talk to his deceased father and grandparents. These were things we had heard before. But this case had something different. His mother was in the room, and he asked her if there was a Jason in their family. She stuttered at first, not finishing her answer before asking him why."

I listened intently as the afternoon breeze tickled my face and laced my lips with a salty aftertaste. "What did he say?" I asked, intrigued by the subject.

"He said the person claimed to be his brother."

"And?" I tried to push the story along.

"His mother fainted."

"It was really his brother?"

"His father had an affair with another woman shortly before he died in a car accident. His mother never told anyone."

I watched Dillon pull the rod back and forth in the water, not overly eager to catch anything. "You believe there is more to it than this?"

"I met dozens of those cases after I started studying the subject. I have no doubts there is a life beyond this. Any doubts I may have had were erased when a man who was blind from birth was brought back from death and began describing things he had never seen before."

"You don't think he was making it up?"

"He described me."

"You're serious?"

"Even told me about the scar at the base of my neck. He never touched me. I spent one minute in the room watching the doctors resuscitate him. And he saw it all. He even asked me how an M&M could have gotten in the light fixture hanging overhead."

"Did you find one?"

"I let Dr. Evans climb up on my shoulders sometime afterwards and he pulled a dust covered green M&M from the fixture. He became a believer also."

"Amazing," I said, hoping my experience with death would be so enjoyable.

"Everybody I interviewed," Charlie continued, "said they lost their fear of death afterwards." Charlie rubbed the back of Dillon's hair and then showed him how to properly drag a fishing line. "But that wasn't the most common thing I heard from these people?"

"What was it?" I asked.

Charlie looked me in the eye. "Once they left their body, they didn't want to come back. They said it was almost intolerable."

"They wanted to stay dead?"

Charlie nodded his head. "They described it as being alive, no pain and no burdens."

I exhaled loudly. "Maybe I should be excited about dying."

"Just don't be afraid of it."

———————————

Under the twilight of night we traveled back to the shoreline. I savored the smells and sounds of the river; nothing was taken for granted.

After Charlie tied the boat to the dock, he asked me if I had finished the list of things I wanted to do before I died.

"I never got past number one," I told him.

"You want to see Wendy again."

I shook my head. "Just to see her from a distance. I know that talking to her would just make things worse."

"How's next Saturday sound?"

"Really?"

"It's what you want."

"It is."

As Dillon climbed out of the boat he tugged on my hand. "Love is what you feel before bad stuff starts to happen."

"Something like that." I knelt down, kissed him on the forehead and said goodnight.

Chapter 52

Preparing yourself to die is a surreal experience. Whereas some people talk about their lives flashing in front of them, when cancer lurks in the dark corners of life, the flashes continually replay themselves. And with each replay, you think of something else you should have done, or wish you could finish. But mostly, you think about your family and wonder if you loved them enough, and if they knew it.

And so my week went, with an epic battle raging in my mind, setting course for an ending that I no longer wanted. Every breath I took, every second I had, became more valuable than all the gifts on earth.

I also took time to count my blessings. I had lived for thirty years with parents who loved me, unconditionally. I had friends who would gladly trade in their time on earth to give me another day. And, of course, there was Dillon. I had never experienced the kind of love he gave me. It was pure and innocent, not understanding that I was just another deprived human soul, moved by the currents of life's sea. But to him I was an unwavering rock, sturdy and sure. I would let him down soon, when I passed through his memory like an ancient chapter you're no longer sure even existed.

And then there was my lost love…Wendy Summers.

———————————

The six hour trip to Charlotte seemed to take twice that long. When we arrived shortly after lunch, we still had no plan, nor were we sure Wendy would even be in town. Dillon was sound asleep in the back seat.

Driving down Maple Street took me back to my first days with Wendy and the nervousness I felt when meeting her parents for the first time. They were always cordial, yet obviously unimpressed by me.

The large brick house sat at the end of the street and had not changed in the years since I last saw it. We stopped fifty yards away and everyone remained silent as I let the waves of emotions crash through me. Wendy's old car was out front, filled with thousands of memories of my younger days. It was unfathomable to me that within the walls of that house was a ghost I could never stop thinking about. I wondered what she was doing. *If I could only walk through that front door and hold her.* If I could have only done that, I could have died a happy man.

It was a half-hour later that the white SUV drove past us and parked in the driveway of Wendy's house. A well dressed gentleman stepped out of the vehicle, walked around to the passenger side and opened the door.

"I wonder who that is," I whispered to Charlie.

Before he could answer my world came to a screeching stop. It was her, Wendy, in the passenger seat. She was every bit as radiant as I remembered. Her smile and sparkling eyes had been frozen in time. She looked wonderful – she also looked happy. Her walk was still more of a glide, something I would imagine from an angel. I understood, as I saw her for the first time again, the reasons she evoked the immediate feelings I felt so many years ago at Jordan Lake. She was a perfect creature.

When they got to her front door, they stopped and he said something to her. She laughed. *Gosh, did I miss that laugh.* They hugged for a long moment and then he backed away a little and looked down at her. When they kissed, I felt the last heartache I would feel in this life. Charlie and I both stared blankly, until he placed his hand on my shoulder.

"You okay?" he asked.

"She looks happy again, doesn't she?"

Charlie looked back at Wendy who was now waving goodbye to her date. "She does look happy," he admitted.

"You know what?" Charlie didn't reply. "This is what I needed to see. I needed to see her smile once more before I go. This is good. Really, it is."

Dillon awoke and crawled into the front seat, taking his place on my lap. He unfastened the seatbelt and then placed it around both of us. "Who is that, Daddy?"

"That's her," I answered for him.

Dillon rubbed his eyes and put his glasses back on. "That's Ms. Wendy?"

"That's her."

"She's pretty, Uncle Chance."

I caught my last glance before she turned her back and disappeared through the front door. "She's beautiful," I said. "I just hope he treats her well. God knows she deserves it."

The SUV passed by us again. "Let's find out," Charlie said, as he circled around and followed it.

We trailed the truck in complete silence. The afternoon sun was magnified through the front windshield, warming my hands and chest. Dillon became tired of the riding and curled himself comfortably in my arms. I leaned my head forward and whispered in his ear, "It's when another person's happiness is more important than your own," I said.

Charlie looked over at me with a confused face. "What?"

"That's what love is," Dillon answered.

Chapter 53

Wendy walked slowly through the foyer, taking a moment to look at her face in the mirror. It should have looked happier, she thought. Scott was a great guy and she was lucky to meet someone like him who wasn't already married. "What's wrong with me?" she said to herself before walking into the living room, taking her usual spot at the far end of the couch.

Mrs. Summers came from the kitchen and sat across from her. "Well? How did it go today?"

"It was good," Wendy said, with a feigned enthusiasm.

Mrs. Summers picked up on her apathy. "Are you not enjoying his company?"

Wendy shifted her weight, not sure how to answer the question, and for good reason; she simply didn't know. "I do, but then…" her voice trailed off. Frustration filled her face; she wiped a stray tear away.

"He's not Chance," Mrs. Summers answered for her.

Wendy fought back any additional emotions. She had come too far since losing her baby. She would not relapse now. "It doesn't feel the same. Maybe I've just lost the ability to feel that way."

Mrs. Summers moved over to the couch and sat next to Wendy. "Maybe those feelings just belong to someone else. It's true you know; you never forget your first love."

Wendy leaned her head on her mother's shoulder. "I know you don't. That's why you're sticking by Dad. And I'm sure things will be great with Scott. I'm just expecting too much too soon."

———————

We watched him walk into the Java House with a book in his hand.

"Look's like a good opportunity to learn a little about this guy," Charlie said. "We'll strike up an innocent conversation, get a feel for him, and be gone. He'll never know better of it."

Once inside we ordered two mocha coffees and a small hot chocolate for Dillon. I spotted him sitting alone in the back, lost in his book. We swiftly took a table next to him, barely beating another couple to the spot.

"I shouldn't talk too much, should I?" Dillon said, sensing our desire to remain anonymous.

"No," Charlie and I answered in unison. Dillon gave us a dirty look and began working on his hot chocolate.

The mystery guy looked up from his book and acknowledged us with a slight nod. He paused, placed his book down on the table, and took a sip of his coffee. He looked over at us again and gave a pleasant smile.

"How are you doing?" I asked.

"I'm doing well, Chance, and you?"

I froze.

"Excuse me?" I replied, glancing at Charlie for an escape plan. We were both jolted.

"I recognize you from some pictures," he continued. Charlie and I were too in shock to respond. We were exposed and there was no need trying to deny our identity.

"I'm Scott," he leaned over the table and held out his hand.

I shook his hand. "No need to introduce myself."

Charlie also shook his hand. "I'm…"

"Charlie," Scott cut him off. "I've heard about you too."

"Look, Scott," I began. "This is not what it looks like." Scott gave me an unconvinced look. "Okay, so it is. But I'm not here to interfere. I just needed to make sure Wendy was happy before I…" Scott waited patiently for my excuses. "Trust me when I say I will not be around to bother you guys in the future."

"Okay," Scott accepted my promise with some obvious skepticism.

There was an awkward silence as the three of us stared at each other. Dillon slurped the last of his chocolate down, ignoring the conversation.

"I just need to know that you will take good care of her."

Scott studied me for a few seconds before responding. "You have my promise."

"And please do not tell Wendy that you saw me."

"She won't hear anything of it," he assured me.

I looked him in the eye one last time, looking for any sign of deception. "That's all I need," I said as I pushed my chair back and began to stand. "And good luck with her father. Let's go, guys."

"He's in prison," Scott said. I paused while his words registered in my head. "He got caught stealing money from some older clients. He's got eight more years to serve." Scott took another drink. "That's all the more reason why I wouldn't hurt her."

"He's in prison," I repeated in disbelief.

"The Raleigh Penitentiary."

I was surprised at my lack of fulfillment after hearing such news. "Now we have something in common - prison," I replied before the three of us got up and walked away.

When we reached the front door, Charlie stopped and looked back. "Dillon, do you need to use the potty before we go?" Dillon nodded his head. "You go ahead, Chance. We'll be out in a second."

Once I was out of view, Charlie walked past the restrooms and stood in front of Scott's table again. "You have a second?"

Scott put his book down. "Sure."

Charlie told Dillon to stand a few feet away so he couldn't hear the conversation. He then pulled a chair out and sat across the table from Scott. "I have a story to tell you."

When Charlie finished, Scott sat in shock, unable to say a word. He looked over at Dillon and then back to Charlie. "Why are you telling me this?"

"I just want you to know what's at stake here. Just give it a few more weeks." Charlie slid the chair back and stood up. He walked over and lifted Dillon in his arms before looking back at Scott. "Thank you, Scott. You've been a gentleman."

Chapter 54

_____

Dear Wendy,

It won't be long now. I can feel the pressure building. Time is moving faster, and my days are growing shorter. I will leave so much undone. I would have done things a lot differently if I could have only known. It's a terrible thing to die knowing you're not leaving this world a better place but instead a more hurtful and dark place. It's the worst reality.

I love you, if only for a short time longer.

Yours

_____

Scotty and Diesel's hugs were becoming progressively stronger as my days began to fade like the mist of a winter's morning. We had finished our goodbyes for the day and were hopeful for the opportunity to meet again. I began to treasure the waning minutes of my life, instead of just the days. Things were coming to an end; we could all sense it. The grass would soon lose its green luster and the air would no longer need to harbor in my lungs. Like a stranger passing through, I would soon be forgotten.

The dark backdrop of the sky was freckled with bright shining stars. Bats performed aerobatics above our heads, seemingly trying to weave themselves between the maze of twinkling lights. Crickets hummed their ancient songs, and were often joined by the crowing of tree frogs. I now appreciated this music of the evening, and I would miss it, too. If it wasn't too late in the game, I would have considered the radiation and chemo treatments to possibly add another year to my life. But like everything else, it was too late.

With everybody gone for the day, Charlie, Dillon and I sat at the edge of the dock, swinging our legs in sequence. Dillon did his best to keep pace with us, but his little legs had to make frequent stops to regain rhythm.

Charlie looked down at him and smiled. "Remember when we were that age?"

I smiled back and nodded yes.

"That really wasn't yesterday," Charlie continued, while looking out at the stars. "I wouldn't trade my childhood for anybody's. My greatest wish in this life is that Dillon can have a little of what we had as kids."

"It was great," I agreed.

"Remember the duck we saved?"

"I do."

"When we let it go that afternoon, and it flew away, that's when I knew I wanted to save lives somehow."

"I guess I've been a difficult case for you," I said, assuming Charlie was thinking about his inability to save me.

Charlie agreed. "If I could only save one more life, it would be yours. I certainly owe you."

"You owe me nothing. You've been the best friend anybody could ask for. If it weren't for you, I'd be dying a lonely and bitter man. Instead you brought some happiness to my life." I looked over at Dillon as he drifted away in Charlie's arms. "You brought me Dillon."

Charlie continued rocking Dillon back and forth. "He thinks the world of you, Chance. Besides me, you're the only other person he really cares about."

I tried to block the emotions out of my mind as I thought about leaving Dillon behind. I never thought I could love anybody more than I loved Wendy, but Dillon changed that. When I saw those innocent little eyes peering through those glasses at me, my heart sank. He was such a precious and loving child. I would miss him more than anything else in life.

Charlie clung tightly to Dillon. It was getting late and we both hated to end the day, fearful it may be the last we spent together.

"I want you to remember something, Chance."

"What's that?"

"I want you to know that I'm going to take care of everything. You'll have nothing to worry about."

"I appreciate that. Mom and Dad are going to need you."

Charlie looked back down at Dillon and whispered, "Right."

Chapter 55

When I opened my eyes on Monday morning I immediately thanked God for another day. There was something weighing on my mind. One more thing that I felt I had to do.

When Charlie arrived he walked inside with Dillon. "Are you feeling up to watching the little man today?" he asked.

"Been looking forward to it all morning," I answered. "Do you think it's safe for me to take him along on a little trip?"

Charlie shrugged his shoulders. "Sure you can. If you start getting a severe headache or feel dizzy, just pull off the road. Dillon knows exactly what to do."

"I dial 9-1-1," Dillon answered loudly.

"Just be careful with the traffic. You know there's a hurricane heading this way."

"Haven't heard," I said.

"The surface pressure is just over nine hundred millibars."

I looked up at Charlie with mild interest. "A category five?"

"Haven't seen one like this since Andrew wiped out Florida."

"How far away is it?"

"About six hundred miles from the Cape. It's probably a couple of days away."

These storms would usually spur a sense of excitement in me. But with potentially only days to live, it was nothing more than a mild aside. I had more important things to worry about than another hurricane barreling down on the North Carolina coast.

––––––––––––––

"Where are we going, Uncle Chance?" Dillon asked as we drove away.

"I need to visit somebody before I go away."

Dillon accepted this answer for only a brief moment. "Is it a friend?"

I looked over at him and smiled. His eyes were magnified through the thick glasses. "I can't say it's a friend."

"Then why are we going?"

"Because I have bad feelings for this person that I need to get rid of."

Dillon looked out the side window, barely able to see over the door frame. "I don't understand."

"One day you're going to get a fish hook in your hand, and when you do you're going to pull it out as soon as possible. I've waited too long to pull this hook out."

Dillon stared at me with a blank look on his face. "I'm not fishing anymore."

––––––––––––––

The three-hour trip passed quickly, and without a hitch. Driving without a license should have made me nervous, but then again, I had nothing to lose. There's some peace in knowing the only thing you can be deprived of is two rocking chairs and a pet crab.

I pulled into the Raleigh Penitentiary and parked in the visitor lot. At the front desk, I checked in and showed my expired license, which the clerk didn't seem to notice. She quickly thumbed through the appointment log and found my name.

"Here to see Tom Summers?"

"Yes."

"Walk through those two doors and have a seat at the second window. Mr. Summers will be out in a few minutes," she said, while turning her attention back to the gossip magazine she was reading.

When Mr. Summers came out he looked much older than I remembered. His hands were cuffed, which was protocol when moving an inmate from the cells to the visitation area. He gave me an embarrassed grin as he waited for the guard to free his hands. I had no expression on my face as I studied the worn portrait of what was once a proud man.

"I was surprised to see your name on my visitation list," he finally broke the awkward silence. "To what do I owe this pleasure?"

"Nothing," I said.

"There must be some reason you came all this way to see me in my new suit."

"I have cancer," I replied. Dillon was sitting next to me on the chair and looked up when he heard that familiar word. "I'm not going to be around much longer."

A frown slid across Mr. Summers face. "Chance..." he began, "I don't know what to say. I'm sorry."

"It's okay, I'm really not here for that reason."

"What can I do for you?"

"I just need you to know that no matter what you think of me, I always loved your daughter and I never meant to hurt her. If there was any way..."

"I know, Chance," he interrupted me. "I'm not the same man you knew." He paused, allowing his eyes to scan the surroundings. "Prison has a way of changing a person."

"I'm sure it does," I admitted.

"Do you know how many visitors I've had the last year and a half?"

I didn't bother guessing the answer.

"Three," he said, with clinched teeth.

"Three," I repeated.

"My wife, my daughter, and now you. Three people."

"I'm sorry to hear that."

"I learned the hard way what's important." He leaned forward and placed his hands on the counter. "I've lived a life of counterfeit values and counterfeit friends. And when it all sizzled out, all I had was my family. If I ever get out of here…" When the tears rushed forward, he was unable to finish his sentence. He attempted to hide his face at first, but instead surrendered his emotions for me to see. Frustrated, he let out a big sigh and looked back at Dillon. "That's what's important, children. Is he yours?"

"No. This is my best friend's son." I glanced down at Dillon who was sitting with a mature reverence for the environment. "He's changed my life."

"I'm sure he has." Mr. Summers glared down at the floor, obviously contemplating his next words. He looked back at me with an intense expression adorning his face. "Chance, I can never make it up to you, but I want you to know, I'm sorry for ruining your life."

I shook my head slowly. "Mr. Summers, I'm the one who ruined my life. You had nothing to do with it."

"I forced Wendy away from you," he replied. "You were a good kid. You were good for her, but I was blind. I'll never forgive myself."

"It's behind me," I assured him. "When I say that I've forgotten those times, I want you to know that I mean it. You'll get out of here one day and Wendy will need you. She needs you now." I put my arm around Dillon and squeezed him closer. "The greatest peace I have is knowing Dillon will have a good life and Wendy will be taken care of." Dillon lifted his head and smiled at me. "I've met Scott, and he's a good guy. I believe he'll take good care of your daughter. Better than I ever did."

Mr. Summers leaned back in his chair. "You listen to me, Chance. Nobody will ever take care of Wendy the way you did. You gave her your heart and you continue to do so. There will never be another Chance Gordon in her life. I mean that."

His words were genuine and sincere. The piercing darkness in his eyes that once intimidated me was now gone, leaving behind a softness and spirit of forgiveness. In that small, empty cell, separated from his worldly possessions, he found himself. And he found that he needed the same basic essentials that we all need. His greed and worldliness had insulated him from the true nourishment of humanity. Now that he had a taste of it, it was obvious he craved it. I sensed his life was turning a corner as sharp as mine; only he would have time to experience that new chapter, while my time neared its culmination.

"I'm glad I did this," I said, as Dillon and I stood up to leave.

"I'm glad you did, too," he said with a sadness draping his face. "I hate that I won't have a chance to get to know you...really get to know you."

"Thank you, Mr. Summers," I said with deep sincerity. "I'm ready to go now."

"Goodbye, Chance," he whispered before placing his hands out for the guard to cuff. I watched as he disappeared behind the thick steel door.

"So long, Mr. Summers."

Chapter 56

Mrs. Summers was finishing up some dishes when Wendy came in and sat quietly on the stool behind her. Her phone conversation with Scott was much shorter than usual.

"How's Scott?" Mrs. Summers inquired.

"He thinks it's best we not see each other for awhile," Wendy said bluntly.

Mrs. Summers put her dish down and removed the gloves from her hands. "What? I thought you guys were enjoying each others company."

"I guess not as much as I thought."

"Did he give you a reason at all?"

Wendy shrugged her shoulders. "He just said it was the right thing to do now."

"That's it?"

Wendy put her head on the table. "That's it."

Back on the coast, businesses were busy boarding up their windows as a massive hurricane packing 160 mile per hour winds churned in the mid-Atlantic. Cooler waters and wind shears from a Canadian front would likely weaken the storm as it approached the coast, but it would certainly remain quite dangerous.

On the beaches, surfers got some last minute joys out of the large waves that were ominously warning of the unseen beast rolling towards land. There's always a daunting calm before a big storm arrives from the ocean. Even people who have not lived on the coast can feel Mother Nature's baneful palpitations.

I always loved the chilling winds before a storm. They reminded me of my simplicity in this world. In early nautical times, a ship at sea that had lost its sails and steering by these storms was said to be "moved." The ship and its crew were moved wherever the sea and its despoiling waves took it. Hundreds of years later I could still imagine that feeling. No amount of technology or sophistication could stand any higher than the bare feet of Mother Nature. She would destroy as she saw fit, and we could only cower beneath her and pray to be spared.

The waves began striking the base of the concrete dock with increasing frequency as the Charlie, Scotty and I sat and watched the dark, thick clouds begin surrounding us. Dillon was busy building a shelter of shells for his pet crab and its friends. There was no rain or thunder yet, just a steadily increasing breeze with gusts that carried pieces of litter across the grass.

"I'm thinking about heading up to Kinston or Goldsboro," Scotty said when the wind lifted his hat and blew it against the wall behind us.

"It's weakening pretty quickly," Charlie replied. "There's probably more chance of flooding inland than here."

"What are you thinking, Chance?" Scotty asked.

"It doesn't make much difference to me. I'd probably stick around for a category five."

"Yeah," Scotty said regretting the question.

"This is the last hurricane I will see. I say bring on the show."

Charlie stood up and inspected the darkening sky. Some faint rumbling stirred off on the horizon. "I just can't risk going inland and getting flooded away from home. I'd rather Dillon and I stick it out here." He looked back at me and asked, "You want to stay at our place?"

"No. I'll be fine here. This place isn't going anywhere."

Gramps had built the oyster shack to withstand the constant threat of hurricanes. It was constructed with concrete blocks and a deep rock foundation. Not even the strongest of hurricanes could budge it. The biggest problem was the threat of storm surges which could wash in up to ten feet of water from the ocean. The house had been flooded up to its roof on multiple occasions. Whenever a storm came to town, Gramps would place all the valuables in the attic, away from the flooding waters. Once it passed he would allow the sunshine to dry the house out and then sprayed bleach to kill the impending mold. It was for this reason that he built the house so simply and with few inner walls. Even the wood floor could come up in just a couple of hours. It was a most efficient turn around from seemingly utter destruction to complete normalcy.

In the distance we heard the stuttering siren of Diesel's truck approaching. He stepped out and jumped up on the dock, trying to conceal the smile on his face. Diesel craved the feeling of importance, and this storm gave him a great outlet.

"I don't like it, guys," he spoke with a slightly deeper voice than usual. "The angle of this hurricane is worrisome."

"What are you talking about Barney?" Scotty asked.

Diesel gave him a "watch it" look and continued, "It's coming at us perpendicular. Usually a hurricane will skirt the coast, but this one is coming straight in." He looked down at the growing waves. "I think it's going to push a lot of water in here."

"I'm sure you'll float," Scotty shot back.

"Be nice, Mr. Scotty," Dillon warned him.

We could hear another car traveling down the shell road, its tires crunching along the way. When Diesel recognized the police car, he rolled his eyes and let out a troubling grunt. Trooper Tim Long stepped out and removed his sunglasses. He looked out across the river as he placed the folded frames in his front pocket. He then gave Diesel a discouraging look before walking over to the idling truck. After reaching in and pulling the wires that connected the lights and siren he smirked and then strutted over to us.

"This is the last time I tell you, Diesel," he began. "You are not to use those lights or that siren. You're not an officer." He tugged at his badge so Diesel could see it. "If you don't have one of these, you don't get one of those," he said while pointing at the lights on the truck.

"Yes, sir," Diesel said, his head hanging low on his chest.

Scotty perked up and walked to the edge of the dock. "Hey, Long, how many criminals have you arrested this month, not including your immediate family?"

"Shut it, Scott."

"I'd feel safer with a pea-shooter and a Chi-wa-wa than having you protect us."

Tim ignored Scotty's comment and instead looked back at Diesel. "No more siren and lights or I'm writing you up."

Chapter 57

Wendy was sitting on her bed thumbing through some old pictures when she heard the knock at her door. Mrs. Summers sat beside her and began brushing the hair from her eyes.

"You feel like talking?"

Wendy forced a smile on her face. "I'm fine, Mom." She grouped the pictures of us together and placed them back in the shoebox. "Isn't it amazing how one moment can change your life so much? I was the happiest girl back then," she said as she paused to look at one of her pregnant pictures. I was sitting beside her with my hand on her stomach, smiling like the proud father-to-be.

Mrs. Summers agreed. "I think you'll be that happy again."

"How can I? I wanted to be a mother so bad. And I felt like Chance took it all away from me."

"I've always wanted to be a wife with a strong family and a beautiful home. And it seemed that your father took that away from me. I'm sixty years old. It's too late to start over." Mrs. Summers put her hand under Wendy's chin and lifted her eyes. "But you know what? Even when I have to sell this house and my belongings and move to an apartment, I will still be a good wife and mother. Just because you lose your dreams doesn't mean you can't be happy with the other things you find along the way."

"What could you possibly find in all this?" Wendy asked.

"I found the man I fell in love with thirty-five years ago. Somewhere along the line I lost him. He got buried beneath all the affluence and money, and I did, too. I got too caught up in that life to realize I no longer knew the man I was sleeping beside." Mrs. Summers pulled a picture of Mr. Summers out from the shoebox. She ran her finger across his face. "Now when I see him, it's like I'm twenty-five again. I've fallen in love with him all over again."

Wendy wiped the tears from her eyes. "I'm sorry we've put you through so much." She wrapped her arms around Mrs. Summers and hugged her tight.

"Nobody has it as good as they want you to think they do. We're a family who's dealing with adversity. I'm proud of us."

Wendy and her mother hugged for a few more minutes, feeling the intense love that can only be felt between a mother and daughter. When they finished, Mrs. Summers walked out of the room momentarily and then returned with a box in her hands.

"I wasn't sure if I should show you this, but your father made me promise to give it to you. I'll leave you alone for awhile."

Wendy opened the box and placed her hand over her mouth. On the top was a letter from Charlie, accompanied by a picture of Dillon. Tears began to flow from her eyes. She put both her hands over her face and said, "Dear God." When she was able to catch her breath, she reached into the box and pulled out some of its contents. The tears continued rolling down her cheeks.

Outside Wendy's door, Mrs. Summers leaned against the wall. She looked up and said a prayer, something she was doing more of those days. She then pulled the collar of her shirt over her mouth and muffled her cry.

Chapter 58

When the wind gusts reached fifty miles per hour, Charlie and Dillon began their walk home. I watched them trudge along the seawall, both struggling to walk a straight line with the force of the wind against them.

I stayed out on the back dock for a couple more hours, watching the orchestra of black clouds grow thicker. The shearing winds began to whistle through the trees and bushes, making them dance to and fro with unerring rhythm. In the distance a lonely chime played its panicked song, warning me of the dangers lurking closer by the minute. Sheets of rain shot across my face and began stinging my eyes. It was already an angry storm and only its outer bands had reached me.

As the afternoon grew older, it quickly began to darken, making the ominous clouds visible only when a bolt of lightening lit up the stormy sky. The wind began its vicious growl as it grew to hurricane force and was steadily becoming stronger. I jumped off the concrete foundation and walked out to the end of the wooden dock. The storm surge was beginning already as white-capped waves began to crash on top of it. The weakening structure began to grate with each attack, disclosing subtly that it, too, may not make it through the night.

I toed the end of the dock and spread my arms out like wings. My clothes whipped wildly against my body, snapping loudly like a kite on a wind filled day. Keeping my legs straight I leaned forward, allowing the strength of the wind to hold me up. I closed my eyes and pretended to fly. My limp body danced back and forth in the changing gusts, never letting up enough to sacrifice me forward into the angry river. It was only after a particularly strong gust of wind shot against my torso and threw me back onto the dock that I decided to seek cover in the house.

Once inside, I pulled a rocking chair in front of the large window overlooking the river. The rain pounded against it while bursts of thunder rattled the edges. I sat there with a glass of tea and watched the conditions deteriorate before me. When a large bolt of lightening lit up the shoreline, I could see the last remains of the dock get washed away.

As expected, the electricity succumbed to the onslaught and the house became filled with darkness. For the next hour I sat there in the dark reliving the days of my life while the wind and rain pounded against the house. During some reminiscence of holding Wendy, I slipped away and slept peacefully in the chair while nature unleashed its wrath against the defenseless coast.

––––––––––––––

I'm not sure if it was the deafening crash of thunder or the airlifted wave against the glass pane that startled me awake. I walked to the window and stared into the vast darkness, awaiting the next flash of lightening to reveal the progression of destruction outside. The waves were beginning to splash against the side of the house, giving rise to a steady flow of water through the cracks of the back door. The storm was in full force and the coastline was no match for its aggression.

The howling winds of a hurricane have a way of playing tricks on your mind, often mimicking the cries of a ghost. It was for this reason that I initially ignored the faint screams that reached my ear. However, when the screams sounded more childlike, I became exceedingly concerned of its possible source. I searched the shoreline in front of the house, unable to recognize any possible explanation. Maybe I was just hearing things. I was sure the brain could do stranger things when under attack by a ravenous tumor.

The screams continued and became slightly more audible with each passing minute. When I finally deciphered the words *Uncle Chance* a chill ran down my spine.

It just couldn't be...

I ran to the side door and had only opened it an inch when a gust of wind tore it from its failing hinges and tumbled it into the dark night. The wind whipped against my face, making it nearly impossible to open my eyes. I squatted down in an effort to stabilize myself and peered down the shoreline. Debris was flying all around, enticing my eyes in every directions. I looked down at the beginning of the seawall, carefully screening as far as my eyes would allow me.

It was after a massive bolt of lightening lit up the shoreline that I noticed the small silhouette a hundred yards down the shoreline. It appeared to be a child during the few seconds it was able to stand. Then the voice struck me.

"Uncle Chance. Help me, Uncle Chance."

My heart stopped as I made the terrifying realization - it was Dillon!

Chapter 59

I kept my eyes fixed on Dillon's shadow as I forced my way through the menacing winds. I could only make it a few feet before a blast tackled me to the ground. Each time I would push myself back up and frantically search for Dillon. I knew he wouldn't last much longer in those gales.

The shortcut from Charlie's house to mine required walking along a concrete sea wall - it was the only path Dillon knew. The waves from the storm surge were crashing over the trounced wall, constantly washing Dillon's feet from under him. With each wave he would roll a few yards away from the seawall and then quickly get up to battle the next one. I knew the consequences if he didn't make it up in time for the next attack.

When I managed to get within twenty yards of him, I began to scream, "Just hold on Dillon. I'll be there in a second. Everything's going to be okay." I could see him clearly, his thin body shaking from the cool water.

The churning river began to wash over his spent body, tossing him precariously to the edge of the seawall. The foaming salt water began to enter his throat, causing him to choke briefly before coughing it out.

And then the nightmare became worse.

A mighty band of wind surged a wall of water toward the shoreline. "Get down, Dillon," I screamed, but it was too late. I watched the swell of water crash easily over the wall and engulf Dillon's helpless body. When it washed back out to sea, Dillon was gone.

"Dillon!" I screamed, but the only answer was the sinister roar of the hurricane. The surge of water forced his feeble body under the black, possessive river. I stabled myself on the wall, ducking beneath the next massive wave and looked out into the merciless sea. Dillon's head bobbed up from the foaming abyss. It was pulling him farther out and I knew there was no time to think.

When I dove into the water, everything suddenly became quiet and peaceful. Beneath the convulsing surface there was no hint of the monster ripping away from the top. I resurfaced and the fury of the hurricane drove needles of rain into my eyes. The salt burned my throat and forced one eye closed. I quickly scanned the surrounding area for any signs of Dillon. A rush of water rolled over me, partially filling my lungs. Gasping for breath, I continued to search for Dillon. *I can't let him die. I just can't.*

I spotted his head for a split second before it disappeared again beneath the battering waves. He was close. *God don't let me lose him.* I dove under and swam in the direction of the current, hoping I would cut him off as the surge pulled him farther out. As my hand stroked forward, it brushed his ankle. I grasped it tight and pulled him to me.

I felt his arms struggling for the surface, his body desperate for air. After managing to fight through the current, I pushed Dillon above the water first. We both gasped for air and tried to keep our heads extended above the marching waves.

"I've got you," I screamed above the roaring wind and rain. "You're gonna be fine." The conviction in my voice was weak. I knew we had a daunting task ahead.

No matter how hard I swam, the shoreline didn't seem to get any closer. My lungs and arms burned. I had never felt such pain. Dillon clung to my side as I tried to kick free from the retreating waves. After a few more minutes of intense fighting, our fate became frighteningly evident. I realized that even if I had the strength, the current was too strong to allow me back to shore with Dillon's added weight. The only chance I had was to let him go, and that was not an option.

Twice more we were sucked under, while the water continued filling my lungs. My grip remained firm on Dillon; if we were going to die, we would do it together. I would not let go until that final breath closed the door of my life. My arms locked around him for the last time. My legs went limp and my body expired itself to the invincible sea. I prayed my last prayer – *God, if there's any way to save this child...*

Lacking sufficient oxygen, I began to black out and my arms gradually loosened their grip on Dillon. My legs were now completely unresponsive. We were on our third submerge and I knew we would not come up again.

It was at that moment that I felt a thick arm wrap around my neck while the other hand pulled Dillon from my grip. My head was thrust above the water and I again gasped air into my lungs. Water purged from my mouth and ears.

"Just a little longer," I heard Diesel's familiar voice scream above the bedlam. I reached over and felt Dillon's head.

Diesel had us both in his firm grip.

After what seemed like an hour of struggling towards the shore, my feet finally touched the sandy bottom and

I did my best to help Diesel fight our way through the pulling current. I began to breathe a little easier and steadily regained consciousness. At the sea wall we timed the incoming waves as Diesel pushed us to the top of the barrier. I pulled Dillon away from the surging water while Diesel also pulled himself up to safety. I continued gasping for air and began slapping Dillon on the back. His coughing became stronger, and he purged out a large amount of seawater. It poured from his mouth as he wrapped his arms around my neck.

Chapter 60

"Dillon, what are you doing out here?" I asked, my chest heaving up and down. "Where's your dad?"

"Daddy won't wake up. He's on the floor and he won't wake up. I was scared," Dillon cried between coughs, his face buried between my neck and shoulder. His teeth chattered loudly and his body shuddered with chills.

Diesel crawled to us and laid on his back, fighting precious air back into his lungs. "What," he huffed before finishing, "happened?"

"I don't know," I screamed above the howling wind. "I think something is wrong with Charlie."

I pulled Dillon off my neck and handed him to Diesel. "You take Dillon and I'll go check." Diesel wrapped his massive paws around Dillon and nodded his head in agreement. He then turned around and started for higher land. I grabbed his shoulder before he could take a step.

"You saved our lives. You're a hero, Diesel."

He smiled broadly and firmed his grip on Dillon. "I was worried about you down here," he replied, water shooting from his mouth. He then placed his hand on the back of Dillon's head. "He'll be safe," he promised. "You be careful. Are you sure you can make it?"

"I'm fine. I'll stay away from the sea wall."

———————————

It took me only a few minutes to reach Charlie's house. Although the storm continued to rage without mercy, the house looked still and lifeless. The front door was left open and swung back and forth against the outside wall. After carefully climbing the steps, I walked in through the living room. The storm shutters blocked out any source of light from the sky, which would have left the house pitch-black except for the flickering of a candle coming from the kitchen. I followed it to its source and then made the horrifying discovery. Charlie's body lay lifeless on the kitchen floor. Blood pooled around his head and drifted down to his waist. I dropped down to my knees and rolled him over.

Frantic, I slapped his face and screamed his name. He showed no signs of movement. I felt his pulses and placed my ear against his mouth. I sensed a light breath against my cheek - he was alive. I knew I had to get him to a doctor, and quickly.

All the roads and bridges leading into Morehead City were surely flooded out by then and the weather was much too severe to even consider an emergency call. The only other option was to take a boat across the river and then walk the short distance into town, but with one-hundred mile per hour winds there would be nearly no chance of staying afloat. I sat down beside Charlie's lifeless body and placed my head between my knees. I did my best to control the panic and to think more clearly. *What could I do?*

It was at that moment that I experienced the most bizarre event I had ever seen. The winds abruptly stopped and everything became quiet. There was no more howling in the dark night or crashing of tree limbs. The rattling of the windows ceased and the bushes returned to their normal shape. It was as if someone just cut the switch and everything froze in time. Like a ton of bricks, it hit me. I had heard of this event before.

It was the eye of the hurricane.

Chapter 61

The eye of a hurricane is one of nature's most bewildering events. Like some mythical wonderland, it lies hidden in the center of the spinning cyclone, calm and peaceful like a cloudless day. I had often heard Gramps tell stories of this weather phenomenon. He told of how the most severe storm conditions, with winds up to one hundred and fifty miles per hour, suddenly became still and eerie. The sun would shine bright and the birds would temporarily rekindle their voices. The eye was typically about twenty miles wide and lasted just a few minutes. Then, as ominously as it arrived, it would vanish, leaving behind the ferocious backside of the hurricane.

———————

The only possibility of getting Charlie to the hospital in time was to travel across the two miles of river that connected to the shore of Morehead City. From there it would be another two mile hike on higher land to the rear entrance of Carteret General. Even if I could make it across the river before the backside of the hurricane reached us, I had no clue how I would carry him through the pounding wind and rain to reach the hospital. I just decided to cross that bridge when I reached it.

304

I ran outside and scanned through the dozens of boats that had been blown into shore. I was certain there would be one that remained functional. The sky was clear and the stars sparkled like a winter's evening, but beyond the eye, more destruction crawled forward. It waited for no one. I had to move now.

Behind a wall of cluttered boats, I spotted a small skiff that somehow remained floating in the still choppy waters. I ran down to the shore and climbed over the other vessels to reach it. After pulling it to a clearing, I tied it to a grounded shrimp boat and then briefly inspected it for damage.

I sprinted to the house and found Charlie still unconscious on the floor. My knees buckled as I lifted him over my shoulder and shuffled my feet towards the door. Time was running out. If the eye passed before we made it across the channel, the skiff would surely sink and I would have no chance of getting Charlie to shore.

I positioned Charlie's head on a life preserver and used my shirt to help control the bleeding. After choking the engine a few times, it reverberated with combustion and sprung to life. I throttled it to rhythm and then untied the rope from the skiff. The waves, although much smaller in the eye, were still imposing, a sure sign that the calm winds were only temporary.

We made it half way across the river without taking on too much water. The skiff was proving to be seaworthy, even with four-foot waves to climb. Above our heads the bright shining stars began to fade and then under a thick curtain of black clouds, disappeared. I knew the back side of the eye wall was near, and its winds would be more devastating than the front side.

The winds began their antagonizing howl with the shoreline only a short distance away. The waves were building, causing the bow of the boat to raise high above the water and then crash down with a loud clap. Charlie's body began sliding freely across the hull, spilling blood throughout the skiff. The shoreline was close and the water was becoming more shallow by the second. We were going to make it, but it would be close.

The rain began just as the boat came to rest on the shore. I ran to the front and pulled the bow up another foot to temporarily lock the skiff down in the mud. I took a deep breath and jumped back in the boat. Charlie's body was cold and wet. I grabbed an arm and struggled to lift him up on my shoulder. The winds suddenly picked up and forced me to put him back down to avoid dropping him. *How am I going to do this*, I asked myself. I turned to study the path up the sand and saw the most glorious sight. A pack of police cars came speeding down the back road and quickly divided to allow an ambulance through to the boat ramp.

I knelt beside Charlie and placed my hand over his cheek. "Hang in there, buddy. Help is here."

As we followed the ambulance through the back streets and into the hospital, Officer Burns explained how Diesel radioed help when he saw me take off in the skiff with Charlie. Before getting out of the car I told him the short version of Diesel coming down to the river to check on us, and how he risked his life to save us.

"I'll be sure the Chief hears about this," he assured me. "The medics said Charlie's vitals were fine; they figure he's probably got a nasty concussion. But he should wake up soon."

"Thanks for your help," I said as I shook his hand and headed for the waiting room.

Chapter 62

I leaned against the cold wall, lost in trance as the fluorescent lights buzzed and flickered from above. Somehow I wasn't overly concerned about Charlie pulling through. I assumed we had weathered the toughest part of this day. I closed my eyes and prayed for his quick recovery. After all, Dillon would need him more than ever with my death. I felt a spell of dizziness coming on so I slid down to the floor and allowed my head to rest against the wall.

"Chance," a voice came from above me. It was Dr. Evans, Charlie's clinic partner. "Let's talk in Charlie's room."

"How is he?" I asked, climbing to a standing position.

Dr. Evans walked ahead of me. "I'll let him tell you."

"So he's awake?" I replied.

He continued walking without answering my question.

When we arrived to the room, I expected to find Charlie sitting up, maybe a little groggy at most. But as I made the corner into his room I found him still unconscious with tubes entering and exiting from all over his body. A ventilator supplied air to his lungs, forcing his chest to move slowly with each cycle.

"What is this?" I exclaimed.

"This is what happens at the end of a battle with GBM," Dr. Evans said while holding back any emotion.

"What are you talking about? What's GBM?" I said in complete confusion.

"I have him on corticosteroids for the cerebral edema, but I don't expect it'll make much of a difference," he said, ignoring my question. "The expansion has likely caused too many strokes by now."

I stared at Dr. Evans as he spoke the words, my body completely insensible and numb. He pulled out an envelope and handed it to me. "Charlie wanted me to give this to you should something like this happen." I took it in my hand and read Charlie's incursive spelling of my name on the front. Dr. Evans patted me on the back and said, "I'll leave you alone for a few minutes."

I looked at Charlie's lifeless body and then back to the envelope. My head began to spin wildly and I felt my stomach turn inside out. I sat beside Charlie and pulled out the letter.

————————————

Dear Chance,

If you're reading this letter, things have not gone exactly the way I had planned. First, I want you to know that all I have done has been with the best of intentions. I trust that you will see this.

All the symptoms you've had over the last couple of months, I've caused. You see, I've given you medications in your food, Ipecac, to cause vomiting and adrenaline to cause headaches, to make you believe that you have cancer. It's hurt me mightily to do this, but in desperation I had no other choice. I didn't plan on it being this difficult. I thought I could simply move home, introduce you to my son, make you fall in love with him and overcome the years of depression. The battle has proven to be as difficult as any I have faced.

Nobody can truly know how valuable his life is until he's dying. I know this well, as do you. At the writing of this letter it has been almost a year since I learned I had GBM – Glioblastoma Multiforme. I fought it with all my power. The radiation and chemo bought me some much needed time, and that's when I moved back home.

But when I got here, your depression had grown so deep I couldn't break through. I was desperate, Chance. Please understand this. I was desperate because I needed you to live, because I can't. And I know that there is only one other person on this earth who can show Dillon the kind of life I planned for him – and that person is you. I want him to have the childhood that we had. This has always been my dream since the day I first held him. I've raised this sweet boy alone. You couldn't imagine how that makes love grow.

So in my desperation, I devised a plan. I knew how much dying made me want to live, and I hoped it would have the same effect on you. Once I told you that your life would soon be over, you began to open up, and that's when I put Dillon in your life. He loves you dearly, Chance, and I know you love him, too. You can hate me for this, but please don't lose your love for my boy. You're all he will have soon. Love him please; love for the times I can't.

I've taken care of everything. The house was built for you and Dillon. Now I want you to build a life together there. My life insurance will give you enough to get out of debt and put some away for Dillon's future. Use what's left at your discretion. Dr. Evans will run my clinic as planned and will pay you for our agreed buyout. He has followed me through my cancer since it was discovered at Hopkins, and has been a good friend to me and will be there for you also.

I've loved Dillon with all my heart since he was a minute old. Not one second have I taken for granted. I held him each night, read him the stories my mother read me, taught him about the coast like Gramps taught us. Knowing my time was short has allowed me to squeeze the love out of every moment with my boy. I've loved every glass of water I've gotten him in the middle of the night and every kiss he has given me for no reason at all. Now I pass his love to you. You will find attached an adoption certificate. All you need to do is sign it, and Pam, the hospital social worker, will take care of the rest. I refuse to think of this as giving Dillon to you. Instead, I am letting you borrow him for a while…until I have him back again.

I love you, Chance. You are my brother. I'm glad you've found life again. Now enjoy the rest of it with Dillon. I'll see you again someday.

Charlie

Epilogue

Three years later...

And so I come back to this old oyster shack on most mornings to reflect on the life that was given back to me three years ago. It's hard to believe Charlie has been gone that long. Those first days were difficult. Dillon cried so much I took him to Dr. Evans to make sure he wasn't dehydrating. It has taken him a while to understand why his daddy didn't tell him he was the one who had to go away and not me. But with time he understood. He still talks about Charlie all the time. I reckon he always will, and so will I.

I never held an ounce of animosity towards Charlie for the way he mislead me. He did what he had to do. In fact, even my family knew the truth when I thought I was dying. They understood Charlie's desires, and though he had to work hard to convince them, deep down they always knew his plan was the only way to get the old me back.

The day of the funeral was filled with mostly horrid emotions. I held Dillon through the service as Charlie's friends told stories of his life. Dillon screamed at the sight of his daddy being locked up in a box. The preacher had to stop the service while I tried to calm Dillon down. And

I did. As the entire church listened, I tried to convince him that there was only a shell in that coffin and that his daddy was up in heaven with Gramps, waiting until the day he could see him again. That was hard for Dillon to understand, but he trusted me. To say there was not a dry eye in the church would be an understatement; every person was sobbing with Dillon. If hearts can really break, they did on that day.

When it was my turn to speak, Dillon wouldn't let me leave him behind with Charlie's parents. So, I took him with me to the pulpit and held him as I began speaking to Charlie's casket. Through tears I told how I had come to believe in angels. I believed that angels walked all around us and that maybe even they didn't know they were angels. I said that maybe God sent angels to earth as everyday people, and that they helped complete his perfect plan as imperfect people. And if that could be the case, Charlie was certainly my angel. Although I know better now, I still believe that in some ways, Charlie was an angel.

When I finished, I looked out at the large crowd and noticed one person in particular. Wendy sat mid-way back, drying her eyes with a tissue. I didn't expect to see her afterward. My attention would be with Dillon as we left Charlie's body behind.

When the burial was complete, the limo carried Dillon and me back to the oyster shack so I could pick up some clothes. Once we got there, I sat down in my usual spot, with Dillon in my arms, and stared out across the river, with newfound heartache and loneliness. I could tell there was a lot going through Dillon's head. He kept looking over at the rocking chair Charlie always sat in, while tears rolled down his cheeks. I watched him with a heavy heart, not noticing the shadow that emerged from behind me.

"Am I interrupting anything?" Wendy's soft voice seemed to come from heaven.

"Wendy," I said with a surprised voice. She put a box down on Charlie's chair and hugged me tightly.

"I'm so sorry," she kept saying.

Dillon walked over and wrapped his arms around both of our knees. Wendy knelt down and hugged him gently. "I got your letters. Thank you for sending them."

"You're welcome," Dillon said with a sad whisper. "My daddy's gone away."

"I know he has," Wendy could only manage to say.

She stood back up and looked deeply in my eyes. She studied the changes in my face over the last five years. "I brought your letters back. I have a feeling you didn't send them to me."

"Daddy did," Dillon informed us. "But I told him to."

"I had no idea," I said. "I haven't checked…"

Wendy gleamed as she showered Dillon with her beautiful smile. He continued to frown deeply, and I could see the mother in Wendy hurt for him. She looked back at me. "If you don't mind, I'd like to keep them."

"They're yours," I said.

That was three years ago, and Wendy never left. In fact, she really enjoys being a preacher's wife. Yes, a preacher's wife. You see, with the extra money Charlie left behind, I decided to build a church around Gramps' old chapel. It's called the Finding Life Center and today we break ground on its first major addition. People come from all over to hear my messages. That's why I always come here, to the oyster shack on Sunday mornings, before the service; it still refocuses me.

I have to admit that I get plenty of help around here. After Diesel's famous heroics faded and his picture stopped appearing on the front of every newspaper in the southeast, he became my assistant pastor. His wife is quite nice and refuses to allow him to bring out that old siren, no matter how much Dillon begs.

And then there is Scotty, who does a hilarious skit for the children each Sunday. It turns out that when you are a child at heart, kids really like that. Last Sunday we had over two hundred children attend our children's church.

People are amazed at how clean the church and its grounds stay. The long hallways around the church never have a piece of lint to show. Nor do the pictures of Gramps and Charlie that hang in the front entrance ever attract dust. Robbie Seffers makes sure of that. He's been our custodian since the first day I moved him back to Carteret County. He's a part of my growing family now. Robbie stays in an apartment over the garage, which he keeps just as clean as the church. I've invited him to stay in the extra room next to the twin's bedroom, but he prefers his independence.

Oh yeah, the twins. That's another story.

It's the funniest thing. Somehow Charlie must have known that he and Dillon's little letter trick would work with Wendy. A couple of months after he passed, I received a phone call from a Dr. Melvin. He said he was an old colleague of Charlie's and that he did a lot of research with trauma induced fertility problems. With Charlie's request, he flew Wendy and me up to see him for a weekend and started us on some experimental treatments. Turns out he does a pretty decent job. On the night Wendy and I remarried, we conceived two little girls; Ema Grace and Leslie Sue. But nobody gets close to them unless they go through big brother Dillon first. That's the law.

Wendy, of course, is a beautiful mother. Even with a painful delivery, she smiled throughout it and has never lost that smile. And as much as she loves those twins, she loves

Dillon the same. He stole her heart from the beginning, just like he did mine.

———————————

Well, it's time to get over to the church. I hope Charlie can see me today. I've been practicing weeks for this day. Let me try it one more time...

———————————

I want to welcome you to this historic day at The Finding Life Center. Many of you will never know Charlie Robbins. But I believe God sent him to help lead me through the darkest days of my life. And today we break ground on a building that will honor his name – The Charlie Robbins Fellowship Hall. Charlie was all about finding life, no matter the events that haunt you. Finding life is for each of us. I trust that those of you who have come here today with pain and disappointment may also find your life this day...

About the Author

James L. Graham has published dozens of articles with a unique combination of science, medical research, and inspirational elements. He has a background in both the science and healthcare professions. He lives with his wife and family in Eastern North Carolina.

Printed in the United States
28125LVS00001B/46-510

9 781420 838664